ABRUPT

KATHY COOPMANS

*Anne,
Expect the Unexpected
Kathy Coopmans*

Abrupt

© 2020 Kathy Coopmans

Cover Design- Jill Sava with Love Affair With Fiction

Editing done by- Ellie McLove with My Brother's Editor

Proofreader- Cat Parisi with Cat's Eye-proofing

Formatting- HJ Bellus/Small Town Girl Formatting

This is a work of fiction. Names, characters, places, and incidents are products of the author's imagination or are used fictitiously and are not to be construed as real.

Any resemblance to actual events, locales, organizations, or persons, living or dead, is entirely coincidental. All rights reserved.

The unauthorized reproduction or distribution of this copyrighted work is illegal. No part of this book may be used or reproduced electronically or in print without written permission by the author. All rights are reserved.

DEDICATION

For Xavier.
"You've got a Friend in me."
Randy Newman
Toy Story.

PROLOGUE

LANE

"Do I look like a man who gives a shit that's a two thousand dollar bottle of bourbon? I told you to give me the whole damn bottle." A breath of disgust passes through my clenched teeth. More of it's about ready to slip out of my lungs if I don't get the hell out of this room to breathe some fresh air.

I'm two point five seconds from causing a scene at this farce of a wedding by reaching across the bar and crushing the bartender's windpipe the minute he turns back around. All the while shouting to everyone that the bride will never love the groom the way she does me.

"Sienna." Her name leaks out of my aching chest in a barely-there whisper.

"And I told you Mr. Ricci said to cut people off if I thought they had too much. You've had enough, pal." He spins on his feet, daring to stare me down.

I'm not this asshole's pal. I'm nothing but a miserable man who needs to drink myself into a stupor. He happens to be in my way.

I contemplate jumping over this bar to take my frustration out on his face or scare the shit out of him.

Either way, I will have that bottle.

"I'll show you, pal, when I ram this down your throat. Do you have a problem with giving me the bourbon now?" I flash my gun, not bothering to thank him when he raises his hands in surrender, grabs my drink of choice, and slides it across the smooth top of the bar.

I hated guns about as much as I hated having to attend this wedding. The problem was, tonight, I wanted to strap it to my side in case I decided to pull the trigger and shoot the groom in the back of the head as he stood at the altar. Now, I wish I had.

Sienna is married, my life, my girl is married.

Fuck.

"Wise choice, asshole." I snatch hold of it, fingers itching like a bitch to walk up to the groom, dump it over his head and light him on fire.

Yeah, I had a problem with the groom.

I hated his guts. He has my only regret, my life, my everything in his arms.

At twenty years old, I had a list a mile long of regrets, most of them having one thing or another to do with the bride.

Regret number one, she was as much the forbidden fruit as tempting, and I was that much of a dumb ass like Adam was with Eve to take a bite. I knew the commandments and broke them anyway by touching the woman with hair the same color as the apple.

Flaming red.

She's poisoned me for life.

The woman should be mine instead of some made man's in her father's mafia. Bastard jumped at the chance to slide a ring on her finger within two months after I made the biggest mistake of my life.

I might be able to handle it if he wasn't a piece of scum, I think, to be a traitor. If only I had the proof to back up my instincts. The only thing I have is how my blood boiled every time he shook my hand and smiled with a sinister look in his eyes.

If I find out he's fucking with my family or trying to destroy what they've built, I'll blow a hole right between those demonic looking eyes.

Taking a swig, I spin around, keeping my eyes on the door, determined to not only look at the bridal table but to take my pity party for one as far away from the glam, glitter, and the celebration as I can get. I need to be drunk and forget about watching the gorgeous woman dressed in white walking down the aisle toward a man I know damn well she doesn't love.

No. That love will always belong to me.

I need to forget the hurt on her face when she found out what I did at Behind Closed Doors; the sex club me and my brothers own. I need to forget how I should have never fallen for a girl years ago when I knew I couldn't keep her.

I need to learn how to live my life full of regrets. I need to forget Sienna Ricci ever existed and move on.

If I don't, I'll likely get us and a slew of other people I care about killed.

CHAPTER ONE

Sienna

"Welcome to Texas, Sienna. Sitting behind that desk suits you. I bet you'd look better spread out on top of it. In fact, I know you would."

I jump, my heart thumping wildly, my finger lifting off the trigger of my 9mm at the sound of that voice. God, talk about deep, as in, confine my heart in a destructive web of delicious sin. I remember it all too well.

It belongs to none other than Lane Mitchell. The man who grabbed hold, seized, and still owns every part of me. It's been over a decade, and I still feel him in my soul. From the first time he spoke to me, he spun a piece of himself into me.

I won't tell him that. Ever again.

Biting my lip, I wondered how long it would take him to make an appearance back into my ungrounded world to tremble it under my feet all the more.

An earthquake that will rattle me before it splits me in half.

My throat goes dry, stomach queasy at the thought of

shooting a man who is physically harmless to me. It's the emotional part of me he'd ripped thousands of moons ago into shreds that concern me. No matter what he has done, I'd never want to shoot him, and I could have.

My heart palpitates with the thought.

"Look at me, Sienna," he demands, causing me to clench my teeth as well as my legs, the man dragging out the 'n's in my name as if he's waited years to say it.

It makes me want to burst out in laughter. A sound that would be so alien coming out of me, I'd up and pass out onto the floor.

I'm relieved and scared at the same time as I holster the gun I keep stored under my desk back where it belongs. I'd pulled it out a few minutes ago when I heard the near soundless footsteps coming down the hall. When you grow up believing boogeymen lives under your bed, then turn around and marry someone far worse than you pictured the Devil himself to be, you can hear a pin drop.

I knew it wasn't my husband, Joseph, coming back to claim the little of my spirit he'd left me to survive with, his footsteps, whether light or heavy, I can hear in my sleep. They've haunted me day and night for years as well as the man standing in my doorway. If I knew I'd be able to get past Lane without the slightest of touch, I would, and then I'd disappear. It wouldn't be by choice either. It would be so I wouldn't have to crush his heart along the same, yet a different reason as he'd done mine.

"When someone receives a compliment, they say thank you while looking the person in the eye. I'm sure your father wouldn't be pleased if he knew his Bell' Angelo was cowering away from me. I have a list of regrets that have trailed me for years when it comes to you. They need rectifying. Look at me, La Mia Vita. I'm not going to ask again," he commands with such a dominant tone. One that hasn't changed a bit. I swear the intensity of it along with the sweltering energy swirling from his presence ricochets from the walls, bouncing right into my chest.

Bastard.

I, too, have a list. The first, how dare he use the two terms of endearment that are permanently attached to my heart. Bell' Angelo means a beautiful angel in Italian. My father has called me that for as long as I can remember. The other? La Mia Vita translates to *my life*. Sometimes I swear I can still hear Lane whisper it in my ear before I fall asleep at night all these years later. It and the things he used to promise, along with doing pleasurable things to my body, do not have a place in this now stifling room. I refuse to show how it's tugging at the strings of my heart.

"He also taught me not to be a hypocrite. When you don't particularly like, nor want to acknowledge someone, you don't. Both apply to you. It's a little too late to right wrongs, Lane."

Trust me, I should know.

Keeping my head down, a hopeless chill raises goosebumps on my arms as I glance at my phone while struggling to wrap my head around that distinctive voice from a past I wish would have gone differently.

It's unforgettable. It is deeply planted in the very pit of my core, and no one in this lifetime will ever uproot it.

"As you can see, I'm busy. What do you want?" I blow out a shaky breath and still my trembling fingers over the keyboard of my laptop.

Closing my eyes, I try to block out the times I've seen Lane's brothers Seth and Logan since I moved to Texas. The heartache is constant after hearing from his brothers that he'd changed. It's what I deserved to hear when I was naïve enough to fall for him long ago, believing he loved me the way I did him when he didn't.

The worst thing about it, I know the hidden truth. Lane might have changed in some ways; in others, he hasn't. Those ways I have to stay clear of, or he'll suck me right back in.

Over the years, I'd ask about him when I'd come home to visit, pretending I wasn't a mixed ball of emotions when I'd walk through the door of my father's home wondering if that would be the time he'd be there.

He never was. I was thankful and disappointed.

What's even harder to think about is when I was fifteen, my father sat me down, along with all three Mitchell brothers, and told them I was forbidden. He made them swear they understood while I sat there mortified and shaking like a leaf. He threatened to kill them and any of his other men if they ever broke his loyalty. Lane did right along with my heart. What my father didn't know then and still doesn't is that Lane and I were already involved.

Breathe, Sienna. It's okay. You knew deep down you'd see him again. Look him in the eyes and get everything you should have said years ago off your chest.

I do as my mind says. Well, the breathing part and all I smell is the scents of citrus and control that to this day slay me.

I hate that Lane's scent comforts me when it shouldn't.

I let out a sigh, everything inside of me trembling.

There are two people I've told about the secret teenage affair that started when Lane and I were fourteen. My husband, who beat it out of me until I gave in, and the only real friend I've ever had, Victoria Hughes.

"I'm not above making you look at me. It'll allow me to touch that silky skin. I can see how soft it still is from here.

Snowy white perfection." Oh, God, he is still a smooth-talker.

Arguing sits on the tip of my tongue. I bite it down, knowing all too well the man is trying to get under my skin. If he only knew he's always been there, Lord knows what he'd do. Probably slam me against the wall, please me in ways my body hasn't been in a long time.

I sit perfectly still, ignoring his loads of bullshit. In between my legs? Well, it pulses with need, remembering how Lane knew my body better than I did. But then reality confronts my mind, recollecting how he used me. Hurt me in ways I've long forgiven him for, yet I haven't been able to forget.

Of course, my despicable husband did the same thing only months after we married. Except he didn't sneak his secret sex-life behind my back. He paraded his whores around if only to humiliate me, broke many of the mafia's codes, as well as the ones set forth when he asked my father for my hand, and throughout the years, I kept my mouth shut out of fear and protectiveness. Letting my father believe his trusted right-hand man running his dirty and criminal dealings in New York was loyal and faithful.

The man I married has a cold-black heart that I hope once he's found, it's cut right out of his chest. The bastard vanished into thin air after he took away the only thing that has kept me from killing myself.

After what my husband did, my uncle and father will castrate him before slicing him from head to toe. I don't care how they kill him. I want him dead.

If only I would have told them what kind of man Joseph is before it was too late. If only the boy I fell in love with didn't come along and break me enough that I ran right into

Joseph's arms after I caught Lane balls deep in a woman while another rode his face.

Those thoughts have me glancing at my phone again. It's a habit, wishing for it to ring and the person on the other end being the one I need to survive. I carry my phone with me wherever I go. I sleep with it close to my ear. It's my lifeline, and one of these days, it has to ring because despite the hell I've lived in, I still believe there's a God out there who will grant me this one blessing. If he doesn't, I don't know how to go on.

"Do you know what I want from you, Sienna? The truth. Let me take you to lunch, and we'll go from there." He sounds completely shattered.

He cannot know the truth, can he? No, he would have tracked me down long before this if he did. I swallow around a ball filled with a treacherous lie.

Lane will find the truth soon enough. When he does, he won't think me anything but the scum of the earth that I am.

"I can't afford you to spend time with you. How did you get in here, Lane?" I reset the alarm when I came into work. I always double, sometimes triple check. If I don't, even knowing that there's security outside, I wouldn't be able to work by myself.

Then I remember just who this man is. He's clever. After all, he'd sneak past my father's soldiers and right into my bed, and I was the stupid girl who spread her legs and gave everything to him.

An infinite amount of emotion rolls through me, approaching the dam surrounding my chest I painstakingly built over the years. They were already close to breaking the walls and drowning me before Lane thought he could waltz back into my life and make demands, bringing emotions I can't afford to harbor when I'm barely afloat. If I cave before screwing my head on straight when it comes to him and the secrets I hold, I will surely drown in the undertow.

"We'll get to that once I see your gorgeous face. Don't play games with me, Sienna. I said lunch, not sex. I haven't taken money for it in years."

That wasn't the afford I meant. I'm talking about what will shift the lives of so many people if it's not done the right way, especially if Lane and I were to be seen in public when I haven't a clue where my husband is.

"Of course, we'll get to it at your convenience. How could I forget that the Mitchell brothers always get what they want?" That's something that will never change. I used to like it that way. With Lane, I got the things I wanted too. We were equals. Or so I thought.

"In most cases, we do. In the one I've always wanted, I didn't. I lost it, and now I want it back." Lane's tone is under control, but his words? They are intense and hungry, hitting where he meant them to, right between my unsatisfied quivering legs.

Don't give into him, Sienna. He's a master at manipulation and lies.

What's left of my heart thumps frantically, as if fighting to find a place to hide. I shouldn't have listened to my uncle and father when they practically dragged me out of my house in New York and gave me a choice to stay at my childhood home or move here where my father bought a house for him and me. I couldn't live in New York any longer, any more than I could sleep in a room in New Orleans that held memories of Lane. I would have died a little more every day than I already am. I chose to move here knowing I'd run into the man who mutilated my heart.

I should have never let excitement get the best of me when I interviewed and got the manager's position at The

Grill House. One of Houston's newest five-star steak restaurants in the heart of the city. It's been open a month, and we're booked six weeks out already.

How my father was able to get me in for an interview, let alone, how I got the job when I have no experience whatsoever except spreading my legs, playing the part of a loyal wife to my husband's power, is beyond me.

Once power, I remind myself. Thanks to what my husband did, it was stripped away by my father. Without it, Joseph is left wide open for any mafia member from all the families to capture and be rewarded once I have back what he took from me.

Now that Lane is a few feet away from me, I'm regretting my decision. As well as so many more I've made.

"I hoped to run into you sooner. Hoped about a lot of things over the years when it came to you." Lane drawls in that Southern Louisiana accent I missed. "The one thing I hoped more than anything is to hear someday you say you loved me again."

Sweet Jesus, help me, please. He says it as if he genuinely means it. I want to believe it, want to one day hear him say it as much as I want to hold on to hope. Hope is the only thing I have to cling to, but not when it comes to Lane. The man is nothing but a liar, a cheat, and a thief.

I can remember as clear as the sky is blue, my mother's words about hope as she gasped and sputtered on her deathbed. Her blood was coating my dress where she laid on top of me, her bullet hole riddled body a shield tucked around me under a table during a family spaghetti dinner shootout. Gunshots were blazing everywhere. I was crying so hard, yet I remember her telling me to never give up on hope.

She said, "Sienna, I'm one of the lucky women in our

world of violence and corruption, I found a man that loves and treats me as his equal as much as a man in our world can. I hope you find true love, health, happiness, and someday a man who loves only you. Who lets you make your own choices while standing behind you in the same way you'd do him? Hold on to hope, hold it close to your heart, my sweet little girl. Promise me you'll never forget what hope can do for you, no matter what."

She died before I could answer. Of course, I was seven at the time, much too young to understand what she meant and scared out of my mind.

Hope has been my friend since.

After my mother died, my father rarely let me out of his, or our family's trusted guard's sight. I felt suffocated. I was homeschooled and guarded as if I were on death row. In a way, I was.

I wasn't allowed to walk through the doors leading to the west wing of our mansion until I was old enough to understand who my father was outside of our home. I wasn't allowed to watch the news. I wasn't allowed to play with other children unless my father, Lorenzo Ricci, the Boss of the Italian-American mafia, deemed them safe and worthy. But I studied every single person from my bedroom window who came to our house. By the time my father sat me down and told me who he was, I knew who was his friend, his enemy, and who would make it back to their car either in a body bag or on their feet.

Some days, I had my aunt Lena, who devoted as much time to me as she could before she too died. I had my uncle Gabe. And my father was an amazing dad when he wasn't tending to business. He made me laugh, he played dolls, and he cooked and watched movies with me. He was my hero in an anti-hero, ugly, ugly world.

And so was Lane. A man I don't dare peek over my lashes to get a look at before I kick his ass out. If I do, the truth will spill right out of my mouth.

"I missed you. Missed you so damn much it hurt. I've lived with the pain I caused you every day. Regret dripping out of me every time I knew you came to town. I heard what happened. I wanted to come to you sooner, kept telling myself to give you a little more time. I'm sorry, Sienna. I can't imagine what you are going through. Let me help you." Everything he said makes my heart bleed, causing it to clench tightly. It forces a tear to fall. A lonely drop that rolls down my face and plops onto the space bar of my laptop.

My gut twists, my teeth grind together, trapping the words I'm so afraid to say.

"I find it hard to believe you missed me every time you whored yourself out. Every time you stepped into a room with a stranger and fucked her. What is it you honestly want, Lane? If you're here to offer me protection, I have plenty of it." I shift in my chair, trying so hard to keep it together.

"To help you get through this." I can hear the underlying pain, the confusion of how my life brought me to this day, trying to claw its way out of his throat.

Oh, God.

"You don't have the first clue about what happened to me or how to help!" I yell. No one knows the depth of hell I went through over the years to lead me here except Victoria. And now, my uncle and father. They are as loyal to me as to the criminal activities they are knee-deep in. So, no, even if I betrayed them by not telling how I lived with abuse, rape, and fear, I don't believe they would deceive me by telling Lane the horrific things I've been through.

It's my story to tell. It's my shame to deal with when I decide to talk.

"I'm not here to be saved by you, Lane. That ship has sailed." But, do I ever want him to, even if it's only to ease the worry, the discomfort slowly eating away at me. I'm afraid he'll hate himself and me. I'm scared I'll see pity in his eyes when he's the last person I ever want it from.

I want to lash out and choke him. I want to with every living, breathing cell in my body. I want to blame him for every wrongful thing that's been done to me.

But I can't. Not when it's my fault.

With a man like Lane Mitchell, what I want is of no significance, and he's not going to leave until he's said everything he came to say. Even after, he's going to do his best to pounce on me like a lion cornering his prey.

Well, I've got news for him, I'm already in a corner hiding while I'll wait for another beast to maul me to death.

"No, Sienna, I've been waiting for you to climb on board so we could sail away together. You were my life once. No. Fuck that. You've always been my life."

I doubt that.

"Still sweet with your words, I see." The man was. He could say the kindest things, then turn around and say something sexual. Both would knock me off my feet.

"If God is real, then you, Sienna, are his masterpiece. Now come here and ride my face."

The flashback causes a shiver to run down my spine.

"I deserve bitterness after what I did to you. After I let you marry a man you didn't love. All these years I thought you'd fell in love with Joseph and you were happily married when you weren't. I want an explanation as to why your husband would cut the brake lines on your car. He tried to kill you. You survived, but your son." He pauses. I imagine he's shaking his head and clenching his fists, unable to process or spit the words out of his mouth.

I'll do it for him because I need him out of here before I fall apart.

"Was kidnapped by my husband." I draw in a breath, inhaling the pain of the past one hundred and eighty-two days since I've seen my son. God, saying that to anyone has been a stab to my heart, but to Lane, it's a thousand times harder.

My son Luca has been missing for six months. The first few days after the car accident that led to his disappearance, I was in and out of it, suffering from a concussion and a broken wrist. When the doctors eased me off the pain meds, and I saw the grief on my father's face, I thought for sure my son didn't survive the wreck that sent me flipping the car over when Luca and I descended the steep hill of our vacation home in Northern Michigan. We landed upside down in a ditch.

What my father told me shouldn't have surprised me, but it did. Joseph and Luca were both missing. I should have known I wouldn't get far after the incident that occurred earlier that evening that had my senses waking up to get my son as far away from Joseph as possible.

They weren't kidnapped by one of my father's enemies like one would think. No, my husband tried to off me, and he took my son away just like he promised since the day Luca was born.

We've heard nothing of their whereabouts. Joseph has no family for him to run and hide to. He was raised in foster care. He hasn't called making demands for money either. Not that he'd need it, he took every bit we had, plus some. Every rumor claiming they were spotted, my uncle and his friends, have dug deep to uncover if it's true. There's not a trace of them anywhere. My son is alive, though. I know he is.

And he has to be going through utter hell.

I close my eyes, searching desperately for a place to hide within my mind. Someplace safe that won't rummage through the painful memories of my child. The problem with that, Luca is my safe place.

I draw strength from Luca, knowing I raised him to be a smart young man and knowing my family will search the ends of the earth to find him. But there's no eluding the grief from me that I'm sure Lane can see even if I haven't yet looked at him.

It surrounds me.

"I have a daughter, the thought of someone taking her from me, let alone by the hands of someone who brought her into this world, I can't begin to understand. Fuck, let me help you the only way I can, Sienna. Talk to me."

Tears burn the back of my eyes, anger simmering in my stomach as the pain consumes me. I won't talk to him about my son or the fact he had a daughter with someone who wasn't me.

I'd heard what happened to Lexi's mother, how she walked away from her newborn days after giving birth. She died years later from a drug overdose. I also know what happened a year or so ago to Logan and his wife, Ellie. How a plan hatched to kidnap Lane's daughter backfired. I hurt for all of them then, and I was grateful when my father told me the masterminded brother and sister behind it was dead, and Lane's daughter was unharmed.

Letting out a long sigh, I save the bar order I was working on, shut my laptop, and strum up the courage to look at Lane. I need him gone. I need him to stay away from me. No matter what I say or don't, I can't risk anything happening to him or his daughter. My family might be powerful. They might have resources from here to the other side of the world searching. Still, they do not know Joseph the way I do. If he's not found before he attacks, he'll kill me and anyone standing in his way.

He's as sneaky as Lane.

Lifting my head, my mouth goes dry as I take him in. His hair is still thick and black as a cloudless night sky, eyes as green as the moss of the earth. He is much taller and muscular than I recall standing against the frame of the door, his legs crossed, one hand tucked in a front pocket of dark jeans, the other rubbing his thumb over his index and middle finger.

Christ Almighty, his arms and thighs are like tree trunks, and with each slow roll of his thumb, his muscles ripple, leaving me momentarily dumbfounded.

I stare at him, holding his gaze until I can almost see into his soul. I want to melt right into him and burn him at the same damn time.

In a few long strides, he's in front of my desk, those big hands of his squeezing the edge. Knuckles are turning white. Jaw clenching so tight, I'm surprised it doesn't break.

The dirty, yet pleasurable things those hands used to do to me scroll through my mind, slowly. They disappear as quickly, knowing Lane learned how to play my body from him being a whore. Knowing those hands more than likely did the same thing to thousands of women.

"You are damn lucky I didn't shoot you in the hallway when I heard you. Get out of my office, and do us both a favor, stay away from me. I'm here to make a fresh start for Luca and me when I get him back. Everything else in my past will stay where it belongs. Dead to me. That includes *you*."

Something close to hurt bursts in his eyes like a bolt of lightning cutting through the darkest sky. It's there for just a brief second before it's gone within a blink of my eyes.

Lane is a schemer. I don't buy his gentleman act for a second.

"There she is, that feisty woman who was everything a man like me wanted. The woman whose body I owned. The woman whose face I saw every time I touched another. You want to forget your past, that's fine with me. I want that for you, Sienna. You will tell me what I want to know before I leave this office."

Nervous dread creeps over me like a blanket of snow, numbing my brain. In this frozen state, my mind offers me only one thought.

I have to tell him.

"I..." Mortification and dread sets in, my mouth hanging open to form some response, but nothing more will come out.

"You what? Need more time? Well, tough shit. You deserve a fresh start. With me, damn it, and when Luca returns, he'll join in. I own this restaurant, sweetheart. I used my keys to get in. I'm your boss, and if you think for one damn second, I won't pluck your sexy ass out of that chair and bring you to my home where I'll protect you under lock and key, you are wrong. Regrettably, on my part, wrong."

CHAPTER TWO

LANE

I was the man Sienna thinks me to be. A whore, a user, a worthless piece of shit. I'm not anymore. What I definitely am not, nor will ever be again, is her past. The minute she stepped foot on Texan soil, she belonged to me.

Now, that's a lie if I've ever told myself one.

Years ago, Sienna was mine. She was everything to me. Despite the fact she's here for a reason I can't begin to fathom, and regardless of how many times I tell myself she's mine, and how many times over the years I'd wished she was, she's not mine.

Not yet, anyway.

Not in the way that counts. Not in the way I've always wanted her to be. Not in the way she should have been. Not until I've righted my wrong, lifted my regrets, and not until she tells me why her husband would do what he did. Then there is no stopping me from taking back what belongs to me.

In return, I am giving her all of me, as I promised years ago.

Christ, *her*. The woman who made me want to be a better man than I thought I could be. The woman who taught me the meaning of deep, soul-penetrating, I'd die, kill, and never give you up kind of love.

I was, and now will be a possessive asshole when it comes to Sienna. She is the only woman who has ever gotten me to drop to my knees and worship at her feet. I'd gladly do it every day if she gave me a chance.

Those truths and regrets don't stop me from wanting to kiss her, hold her, walk through hell with her, fuck her. It doesn't stop me imagining it's her hands on me every time I stroke my cock. I've done that enough. The next time I do, it will be with her baby blues on me while she fingers herself until we're both close to the edge. Then I'm going to fuck her until I erase the years without her I let piss away.

I was captivated by Sienna Ricci before her uncle Gabe took me and my brothers in raising us as his own after our shit for a mother killed herself. I will always be bound to this woman who doesn't have a clue that she owns one half of my soul. No, she thinks I used her.

That is far from the truth.

I might not know the woman before me as I did, but I loved her. I always have. I always will.

Even after she'd caught me in the act of regret, I loved her. After she married Joseph, I loved her. Losing her had me falling as deep as I could get into a lifestyle I enjoyed yet felt shame until my daughter, Lexi's mother, became pregnant.

And now, after avoiding Sienna for years when she'd come to visit her father, I'm at the breaking point of breaching a promise I made to my daughter the day her worthless mother walked away.

To never take a woman to bed until Lexi was old

enough to live on her own. I made that promise to keep my ass out of the club. To become the best parent, I could be to a little girl who deserved my undivided attention. I want my daughter proud of me as much as I am of her. There wasn't a chance in hell I was having her ashamed over what I did for a living in a place where craving sex lived like a virus in my veins.

The problem with a craving? When what you want is out of reach, you settle for sloppy seconds, and they do nothing to satiate what you know to be the best you've had.

Fucking someone you don't know is merely a release. Fucking someone you love is a pleasurable one right down to the bone. It's a high like no other.

I miss that kind of sex with Sienna. I miss it about as much as I missed this woman who, despite me hurting her, wants me as much as I do her. No matter how much she denies it and she will. She'll challenge me until she gives because Sienna remembers just how much our bodies pleased one another in both vanilla and the filthiest of flavors as our hearts entwined.

We were volatile together. An explosion from a simple touch. A torch to a flame. White-hot smoke and being with or inside of anyone else has ever come close to what we've shared.

And I'm enough of a son of a bitch to remind her how good we are together.

I miss teaching and watching her suck my cock while I ate her pussy. I miss taking her from behind while fisting that flaming red hair. I miss the way she arches her back while squeezing every drop of cum out of me. I miss talking to her, watching her do the simplest task when she doesn't know I am. I miss hearing the sound of her voice, cheering her up when she was down with a back rub, a kiss, or whatever the hell she needed at the time. I miss everything about Sienna that a man who years later still loves her could. Mostly, I miss the spark I can't seem to find in her eyes.

I suppose if she looked deep into mine, she wouldn't find even a flicker. I've kept it hidden well—the same as I've hidden our past from everyone. Including my brothers and we don't keep secrets.

"You're lying," she challenges in that feisty, sassy sound that she used to taunt me with. Fire shoots out of her eyes as she pushes herself to stand, leans close enough to me that all I'd have to do is move an inch, and my mouth would be one with hers.

Fuck. Me. That mouth.

Instead, I do what any man in their right mind would do when beauty is in front of him. I look down her body. My cock strains all the more when I get a close-up. Jesus, she is sexy as hell.

Deep scorching, thick waves in oranges and fiery red, hair hangs midway down her back. It looks as if it would burn to the touch. Not even close. I know exactly how it feels sliding through my fingers.

Silk and smooth.

Her breasts are ones of a woman now—pert. More than enough for my greedy hands—the nipples, hard, and pushing through her bra and against her blouse. Shit, my fingers twitch to pinch the tight buds before pulling them into my mouth.

"Lying about what, that I'm your boss, or that I want you back? I've changed in some ways, Sienna. Tying you up to get what I want under any circumstance isn't one of them." Provoking and craving slide off my tongue, with her, I'll never hide it. "Nothing more would please me right now than to tie you up, spank your ass and explore your body."

Except to know why your husband tried to kill you and kidnapped your son.

Her eyes change from flaming to ice. Skin beginning to turn red.

Goddamn, I loved it when she switches from hot to cold and vice versa. It shows me parts of her haven't changed at all. It makes me take a trip down memory lane.

"Stop trying to make things better. My father is never going to get over us being together if he finds out we're sneaking around. Why can't we go to him and tell him we fell in love? The heart is going to love who it wants. I love the choice mine made for me, and so do you. He's my father, surely once he sees us together, he'll understand."

She lifts my head from where I'd just dipped down to take one of her nipples in my mouth through her shirt, hoping she'd stop the rant she'd been going on about for the last ten minutes. Face as red as her hair, eyes shooting daggers. Now she's shoving me away, ready to argue more.

Swear to God; this touchy subject is the only time we fight. She doesn't know the real reason why we can't sit in front of Lorenzo and tell him about us, why I can't take her out on a date and show her off. Why we can't be an ordinary couple, but I sure did, and even though I love her, and would fight my way back to her no matter where I was. Many people will suffer because I couldn't stay away.

"I'll never stop trying to calm you down. If I have to play dirty by getting up close and personal with your nipples, then so be it. I'll do anything to make sure you are happy. What we have is permanent between us, Sienna, as in forever. We'll find a way, I promise."

Regret and lies. I'd have found a way to be with her no matter what I would have had to do.

"Cold?" I swallow my groan as I flick my gaze at her

nipples and right back to her striking face. It gets me an eye roll and the crossing of her arms. Which I fully take advantage of by eyeing her cleavage.

My dick screams to slide between those tits.

"You're an asshole. My son is missing, and you have sex on your mind. Unbelievable yet typical." A sad expression dances across her face.

My lungs clamp, insides yelling for me to shut the fuck up and give her some room when she glances at her phone. She's done that half a dozen times in the few minutes I've been here.

She's hoping her son will call. It makes me loathe Joseph all the more for hurting her and, no doubt, their son too.

Dirty rotten bastard, and here I am, acting like one. I can't seem to help it when it comes to Sienna Ricci. To me, that's who she'll always be. Not Sienna Bennett. Joseph doesn't deserve the honor to have a woman as beautiful on the inside as she is on the out to carry his last name.

The thing is, she isn't letting that beauty on the inside out, it's concealed underneath years' worth of scars and pain.

My regret decides to lay a blow to my chest. The way I hurt her, striking me upside my temple.

My fault.

"That's not all I have on my mind, Sienna. Not when it comes to you. I want all of you. I want you safe and secure in my arms, right where you belong. I want to talk to you for hours. I want to get to know your son through you and take our time getting to know one another again. I want to take you on a proper date. Anywhere you want to go," I whisper. That is all the God's honest truth, whether she believes it or not.

I've sat around with my thumbs shoved up my ass long enough, biding my time while she settled in as best as a woman with a missing child can. She needs to know I mean what I say and that I have the upper hand when it comes to her protection as well. If I didn't, the men sitting in cars in the parking lot, and the sniper on the roof of the building across the street wouldn't be there. They are the best. Give zero fucks who they kill. Her father permitted me to handle covering her safety. I've left no stone unturned.

"Now, sit down and hear me out, Sienna."

We have unfinished business as well as new, and she will listen to me. I know Sienna. For some goddamn reason, she wants to protect me. It's the caring blood in her veins. The blood her husband likely tried to drain until there was nothing left. If she needs a transfusion, I'm the man who matches. I know that with every aching bone in my body. What I don't understand is why she feels that need when it comes to me. If she thinks I'm afraid of Joseph, then she needs a reminder of who I am.

"You lying piece of shit. I'm calling my father."

Shrugging, I challenge. "Go ahead. It'll be a waste of your time." I draw in her rose scent, sucking the intoxication into my lungs.

Goddamn. I missed that scent too.

She puffs out a breath before sitting, starts to pick up her phone only to place it back down and snatch what appears to be a picture frame before spinning away from me. Yeah, that will stop quickly. The only time she'll turn her back on me again is when I'm holding her while she sleeps.

It's been years since I set eyes on this beauty, I've seen her from afar since she's been here. It didn't do a thing for my craving. Seeing her close doesn't either, only touching, tasting, and getting that spark of life back into her will.

"I'll give you a few minutes to collect yourself. After, you will turn around and face me."

"Fuck you, Lane."

"I'm quite capable of fucking you, La Mia Vita. You have no idea how much I want that right now. How many nights I've pictured sitting you on top of this desk, spreading you wide and feasting before I bend you over it and bring you more pleasure than that animal you married ever did." My body pulsates with an abundance of lust mixed with anger.

The thought of him touching her has always felt like liquid nitrogen running through my veins.

Now that he's taken her son, I want to smother him with the coolant and freeze him to death. Guarantee he's stolen more from Sienna than her son. Guarantee that photo she's clinging to is a picture of Luca too. The boy I've avoided looking at in Lorenzo's home over the years like the plague.

Because he isn't mine, he's the son of an undeserving psychopath.

Death is too good for Joseph. He needs to be bent over permanently, hands shackled to his ankles, and become someone's bitch.

"You can trust me, Sienna. You have every right not to believe it, but you can. I'm here to help you."

When I heard about her son, I wanted to go to her, but I had to ground myself. Once I did, I bought the home she shares with her father. She doesn't have a clue I own it.

I wanted Sienna here once she'd been convinced staying in New York wasn't going to bring her son back. I wanted her close to me so my brothers and I could keep an eye on her while Gabe went on his hunt to find Joseph. Not to mention, Lorenzo would have peace of mind that her security was meted out by someone he trusted.

Loyalty and trust are everything in the mafia, and Lorenzo thought he had it with Joseph. Who's to say anyone else on his payroll wasn't part of the plan. So far, everyone is in the clear. If I find out otherwise, they will die. Plain and simple.

Guilt licks up my spine. I might have betrayed Lorenzo years ago. I'll ask forgiveness and pay the price when the time comes, but I'd never take a child away from their mother.

It's an unforgiving sin.

It kills me, seeing her twisted up with worry. Every night I lay in bed and wonder if she's sleeping, crying, is she eating, losing her mind.

"I won't let you go through this alone, no matter how hard you try to push me away."

"You want to fuck me, Lane. That's all you want from me."

She thinks I want sex, she's right. There's no better woman than *her* for me to sink my nearly eight-year abstinent cock inside of. Shit, I can almost feel her tightening around me. Can picture her back bowing, her neck angling, and her lips parting.

I'm hard as granite thinking about it. But she'll come to me when ready. That's the only way I'll have her sexually again.

She whirls on me and, we stare at one another, the tracking of her eyes over my face tells me she's searching to see if I'm lying about owning this place.

I'm not. It's mine.

My older brother Logan designed it.

Dim lighting with exposed brick on the inside, white

starch linens, and some of the best steak this side of the Mississippi. Scenic euphoria from dining on the rooftop, which offers a skyline view right in the heart of Houston's busiest district.

It's something I wanted to leave for Lexi to have as her own. My daughter is not only into swimming and anything else she can get me to agree to, but she's also into cooking and baking. Lexi took that up with Ellie. At seven years old, my little girl has the mind of a twenty-year-old. I swear she does. For now, this restaurant's in the hands of an incredible woman. Regardless of what spits out of her mouth, it's hers to do as she pleases.

I take a seat in the plush green chair across from her desk. I had my sister-in-law, Ellie, decorate this office in green and white with hints of pink. Green to match the lightest shade of the color I've ever seen—Sienna's eyes. White for the color of her snowy skin. Pink because when she's turned on, her skin flushes, it made my cock weep every time I ran my fingers across her throat to her ears.

Beautiful.

"I don't want anything from you, just your help. Tell me, is this the ever-changed Lane Mitchell's way of making himself feel better for being lower than low by making promises to me he knew he would never keep? Either way, I quit. I'll have my bags packed and move back to New Orleans. I'll leave all of you behind. Especially the loyalty my father seemed to have forgotten when it comes to me."

We will see about that.

"You're safer here than anywhere you go. And..." I pause, pushing back up to lean into her space again. Fuck, I'm slipping. I want to kiss her so damn bad. She has the poutiest plump lips I've ever seen. "Your father raised you to know loyalty doesn't always mean blood."

She flinches as if I'd slapped her. I study her for a moment. There's something about that word loyalty that bothers her, and it doesn't have a thing to do with her Father.

Why?

I decide to change the subject. To remind that no matter how scared she might be, she's thinking with her head.

"It pleased me to know you heard me as I came down the hall. Why didn't you pull the trigger if you hate me so much?" Having a gun stashed speaks volumes to me. I'm a sneaky bastard when I want to be, and I was.

Growing up the way Sienna did, she'd been trained to watch her back. She had a wicked backhand, and she could strike someone in the throat with her elbow before they saw it coming. Her father taught her that. It is the quickest way to drop a man if given the opportunity.

That was one of the first things Lorenzo and Gabe taught my brothers and me when we were initiated as associates into the mafia. How to kill someone with your bare hands. Also, always have your eyes trained in every direction, keep your guard up, ears perked, and watch people around you. Trust very few.

"Please, you? I'm not here to please you, Lane. Do you want me to shoot you? I'll pull it out and shoot you in the mouth so you'll shut up."

And there went my cock, twitching to be freed. At least she still has that sassy mouth.

My gaze trails down Sienna's neck, where I'm hypnotized as I watch her skin change to a light shade of pink right in front of my eyes. I can't help it; my lips kick up into a half-smile.

I'd love to ask if being this close to me is turning her on. I want to know if she's wet. Is she thinking about lying spread eagle on this desk waiting, begging, and getting angry while she waits for me to make her scream.

I won't. I'm here to gain trust, to make demands she'll follow.

"The sooner you tell me what I want to know, the quicker you can get back to work. You aren't moving anywhere, Sienna. Understand that now."

She gasps, tears forming in her eyes.

I lift a hand to wipe them away when they fall, they never do. But she flinches, takes a few steps back, far enough to be out of my reach.

Fucking Joseph. He's terrorized her. He deserves to have his head severed and placed on the flaming gates of hell for all to see as they enter.

"I don't owe you a thing. My life is none of your business, Lane. You gave up that right when you screwed other women the same time you were screwing me. My son is missing because..." She takes a deep breath and shakes her head, stiffens her shoulders, and locks her jaw as she swallows her pain. Christ, there's so much more of it in her eyes than the day she caught me with two women. "No, I won't give in. You asked me not to play games; I don't want to play yours either, Lane."

"This isn't a game, Sienna. You were never one." If she were, I'd have won her years ago.

She's breaking. I hate myself all the more for it. But I need to know what I'm dealing with when it comes to helping her the only way I can. If it weren't for Lexi, I'd be with Gabe right now. Instead, when we heard about the kidnapping, my younger brother Seth took off in the middle of the night to meet up with Gabe.

"That was before." She pauses, tilts her head, leaving me to connect the dots. I can't when I don't know what's going on, and my patience is thinning by the second. When I asked why Joseph would do this, Gabe said no one knew. Not even Sienna. That's a damn lie.

"I'm not that girl you used. You don't control me, not anymore."

I never used her. That subject is for another day. Right now, I want to dig the truth out of her so I can help her escape the confines of her mind. Parts of Sienna are hiding in there. Parts I heard in her angered tone that want out. She's holding things in. No one knows better than me how those things eat away at you until there's nothing left.

"Did you let Joseph control you? Did he hit you?"

"No, I loved him, and he loved me."

That was a purposeful stab to my chest. It's also a goddamn lie, as well as a subtle way of telling me to fuck off.

I don't bother to bite back my smirk even though I'm raging inside. I'm going to get her to tell me why Joseph would be stupid enough to kidnap Lorenzo's grandson, attempt to kill his daughter, and think he can get away with it.

Every time I think about what Joseph is putting Sienna through, I want in on the settling of serving revenge bloody and cold. I hope whoever finds him cuts out his heart.

"I will push until you break. What does Joseph have on you, Sienna? It must be something you'd risk living in hell for not to tell your father your husband abused you."

I will beat Joseph until the flesh falls off his body.

"Fine, I'll tell you if it makes you go away. It's my fault Luca is missing. He didn't want to follow in Joseph's footsteps. My father wasn't happy about it at first. He grew to accept it; Joseph did not."

That's what I thought, but there's more.

"You stayed with Joseph to protect your son, Sienna,

that's a mother's love. Not fault." That's a saint—a woman who puts her child first.

Her hands shake profusely. Tears well in her eyes again, and fear builds across her face as she holds the picture up in front of me. I want to close my eyes, but nothing could tear them away from the boy staring back at me.

Luca's hair is as dark as mine, eyes the same color as Sienna's, and a smile that reminds me of Lexi. Every feature a mixture of Sienna and me.

Air juts out of my nose. My breath catching in the bubble of anger lodged in my throat. I grip the back of my head with both hands, and I squeeze.

Turmoil and pain slam me in my chest. I can feel it course right through me, hitting every extremity in my body.

"The fuck? No. Tell me it's not true. Tell me you did not keep me from my son." A growl burst that bubble, rage tightening my windpipe. I need to get out of here before I shake the ever-loving hell out of her.

The tables have turned, and I had no idea. Not one clue had dropped in all these years that Luca was mine.

"I'm sorry, I had to. I stayed with Joseph to protect our son, Lane."

Ours.

My regret sits itself smugly on my chest—guilt sloshing around like gasoline in my guts. I had a lot to repent for, sins up the ass, but this, I can't make heads or tails of it.

"You're sorry. You deny me years of being able to know my son, miss all of his firsts, and all you have is your sorry. Luca is mine to protect—the same as you were. You took choices away from me for what, revenge? Is that why? Fuck you, Sienna. You can go to hell. Does your father know?

Gabe?" There's not a chance they do. I'll unhinge if they've kept this from me.

How could they not see me in him? How the fuck can this even be? I have a son. Luca is mine.

"No. Joseph said he'd kill Luca if I told anyone. You don't understand what it was like for me. You'll never understand." Her lips tremble, eyes going wide and clouding over with the hell she's gone through as we stare at one another.

My pain rotates in my stomach, a spinning wheel with emotions I can't quite grasp due to a shit ton of anger threatening to swallow me whole, and my face burns with the hot blood rushing through my veins.

Murder. I will commit it in a hundred ways.

"I'm going to kill him. Joseph is a dead fucking man." My voice thrashes out hoarse, no doubt strangled by the stiffness in my neck and the firm clench of my jaw.

Blood is all I see. Joseph's bright red blood dripping off my fingers as I cut out his soul.

"You wanted me to stay away, Sienna. You got it. Unfucking-believable." He may have put her through hell on earth. I would have brought her to heaven while protecting our child.

I grab the photo and bolt, slamming the door behind me.

There's only one person who can calm the rage flowing through me like a river gone wild.

My daughter, with the most angelic smile. My daughter, who doesn't like it when I swear. My daughter, who wants to be a mermaid. My princess.

I need her sweetness to control the beast in me.

CHAPTER THREE

SIENNA

If I'd stopped to dwell even a fraction of a second today, I would have found myself rocking in a corner somewhere, letting the tears that threaten to fall streak down my face. I don't know why I hold them in. It's a riddle I can't figure out. It's like my glands are storing them in a large reservoir, waiting for my insides to collapse before they flood me out.

A burst to open up my wounds and kill me.

I haven't had a good cry in months. It does not make me feel any better. It adds to what's mincing me up inside. One of these days it's going to, and I'm going to drown in a flash flood of despair and grief.

Instead, I kept busy doing jobs at the restaurant that weren't mine. I wiped down tables to try to wipe away the shame that lives inside me. I scrubbed toilets on my hands and knees, trying to scour the filth from my soul.

I came home early and made dinner for my father like I do every night when I'm not working. I tried watching television, flipping through channels in search of something to make me laugh. I even tried taking a long relaxing bath. I've done everything to keep my mind off Lane and what's coming now that he knows the truth.

I've never felt so bad about hurting a person in my life, except Luca. And there's so much more for Lane to find out.

His reaction left me in an abrupt upheave. Raw and achy with a need to go to him. That wasn't the way I wanted him to learn the truth, but he kept pushing. I knew it would come out sooner rather than later.

If only I could turn back time to the day I found out I was pregnant. But time won't stop in this cruel world. It's the one thing that keeps on.

It can deteriorate you as slow or as fast as it wants when you've made the biggest mistake of your life.

Right now, I can't think about how I want to run to Lane and give him the full explanation as to why I didn't tell him. Not when I'm attached to the wall outside my father's office as if I've been nailed to it when I need to be a woman with guts to stand and put one foot in front of the other to face him.

You'd think I'd have the courage to do so when every day for years, that's all I did was wake and put my feet to the floor, give myself an inner pep talk, place on my mask, and put one foot in front of the other.

God, why didn't I grab my son and run to my father? Now my child is paying for my sins when he shouldn't be.

My father is going to come unglued along with a heap of disappointment and hurt in me. Then there's the wrath he will rein down on Lane. It's wrapping around my neck like a noose. All it will take is a little yank, and I'll choke.

I have to believe the love my father has for me is much stronger than his hate toward disloyalty. If not, I don't know what will happen. The thought of it makes me want to hunch over and heave.

My knees tremble until they can no longer support my weight. I grip the edge of the door to stop myself from slumping to the floor.

Maybe I should go back to my room. It's been a long, trying day, and facing Lane has taken enough out of me. Beaten what little fight I had left.

No. I have to do this. I have to prove I'm not as helpless as Joseph made me feel. I have to protect Lane any and every way I can.

Joseph's cold and heartless words of killing Luca echo in my ears. He said Luca would die if I ever told anyone he wasn't his son. The way he used to describe in horrifying detail of how he'd snap my boy's neck or blow his brains all over the wall while making me watch squeezes pain through my ribcage, pressing those toxic words into my heart. He has to know that after all this time I'd tell the truth.

I can't help but wonder if Luca will come back to me hurt in a way he'll never recover from over Joseph knowing I'd finally speak the truth.

It's in moments like this, and today with Lane, I am least proud of the woman I turned out to be. A woman who betrayed so many people instead of trusting them. I didn't think I could survive any other way, and that shames me to admit that I let Joseph put this fear inside me that doesn't seem to fade away. It's a blood-sucking parasite.

I never wanted life to turn out this way. I never wanted to hurt anyone. I just tried to exist while protecting the greatest gift Lane Mitchell could ever give me.

God, help me before I go insane. My son is alive. I'll get through this with my father, and then I'll deal with Lane.

Hope, hold on to it, Sienna.

"Can I come in?" Not waiting for my father to answer, I enter his office, gripping my phone tightly in my hand as if it will give me strength, and take a seat on the couch, ignoring the wall of monitors that cover every square inch of this place. Even my bedroom and bathroom are under constant surveillance. The only time I have privacy is when I'm in the shower. In a way, I feel like I'm back in New York living in an asylum.

I understand, but I despise it. I want to roam *free* in every meaning of the word. I'll always have someone watching out for me, and honestly, I don't even know they are there. I want to be free to live, love, laugh. To not wonder if Joseph is lurking in the shadows waiting to slit throats to get to me.

Without acknowledging me, my father rolls the tips of his fingers over his temples. He'd been doing that during dinner too. I asked him if everything was okay, and he answered by asking me to bring him some pain reliever for his headache.

Is he becoming ill or has something happened and he doesn't want to tell me? Don't let it be either. A possible stress headache I can handle. Anything else I can't.

"Does your head hurting have anything to do with whatever you're keeping from me?" I ask, a headache of my own brewing in my skull as my thoughts crash against it.

I suck down the lump of panic in my throat when he lifts his head, and I take a good look at him. His natural olive tan skin is as white as mine. One wouldn't think I was his blood daughter by our complexion difference. His skin color is naturally tan, where mine is as light as can be. His hair used to be dark brown. Now it's peppered with gray. Just one look at our eyes, and you know I'm Lorenzo Ricci's daughter. Everything else about me comes from my mother, right down to the color of our hair.

"You're pale. Did you take your blood pressure medicine?" I do my best to read him. He looks like he's going to vomit at any time. My father isn't the type to wear his worrisome emotions on his sleeve. Not even in front of me.

Since Luca's disappearance, I've seen them more times than I care to count. It has my guilt licking a hot shameful trail up my legs.

Green eyes study me, a mask of worry swirling in the age lines on his face.

"I did. It's after midnight. You should be in bed, Sienna." I hate it when he speaks to me as if I were a child. He's not going to get away with it this time. He will leave me in the dark when it comes to my son.

"As should you. What are you keeping from me? Please, if you've heard anything, tell me." My tone leaves no room for negotiation.

Stress lines slat across his forehead as he tilts his head slightly. They've grown deeper since Luca went missing. Before, I never thought my father to look like he was approaching sixty. Every time I walk into the house, he appears to be older with bags under his eyes and blame resting on his shoulders. Luca's disappearance isn't good for his high blood pressure. Here I am about to add to it.

Seeing him this way takes a little more out of me.

My father is guilty of a lot of things. Murder, weapons trafficking, illegal gambling, law and government corruption. An endless list of unlawful activities, but not this. The weighed down blame sits on my shoulders.

It's long past time to be honest with my father. He should hear it from me and not Lane. I know he'll confess, and it worries me that my father will lift the blame and place it on Lane.

I won't allow that to happen. It's the only way I can

make a scratch into denying Lane nearly the first ten years of Luca's life.

If my father is going to punish anyone, it will be me.

"Sienna, I promised to tell you of accuracies, not falsities. Every time we hear something, you get your hopes up. I won't subject you to that anymore." I don't like how those words come out of his mouth. He's lying right to my face.

I have nothing if I don't have hope. I'm not about to share that with him. Men like my father would never admit they believe in it. The mafia uses the word out of context, not taking into consideration what the word means. I think that's one of the reasons why my mother brought up hope. She had to have had it to keep her strength at his side.

"That's not your choice to make." Anger intensifies the emotion in his words.

"It is my choice. I make the decisions. I have the final say. I rule this family, now go to bed." His voice is firm and demanding. I don't like it when he throws his control at me. Yet, I know what battles I'm going to win with him and what ones will be like talking to a wall, and this is a wall made out of solid brick.

I don't care. I'm not giving up.

"No. I'm not a child. I can come and go, stay up as late as I please. You rule a kingdom, not me. Luca is your grandson, but he's my son. If you know something, then you tell me. You don't have the right to keep anything from me when it comes to him," I say with frustration, doing my best not to beg.

"And you are my daughter, my Bell' Angelo. I'm the man who is supposed to shield you from any harm until the day I'm unable to any longer, the same as I should have your mother. That should have been my top priority in life. Instead, I put her, you, my grandson in jeopardy. I put the world I was born into before my family. Look where that got me. My only child didn't trust me enough to tell me her husband did things to her that no woman should go through. You married into this world, flew miles away to where I couldn't see what was happening when I should have seen a man like Joseph a mile away. So, yes, this rests on my shoulders. Christ, your mother must be rolling in her grave." He clenches his fists, his frustration leaking through his clipped words.

"It was my choice to marry Joseph." He wouldn't have stopped me, no matter what. I knew Joseph was being sent to New York. He was my escape from Lane.

"I gave him my blessing to marry you. I put trust in him to take care of you. I trusted you to tell me if he didn't. Somewhere I failed."

His face goes hard; I'd injured my father. I've known this all along. This is the first time he's brought up how much, and I'm about to do it again.

It has my heart rumbling like it's going to pound right out of my chest as I witness a slew of remorse gather at the corners of his eyes.

He swallows and drags his palms down his face.

Memories of my past gather in my mind. My hands trembling as I squeeze my free hand to stop myself from scratching my skin as the unthinkable things Joseph did to me crawl across me like dirty little fire ants that grip and sting.

"I do trust you. I always have. You didn't fail me, yourself, or anyone. You are a good father. Please don't ever let me hear you blame yourself again for the actions of others. Joseph is to blame for kidnapping Luca. No one forced his hand. I had to do what I had to do. Please tell me what you know."

Even Luca not being Joseph's is no excuse for the man doing what he did. Luca is a child. He is innocent in the mess I made.

I didn't know I was pregnant when we married. If I did, I'd like to think I wouldn't have married the monster I never knew him to be. Then again, who knows what I would have done to get away from Lane at the time.

I was a stupid, naive girl with foolish dreams that ended up running straight into a nightmare that never ends.

A vicious loop.

I could go on for hours about how unfair life is, how we are born into cruelty—delivering it onto those that we deem deserve it. Our lives are what they are. We are criminals. It was me who chose to continue to live a lifestyle my father promised wouldn't touch Luca if taking over wasn't something he didn't want to do. My boy wanted nothing to do with it. He's into numbers. A math genius like Lane. I love that he's like his dad in so many ways. Ways that will unleash those tears and shove me farther into darkness if I think too long about them.

Maybe that's what I need is to let loose and cry.

"I hate myself for being weak and timid more than ever over the choice I made, Father. It has affected our boy." My father, at times, can be harsh like he is right now. He never was with Luca. He adores that kid.

"I'm proud of you for putting Luca above yourself. It still doesn't make it easy for me." He stares at me a moment, the veins in his temples protruding. I can see his pulse beating in them from here. A sure sign he knows something, and I could scream until I'm blue in the face, and he won't tell me. I have to trust that if anyone catches a lead that they believe to be true, he will.

My stomach roils with guilt as I watch the breaking of

his heart all over again. It's a horror show that comes to life. It has to end with the people I love staying alive. If I die, then so be it, but not my father, my son, or anyone else.

"I love you, Father. I would think you're heartless if you didn't worry about me." My voice breaks, but I do my best to swallow down my grief and not add to his level of stress by arguing anymore.

"I love you too, Sienna. There isn't anything I wouldn't do for you, for Luca, for those I love. I want my girl happy; I want our boy safe and happy too. I want him to grow up to be a good man. It saddens me, knowing the two of you weren't happy. I want to know something, was Luca born prematurely because Joseph beat you?"

I blink. The question is coming directly at me out of left field. Unexpected. It has my heart struggling to beat as if Joseph has his fist around it again, squeezing tight enough to cut off the air supply to my brain.

Joseph and I told everyone Luca was born two months early. It was the only way to keep the truth hidden. There was a point in my pregnancy where I thought I was going into labor after Joseph wrapped his hands around my neck, squeezing while I gasped and choked until I passed out. I woke with the worst cramps. They had me doubled over with fear strumming through my veins. I wanted to call my doctor, but Joseph wouldn't let me. He worked from home for days after that to make sure I didn't disobey. I never told a soul about that. I never will.

"No, that's not why. I'm not the angel you think I am, Father. I've done a horrible thing. Something you don't know. It's unforgivable. It's the reason I stayed with Joseph, the reason he took Luca, it's the reason for everything."

Father's eyes glass over with a myriad of mixed

emotions. As soon as he learns the truth, anger will take over enough to shoot his blood pressure through the roof.

A sudden flash of nervousness tumbles in my stomach. I want my father to think of me as he always has. I'll never forgive myself if he didn't look at me again the way he is now with so much proudness and respect despite what I just said. But I'm going to stand up and do the right thing for once in my life, no matter how much it pains me to say it and him to hear.

"None of us are perfect, Sienna. Although, in my eyes, you come close. Whatever it is you've done would never be a good enough reason for a man to force himself on his wife or to up and decide he has the right to run off with their child."

No, it's not, especially to a man like Lorenzo Ricci. The only thing my father is against is harming women and children. He's worked years to take down as many of the cartels, gangs, and smaller branches of the mafia who traffic children and women in the US and Mexico down. I've overheard him telling Joseph how he and his good friend Roan Diamond who runs an Empire in New York, has beaten a few of his soldiers to a pulp when they've found out they abused their wives.

Him being friends with Roan Diamond. The boss of The Diamond Empire is how I met Victoria. Her father, Aidan, works for Roan. If it weren't for who they are, Joseph would have forbidden me to remain friends with her. He's beaten me plenty for not having the upper hand when it came to Victoria. I took it to save her from the vile things he said he'd do to her.

Aidan happens to be one of the many people searching for my son. I'm so thankful and undeserving that no one I care about has turned their back on me for not speaking up when I should have. I'll never stand tall again if something happens to any of the men out in the world digging through danger.

"My past is ugly. There are things Joseph did; I don't think anyone could pry out of me no matter how much torture they were to conflict. I chose to stay with him, not as much out of fear for me as for Luca. Now he's taken him, and we are all suffering the consequences. My son and..." I pause, wanting to finish with my son and Lane especially. The words launch my heart into my throat, blocking off my ability to speak.

My body jolts forward as if it had been sitting idle for years, and I bury my face in my hands. I shake my head, not quite having the courage to release the secret out of my mouth.

The room spins, and a sour taste sits on my tongue. A jagged little pill, you know you have to spit out, but you wish with all you had you could swallow it down.

"What are you not telling me, Sienna?" He's becoming furious. I've not once in my life been afraid of my father. He's feared by many, respected by more, to me he's my father—the man I admire. The man whose bark has always been much worse than his bite when it comes to me. The man who taught me so much, and I need to remind myself of the woman he taught me to be.

To have strength. I wouldn't have survived the torture I went through, no matter how much I love my son, if it weren't for that word sticking in my head with every punch Joseph delivered.

How can I take brutal beatings to my body and not tell him what he deserves to hear?

"What she's afraid to say is Luca is my son, not Joseph's. Sienna didn't make the wrong choice. She made the only one she could to look after our son. I made the wrong choice years ago when she found out about the club. The blame is on me."

Inhaling a sharp breath, I look to my right at Lane, paused in the doorway, his jaw set tight. Eyes determined. His clothes are wrinkled. The man anchored down with so much remorse it's crushing to witness. All I want to do is run and fold myself into the safety of his arms.

If this situation weren't life-threatening, I'd laugh that Lane snuck in without either of us hearing him.

My heart races as my father stands, his chair crashing to the floor as he glares at Lane.

"Is this true, Sienna?" he demands an answer in an angry tenor that has me hearing that disappointment.

My lips quiver as I flick my gaze to my father. Hard lines form on his face, nostrils flaring as betrayal etches across his every feature.

"Yes. Before you go off, please know Lane didn't find out until this morning." I want to tell my father this is my cross to bear. Then I want to turn around and yell at Lane for undoubtedly knowing me well enough to show up to defend me. He knew I'd tell my father and try to talk him out of punishing him for being disloyal.

"For fuck's sake, Sienna, do not try to protect me. Let me take responsibility for once. You owe me that much."

I hear Lane, but my gaze remains fixated on my father.

"I'm sorry. I'm sorry you both found out the way you did. I'm sorry I was a coward. I'm sorry, my son is where I can't protect him. I'm so sorry." My voice cracks. The words are barely out of my mouth before a wail shrieks out of me. Each heart-wrenching scream takes another piece of my soul.

God, I want to cry. Please let me.

"Sienna, stop it now. You are my brave girl. I would be lying if I said I wasn't let down by you. It hurts me more to think that the son of a bitch took his hands to you. You lied to me multiple times. I forgive you, but you will stand down when it comes to Lane. He went against an order. I will handle him the way I want to. Do I make myself clear?" My father squats in front of me, stroking my hair, and gently places his hands on my cheeks, forcing me to look at him. My father's hands used to be warm and gentle. Now they feel as icy as his words.

"No, I won't stand down. If Lane betrayed you, then so did I. Whatever you do to him should be done to me."

I don't know what he'll do to Lane. He won't let him off with just a tongue lashing. That's not how the code works. He'll have Matteo hurt him.

"Leave us, Sienna. You are my child, but you are not in control here."

"Stop talking to me like I am a child then. You do it all the time, and it's maddening. You will not harm a hair on Lane. He's a good man, a good dad. It was you who told me that. He didn't take things from me as Joseph did. He's Luca's father. I will not have my son come back to me and have to tell him I kept this from him and then turn around and tell him you are not the man he thinks you are."

Luca might know what my father does, but he thinks the world of him. I won't taint nor keep anything from my son more than I already have. I want my boy's forgiveness, not his hatred.

My stomach clenches when I peer back at Lane. His eyes are boring into mine. The man is begging me to shut my mouth. To leave this be and let him take what he has coming.

He doesn't have anything coming to him as far as I'm

concerned. He broke my heart, but he gave me the greatest gift I could ever ask for, and I kept it from him.

The wrong is on me.

My father takes hold of my shoulders and starts to shake me. I flinch and retract from his touch, sliding down to the opposite end of the couch, fear swelling harshly inside me. All I can picture is how Joseph would shake me until my brain rattled. I squeeze my eyes shut as I remember Joseph's raised fists. The memories hit me fresh and deep.

I shake worse than dried leaves in a windstorm on trees, holding on to the last bit of life before they fall to the ground.

"Jesus, sweetheart, I'm sorry. I would never hurt you. I cannot let a man betray me and get away with it no matter who he is to me. You will not interject, Sienna. It isn't your call. Lane, I want you to leave us. I will deal with you as soon as I sort out Sienna."

By taking this out on Lane, he is hurting me. Why can't he see that? God, I hate this life as much as I hate violence.

Father stands, holding his palms out in front of him, looking at them in disgust before moving back to his desk, pressing his palms to it, and lowering his head.

I remind myself who this man is. He would have someone cut off his hands before he would ever hurt me with them. If he carries this through with Lane, he will hurt me much worse than any physical blow I've taken.

I push up to stand, my legs wobbling as I ready to go to battle with him. "You sat me down with Lane and his brothers too. I'm not going to allow you to treat me special because I'm your flesh and blood." I start to say more when Lane cuts me off.

"Blood or not, Sienna doesn't deserve punishment, she's been through enough. I'm not going anywhere. I will pay for my crime against you. Then I'm taking back what's mine. I've called a meeting between you, me, my brothers, and Gabe. They should be here within the hour. In the meantime, I'm warning you once, Lorenzo. Daughter or not, if you ever put your hands on Sienna again with anger behind it, anger that you should direct at me, I will cut them off."

CHAPTER FOUR

Lane

Regret and remorse. Shame and blame. Those words make up a second chance at love. After all, people who get that chance wouldn't have it if those feelings didn't play a part in their breakup to begin with. They place themselves in the middle of Sienna and me. Continuing to spin in agony until we decide to stop them. For now, their dust and debris fly all over the place.

A dark and dreary cloud.

I want to throw them against the wall and smash them to smithereens.

Our love story deserves a fresh start to build on the love we still have for one another, just waiting for us to snatch it out of thin air when the time is right. We aren't instant-love. We are a forever one. A painful love that will grow, but there's a general in my way at the moment. One who thinks he needs to make me an example, if only to hold on to his pride for disobeying an order.

It's a crock of bullshit that's starting to smell like desperation. We all have it. Only Lorenzo's is worse.

For the past half hour or so, he's gone off with a piss poor excuse about holding onto his leadership if he lets me off. He isn't fooling anyone in this room. Most of his soldiers weren't even here at the time we were told Sienna was forbidden. And who gives a rat's ass if they were. A child is missing. That should be the end of it.

Sienna is thirty-years-old. A grown woman going through hell. Lorenzo's attitude toward me is only throwing her farther into the fire.

I won't stand for it.

"It's my God-given right to get to know my son, damn it. Unless you plan on having my brothers carry me out of here in a body bag, I think I've paid the price by missing years of Luca's life." I grit my teeth. Already felt the knives in my heart from Sienna keeping Luca from me, now I sit here waiting on Lorenzo to shit or get off the pot.

I care for Lorenzo, deeply, but he is wasting my time.

I told myself my decision to come here without letting anyone know the reason could leave a ripple effect across everyone I care about, like a stone skipping across water. Mostly, my daughter, if I was hurt. But I'd be a shit parent to her and Luca when the time comes to discuss the events leading up to this day if I didn't face what I'd done.

I left Sienna earlier and went straight home, relieved Lexi's babysitter, then stared at my son's photo as I called Seth. Without explaining, I said I needed him and Gabe to meet me here as soon as possible. Then I called Logan, ignoring his infuriating ass when he asked what was going on. Then my girl and I spent the day at the park near our house. I watched her play with the neighbors, took a walk with her, fed the ducks, and thought about nothing else except righting my wrongs toward Sienna, my son, along with the hundreds of ways I want to kill Joseph.

I'll gladly start with his fingers.

I blow out a straining breath, still trying to work through the fact that Sienna and I have a son. That missing boy is mine, and I'm lost and helpless. My heart is going through torture as if someone were driving nails right through my chest. It's an indescribable pain.

If I thought I was hurting for Sienna and Luca before, I'm burning in hell now. For many reasons.

"I'll decide your fate. I should have Matteo pull the trigger and blow your head off. You took many oaths when I allowed you to become an associate of my organization. Do you not recall what happens to men when they are disloyal to me? Let me remind you, death happens," Lorenzo shouts, veins protruding at the side of his neck. He keeps on, it won't be long before he goes into cardiac arrest.

That is not something I want to happen.

Coming from someone else, I'd have already pummeled them into the ground. But this is a man I care about regardless of him treating me like the enemy in this heartbreaking situation.

He's taking Joseph's disloyalty out on me. I can take it if it makes him feel better. It's Sienna's reaction to his behavior that concerns me.

"So you keep saying." I'm not going to hide being pissed off and agitated from him anymore. Screw that shit.

Lorenzo stiffens, while the bastard holding the gun to my head growls in my ear, becoming a little more irritated.

"You watch how you talk to me, boy." Lorenzo's response flicks a lighter under my ass. If the flame touches me, it'll be his fault if I knock some sense into him.

I clear my throat, wanting to tell him he's in no position to tell me what to do, let alone calling me a boy. I'm a man standing up for what's mine. The problem with doing so,

I'm wound up about having a gun that Lorenzo isn't planning on giving the order to use sitting at my temple, especially by a man who wouldn't blink an eye at pulling the trigger if he were told.

Another problem. It would turn this room into a bloodbath if that were to happen. I can already feel my brothers heating up at my back. Surprised, they've allowed Matteo to hold the gun for this long. Gabe, too, for that matter.

"You know, for a man I once respected, I have to say I lost what I had the minute you brought your puppet in here and had him wrap his arm around my neck and put his gun to my head."

I wasn't sure what to expect. Maybe a little compassion since we're all wandering around in the same kind of hell.

I glance at Sienna. She is shaking as if she's spent hours in a snowstorm without proper clothes to keep her warm. Her father has her scared to death. I'm sure I'm not helping by arguing, but I'm not sitting here listening to Lorenzo treat me like I'm the one who committed a crime.

In a way, I don't blame him for his reaction. None of us would be here if it weren't for me. Still, this is wrong on many levels.

You'd have thought the remorse he felt at himself would have lasted more than five fucking minutes, after he grabbed hold of Sienna before he had his pet in here aiming a gun in my direction, snarling in my ear while Lorenzo tried to make things right with her. She wouldn't listen to him, and she has every right not to.

Violence is Sienna's trigger, and here he is, trying to prove a point. He's taken it too far. Up till now, I've remained calm. But a man can only take so much, and I'm past it. I need to take care of Sienna, then get back to Lexi.

Sienna won't look my way either, hasn't looked at

anyone. No, she's sat on the couch with her head aimed at the floor like some obedient servant. She's doing it out of living in fear. I feel it leaking out of her.

No woman should feel she can't look someone in the eye. No woman should be afraid of a man who took a vow to treat his wife with love and respect while making her obey in any other way than to please her. And no woman in Sienna's position as Luca's mother should have to be talked to like what she has to say doesn't matter.

Because it fucking does. She matters. Every woman matters.

The woman was so brave going into a battle with Lorenzo, trying to get him to back off me before Matteo walked in. She shouldn't have had to. She's his daughter, for fuck's sake. None of us in this room should be at war with one another.

We're family.

Yet, here we are, me with a gun to my head and him acting like a ruthless asshole.

I'm proud of her for standing up to Lorenzo, not many do. I was close to decking the man when he kept telling her to shut her mouth. I wanted to shove my fist down his throat. I didn't. One, I'd be dead right now. Two, he'd probably be along with me. Three, even with the way Lorenzo is treating Sienna, she loves him, and once he calms, he'll regret his wrong, and four, I won't take her voice away from her, as Joseph did. She has a right to speak her mind about anything.

I won't treat her like a fragile, broken doll either. That's not what she needs. I've yet to figure out what could help her heal, but I will. Even if I have to break my own damn heart, I will get her back to solid ground. She's closer than she thinks. With a little encouragement, and a whole lot of kissing, touching and fucking, she'll be right back to that feisty woman she used to be.

It all makes a man wonder how Joseph got away with treating her the way he did without anyone noticing. It makes me wonder about my son too. Did he witness Sienna being abused? Is he a mess over it? Was he abused?

I have questions coming out of my ass, and they are piling the longer we sit here.

Lorenzo shifts in his seat, pulse ticking at his jaw. "I don't give a fuck if you've lost respect or not, Lane. This is my kingdom. These are my rules. There are no exceptions, not even for you."

For fuck's sake, we all know the rules. It's why my brothers and Gabe have remained quiet. I respect them all the more for it. I know they are likely boiling with anger at Lorenzo and me. Their time will come to lay into my ass. I won't take it the same as I'm not taking it from Lorenzo. He doesn't scare me. What does, is the man holding the gun, and the thought his patience is wearing as thin as mine. If he decides to pull the trigger, where does that leave my daughter and Sienna? Where does that place my son's way of thinking when he returns? I'll never meet him, never get to know him, and that pisses me the fuck right off.

"Why the hell do you think I'm here? I know I'm not an exception. I told you I came here once I got Lexi settled with Ellie to take my punishment. You're the one who insisted on dragging this out by asking me to tell you what happened back then to cause me and Sienna to split." That was one of the hardest things to do. Stand here in front of my brothers and Gabe and tell them how I destroyed a woman they'd defend with their lives over some club. Rehashing old wounds in Sienna and me that are raw as hell.

"You have some balls coming in here the way you did making demands to me regarding my daughter. She isn't yours. She is my daughter. I listen to her yell in her sleep for Luca almost every night. I watch her walk around with her phone glued to her hand as I sit here, blaming myself when it's you to blame. You tell me what you would do if someone did what you did to Lexi?"

"I'd kill them," I answer without hesitation. There's no doubt about it. "You have a right to lay blame at my feet for what I did to Sienna, what you don't have the right to do, is call me disloyal. That right belongs to Sienna and no one else. I've brought in men to watch her every move. I gave her space to get back on her feet. I've done all I can do to help Sienna except searching for Luca. I'd give up my life right now if it meant it would take away her pain. One more thing, I own this house, in case you forgot. I bought it for you and Sienna. If I want to come here any damn time I want, say anything I want, then I will."

I can go on about how loyal I've been. I've killed for him to prove my loyalty. I've kept his name hidden when we owned the club, and I've risked going to prison by keeping his books. I can say my daughter's name to prove how loyal I am. I'd prefer not to throw that card on the table with Sienna present. There are things my brothers told me they told her over the years, but they didn't tell her I hadn't had sex since well before Lexi was born.

That's not something you go tossing around, but Lorenzo knows. So fuck him and loyalty.

A gasp coming from Sienna sucks the air from my lungs. I'm not sure if her reaction is from having no idea this house is in my name. Or me saying I'd die for her. It doesn't matter. A response out of her calms me a bit.

I blow out a breath when affection coming from those

eyes of hers stare back at me. After all this time, perhaps it bleeds from us both.

"Right. How could I forget you bought this house with whore money." Ouch. That remark dug its claws into me deep. He just cut me to my core on top of adding more tension to the room. Enough that I'm surprised the glass on the windows behind him isn't frosting from the death stare I've no doubt my brothers are giving him.

"Father, stop. You are unfair, and I won't sit here and listen to it anymore," Sienna says, defending me once again. I don't deserve it, never did. I'll be damned if I don't deserve her now, and I'm taking as good as I give.

Proud of you for opening your mouth, my eyes say to her.

Lorenzo ignores her like he's been doing since everyone got here. That heats my blood until I feel it boil—a sizzle popping at my heated flesh before it soaks in.

"That comment, along with the way you are treating Sienna, should break me away from this family quicker than flies on shit. Since you're judging me, you are the judge on whether I stay or go. Need I remind you of the things you do, Lorenzo? You are a criminal. No better a man than me."

He keeps rattling my cage, and our relationship will be unsalvageable. He'll be dead to me. That is the last thing any of us needs. Regardless of the degrading way he's throwing his weight around, I care about him. I know he cares for me. He might want to consider that before he tosses anything else in my face.

I take a deep breath, reminding myself Lorenzo is under as much stress as the rest of us. Quite possibly more. He's tired, worried, and yes, he has a right to be angry with me. He's going about it all wrong.

"I don't want mercy. I want respect as a man who would

give his life if it meant my son came home to his mother." My throat bobs with thick emotion. Don't think I'll swallow it until Luca is in her arms.

If I hadn't known Lorenzo most of my life, know right down to my bones he isn't going to have Matteo shoot me, I'd have already shit my pants or begged for mercy over having a gun pressed into the side of my head. Most men would.

I'm not most men.

I'm a pissed off; patience flew out the door the minute I stepped out of the restaurant man who wants to kill the monster who dared kidnap our son.

Ours. It still has my head spinning.

I knew Joseph was a piece of shit, guess I didn't understand how much until I found out I have a son.

That thought pisses me off all the more. Only who I'm angry at beside Joseph, I haven't a clue. It has me torn. Frustrated and until I get a grip, I'll never know.

Silence fills the room as Matteo presses the muzzle of his pistol into my temple a little further. Blood, fear, and annoyance rush through my ears enough to deafen me. This son of a bitch keeps it up, and he better sleep with one eye open. Sienna isn't the only one who can elbow someone in the throat. Mine would crush several parts before he hit the floor.

"We are wasting time finding my son by sitting here. Have him pull the goddamn trigger and get it over with or get the hell away from me. Know this, you shoot me in front of Sienna, and you'll pay the price far worse than the guilt running through my veins. I don't expect to go unpunished, but Sienna and my son, they've been through enough." I fight the quiver in my jaw when I think about what Sienna has been through, hell and back daily, I'm sure.

It makes me realize how much of an uncompassionate prick I was in her office. I owe her an apology.

I don't voice how Matteo has seconds to drop his weapon, or he'll be the one dropping. The only reason I haven't done it yet is Sienna doesn't need to see any more violence.

I learned long before Gabe and Lorenzo taught me how to defend myself after one sick and twisted asshole fuck buddy of my dead Mother's tried to rape me—bastard eyeballing me like a piece of candy at my dad's funeral. My brother Logan saw it. He tensed next to me. It's what made him become the protector he is. It's what made us protect Seth like there'd be no tomorrow.

I was a kid when the prick tried sneaking into my room. I heard him from a mile away. Smelled his sickness every time he came to pick our mother up. I busted him in the balls with a kick so hard it knocked him to the ground. It wasn't until that night I understood something my dad tried to teach me—the meaning of loyalty.

Regret and loyalty define a man my father told me the only time he caught me sneaking around. I snuck out of our house and climbed in the back of my dad's car. This curious kid who wanted to know why most weekend nights my mom and dad would take off after my brothers and I went to bed.

What I saw when I slipped into the building through a window in the basement wasn't what I expected.

I saw my father kissing another woman, his hands all over her ass, and like an angry kid, I ran straight at him, nailing him in the gut with my fist.

He was pissed.

Dad grabbed me by the back of my neck, dragged me into a room, and after spanking my ass, he sat me down and said, amongst other things, this one in particular I remember, "what goes on in our family stays behind the walls of our house. We don't ever talk about it to anyone else. That means you don't tell your brothers about this. Consider this your first lesson in loyalty. There will come a day when you'll understand what goes on in this club as well as what I mean about loyalty, Lane. Know though, no matter what, your mother and I love you and your brothers. We will always take care of you." Little did he know my mother tapped out on taking care of us.

I never told my brothers that was the first time I entered Behind Closed Doors. I never will.

Even though I loved my parents at the time, I hated them for being different. I hated that I grew up like them, and to this day, the only other time I've kept a secret from my brothers was about Sienna, but I've remained loyal to them. Faithful to the promise to Lexi. Loyal to Gabe as well as trustful to Lorenzo.

So, yeah, fuck him and his loyalty bullshit.

"Enough. Drop your gun and get out of here, Matteo. You'll keep your mouth shut about every word you heard in here or I'll carve out your spine and watch you wiggle like a worm," Gabe says with authority he holds over Matteo etching from his tone. I should have known he'd only take so much before he stepped in. Wished he wouldn't, yet the part of me that wants to get Sienna out of here is glad he did.

She and I need to get square with one another. I need to know for sure if she's stable or putting on an act.

Lorenzo nods, and I swear to God the room turns from chilled to stifling the minute he lowers his gun and walks away.

"Don't speak to our most trusted man like that, Gabriel," Lorenzo growls with unapologetic anger.

"Don't start with me, Lorenzo, you are my brother, my blood. I've stood here and listened to you long enough. These three men are family, they are my sons, whether my blood runs through their veins or not. I took them in when their parents died, and so did you. Lane might have gone against your wishes. In doing so, it brought us Luca. You want to make my son pay by throwing around power you don't need when you're with family; then you'll be a lonely man. Meaning, you'll lose the five people in this room who love you even with you being an over-stressed son of a bitch. I won't allow what Joseph has done to rip my family apart."

Lorenzo's eyes dart around the room until they land on mine. This time when I look deep, I catch his exhaustion along with that desperation I saw. He's hiding something.

Something that has his face twisted in in a tortured expression.

Whatever is going on, I best be included, or someone will catch my unrestrained rage.

"This puts me in between a rock and a hard place. You know this, all of you know this."

I want to ask him 'this is my problem because?' I don't. It's not my problem. I get this makes me look like Lorenzo is favoring me to his people even if they haven't a clue Lorenzo didn't know about Sienna and me. I'm the one who will look like a lowlife father who didn't give a shit. Not that I care what his people think. I don't run in their circle to give a fuck.

We're talking about his daughter, his grandson, and the power of a family bond. His soldiers can screw right off.

Instead of answering, I scratch at the scruff on my jaw,

fingers twitching to get Sienna some air. I start to stand when Gabe places a hand on my shoulder.

"Then I suggest you climb out from under the rock. You've sat in that very chair and told me how guilty you feel for putting the organization before anything else. In certain circumstances, you do, you should, and we understand. You won't on this. Sienna is a grown woman going through utter hell because of Joseph, not because of Lane. Take a look at what you've done."

I follow Lorenzo's gaze as he turns toward Sienna. His eyes close the second he does. Mine are wide open as I stare. Her skin is pasty, she's sweating, no longer shaking, but her eyes are void as if she's zoned herself out.

Shit.

"La Mia Vita, look at me." My chest stings like a bitch when she won't. I don't know if I should get up and touch her, soothe her, and tell her she doesn't have to worry about a damn thing when it comes to anyone hurting her again or sit here and wonder if she's going to flip the hell out.

Finally, after what feels like years, she looks over at me as if she senses my presence for the first time in the few hours I've been here. Her eyes searching mine and hold for a few moments before she slinks down to the floor and passes out.

CHAPTER FIVE

Sienna

I'm dreaming again. This dream is more of a night terror because it feels as if I might die from the ache in my brain. It feels like someone is poking me with tiny needles. So many pricks to remind me of who I am. A woman who has lost so much, yet trying to get by.

To continue living in a survival mode of a different kind.

I try gasping in a breath, but there is no air, and I choke on my dry tongue. The lack of oxygen surrounds my mind, and in a panic, I suck in another breath. It burns my lungs with a ferocity that terrorizes me.

"I am your worst nightmare, Sienna, because I know it isn't your pain you fear. You fear what I can do to Luca more than anything. You were once a strong woman. Now, because you are weak, pathetic, and pitiful, you fear I'll snatch Luca right before your very eyes, and you'll never know what kind of man I raise him to be. You're right about that. I will train him to kill anyone he deems a threat. He might not have my

blood, but he's mine. You are too. Fear it, sweetheart. If you ever try to leave me, you better wear the smell of it daily."

The never-ending tears blur my vision. "He will hate you." Tonight, for some reason unknown to me, I stand up for myself.

"Nah, baby. I won't treat him the way I do you."

Blood blends in with the tears as a fist slams into my nose.

"I didn't tell you to speak. Perhaps I should put a gun in Luca's hand and force him to kill you or die himself. Maybe I should kill Lane? Your father, or should I kill you myself? The list is endless for me. So many people my whore of a wife cares about. Except you never cared for me. Not like you do that bastard Lane. Burning you at the stake is what you need. A witch who trances then cast her wicked fucking spell. I loathe you."

Lane isn't a bastard. My husband is.

I try waking up, but I can't. I still feel the presence of Joseph's cold hands around my throat the night I left, his voice as he said those evil things, and so much more as he slammed me into the wall. His fingers were digging deeper around my throat. The sharp edges of his fingernails threatening to break through my skin, ready to pierce.

I hear my heavy breathing screaming for Luca if only to hold him again. To make promises this time that I'll be able to keep, but all I see is my shaky hands as I fumble with my car keys trying to get them in the ignition.

"Mom, are you okay?" Luca asks, his voice trembling, yet comforting knowing we were getting the hell away from Joseph once and for all.

I wanted to scream that I was more than okay, that I was going to make my son understand instead of scared out of his mind for what he saw. I just had to stop shaking. I had to pull myself together for my son.

Always for him.

"I will be, buckle up, sweetheart." Panic rides up my legs when, of course, I have to turn around to make sure Joseph isn't following us with a gun in his hand, aiming it at the back of mine or Luca's head. I pull in a few calming breaths and start the car when I see he's not.

God, I'm doing this. I'm conquering my greatest fear that's been staring me in the face for a decade. I'm getting my son out of here before he's turned into a monster with no compassion. And, Lane. I can't let Joseph get to him. I can't ever tell Lane Luca is his.

But I can. As soon as we get to safety, I can let everything out. I won't have to live this way anymore. I won't have to suffer to save my flesh and blood.

"Okay, but listen, Mom. The driveway was super icy when I was outside earlier. You have plenty of time to get us out of here before Dad gets out of the shower. Go slow, or we'll crash. Here, put this in your nose. It's bleeding bad."

Luca's angry and scared trembling voice forces my attention to the blood dripping down my face as I take the wad of tissue from his outstretched hand and stuff it into my nose. I'd forgotten I was bleeding. I'm used to it after all. But this was the first time I'd talked back in years as well as the only time Joseph had taken his fists to my face.

"Thank you." My words come out on an unstable breath. I'm such a terrible mother if ever there was one. I will beg forever for Luca to forgive me.

"God, I hate Dad. How could you let him do that to you? I don't understand how he could hit you like that? For how long, Mom? How long have you been hiding that from me? I hope Grandpa severs that prick's hands off his body. I hope he hurts him badly. I don't care that you've told me hurting others isn't right. He deserves whatever Grandpa does to him. He should sic Uncle Gabe on him."

My lips quiver as I watch concern form on Luca's face, tears are in his eyes as those horrific scenes he witnessed minutes ago must be playing in slow motion behind them.

I'd never seen Joseph's eyes so manic and murderous before. They were unblinking slits spinning with death as he screamed for me to die.

It's not funny that my nine-year-old knows what my father and uncle do. He chooses not to be a part of it. I couldn't be more thankful for that. I'd love him the same if he decides in the future he does. It's his choice as much as there's no changing who we are.

He's sitting only a foot away, and it feels like an entire world is separating us. I try to push away the fact I chose the wrong path in my life before I speak. That mine and Luca's lives would be different if I'd been honest and brave and not angry and full of revenge. It's hard to do when I don't even know where to start, let alone what to say.

"Hey, I'm okay. We're going to be okay. I love you so much, tell me you know that." I yank my boy into my body, swallowing him in a hug as I stroke the silky strands of his hair.

I never wanted my son to see me like this. Joseph has always been good about hitting me where no one would notice the marks he left. Luca saw the vicious act tonight. He jumped on top of Joseph and pulled a chunk of his hair out as he beat and scratched and clawed him in the face.

When Joseph threw Luca to the ground and kicked him in the stomach, I knew then I had to leave. Laying a hand on me is one thing, on Luca, that's another. He does not get to harm my kid.

I don't know what got into Joseph tonight. In a way, I'm glad Luca saw, it's what I needed to rise above my fear. But Luca loves Joseph, and this has got to be hurting my confused boy awfully.

My heart is in my throat, making it hard to breathe. That's what Luca is. He's my heart. The only good thing I've ever done. The greatest joy.

It's a stab to my chest that I'm the cause of Luca hurting.

Please let me catch my breath. Please let me figure out a way, so Luca doesn't suffer for my mistakes.

Sighing, I do my best to remember what's important. We're both going to be okay. It'll take time for Luca to heal and understand, but he'll forever be safe, and no matter what happens from here on out, that's the most important thing.

His safety. His health. His happiness. All the things a parent wants. All the things I will pull my head out of my depressed state and make sure he has.

"I know you do, Mom. I love you too. He hurt you. My dad hurt you, and I hate him. Get us to Victoria's house, please." His body shudders in my grasp, and I hold him tighter, kissing the top of his head. So thankful to hear he loves me.

"You remember how much you love me next time I tell you to go to bed and shut down your video games." I get a tight smile, which for now is good enough.

Badly I want to tell him that Joseph isn't his dad, that things might not have worked out between the man who helped create Luca and me, but he's a good man, and he'd help raise Luca to be one too.

Soon.

Soon I will right all my heartbreaking wrongs.

It won't be long now when the disappointment and hate clear from everyone's mind that Lane and Luca will be father and son. That is, if and when I can strike up the nerve to tell them both.

Lane may hate me, but he'll never turn his back on Luca, never make him into a man he doesn't want to be. He'll never stop loving our son, no matter how he feels about me. And, Luca will come to forgive me. He has to, or I will surely die.

I clear my throat, pulling back to look Luca in the eyes and try pretending that seeing him hurt, knowing I was too weak to leave, doesn't slice up the middle of my heart.

"He hurt you too. I'll never forgive myself for it, Luca. Never. I'll tell you everything once we get to Victoria's. I promise."

Putting the SUV into four-wheel drive, I head toward the tree-lined narrowed driveway that leads to the steep decline.

"We're going to be fine. I'll find a job. You and I will start over, and once we're settled, we'll get your things from the house in New York. It's going to be great, you'll see," I deflect, hoping to lift, if even only a little, of his fright.

"I don't give a crap about my things at home. Starting over means starting over. Let that asshole keep it all."

"Luca, I'll let that one slide because it's true. Don't make swearing a habit, buddy." At least not in front of me.

Hesitating, along with despising my past actions all the more, and because I don't trust Joseph whatsoever, I decide to add a bit more confusion onto my son's heaping plate.

"Hold on to the grip bar, and if anything happens before we get to safety, you run, Luca. You get somewhere safe and call your grandfather, Uncle Gabe, Victoria. You tell him I said to take you to Lane Mitchell. Do you hear me? Lane. Don't forget that name, ever, Luca." A few years ago, I drilled four phone numbers into Luca's head. Telling him they were emergency numbers that he can never forget: my father, my uncle, Victoria's, and mine.

"You remember everyone's number, right?"

Sheer panic washes over me as the vehicle starts to accelerate, and the brake pedal seems to have more play than usual.

"Yes. Nothing's going to happen to us except ramming into a tree if you don't slow down."

I try to, except I can't as I pump the brakes with all my might at the same time I try to control the steering wheel as the car accelerates and veers from one side to the other.

Panic, it's alive inside of me, breathing down my neck with the stench of Joseph.

"Luca, I love you," I scream. "Run."

CHAPTER SIX

Lane

My spine stiffens when Sienna's body starts thrashing, the back of her head nearly colliding with my face. A blood-curdling cry for help drags through her throat and rips across my flesh like a slow drag of barb-wire. Each pointed interval is piercing me deeply.

The painful hard-on I had from lying next to her goes slack. Before I can make a sensible decision through my tired and wired brain, I wrap my arms around her waist, pulling her into my body. Her entire frame goes into self-protection mode as she kicks at my legs, drags her nails down my arms, and belts out Luca's name so loud it tears through me like a shard of glass. My eyes widen, pulse jumps, heart thudding like a rock rattling inside a box.

Shit. Is this what Lorenzo meant by hearing her scream?

I feel each cry out for him slashing right through me—that barb-wire reaching and slowly dragging across my heart.

It's excruciating to witness and hear.

"Sienna, you're having a nightmare. Wake up." I apply the slightest pressure into my squeeze, hoping like hell it's enough to snap her out of it. Weight crushes down on my ribs as her arms continue to fly all over the place. It's like she's fighting someone off and reaching for someone at the same time.

She's going to hurt herself if she doesn't stop.

"Luca, I'm sorry. I tried to escape. All I ever wanted was to protect you. Come back to me, please. I'm a good mother. No matter what anyone thinks. I am a good mother," she drones, voice carrying a painful pitch of terror.

Hearing her cuts me wide open and bleeds my damn sins into every cell.

"Run, Luca," she says fretfully, her hand grasping hold of my wrist, nails digging so deep I feel them puncture through my skin.

Christ, I want to shake her awake. I don't dare to after watching her shrink into herself when Lorenzo grabbed hold of her. Hopefully, after what went down, he opens his eyes. He owes Sienna an apology as far as I'm concerned.

Mafia king or not, I don't give a flying fuck.

"Don't touch me. You will never take something from me again. You are a raping son of a bitch." She yells those words in her deep sleep. Unconsciously tearing out my soul or charring it blacker. Not sure which, but I feel every painful word she says right in the center of me.

An arrow stuck right in between the cage of my ribs.

That motherfucker raped her?

Blood thunders in my ears and my guilt, my regrets take hold with a claw and sink into my stomach.

They graft some slow and nasty gashes.

Me flipping my shit when she wakes isn't wise. I take

several breaths to control my breathing. Telling myself to get her awake, get her talking, and deal with my emotions at another time.

And so I do. Can't help to think of Sienna living years with a man she hated, doing things to her that no woman should have done. It has me wanting to leave her and Lexi here and take off on the hunt myself.

I'm unable to help rescue my son. I need to remind myself I'm where I'm supposed to be to keep Lexi from the possibility of losing me while my fatherly instincts are choking the life out of me by not helping find Luca. That's a promise I have to honor, no matter how much it kills me inside.

"It's me, La Mia Vita. You're safe," I whisper into her ear, press my forehead into the back of her head, locking her hands loosely in mine.

"Lane, oh, God. I tried escaping; I did. Joseph set Luca and me up that night. I know he meant for Luca to see." Her breathing hitches and sobs wrack through her frame, shoulders shaking, but she doesn't cry.

She's holding it in. I'm in no place to tell her to let it out. Not yet.

It's evident by the cutting of her brake lines; it was a set-up. What I don't understand is what she means by Luca seeing.

Anger shoots poison through my veins. I can already feel the fork-like tongue licking at my blood. Its venom turning me into a deadly beast. At the same time visions so severe of Luca witnessing things a kid his age can never unsee assault my brain.

"Where's my phone? My phone. I need my phone. I can't miss Luca's call." Raw and brutal pain scrapes from her throat.

Good God Almighty.

"Your phone is on the nightstand in front of you. I've got you, Sienna. You're safe in my bed. I've been here the entire time, so has your phone. You are not only safe here, but also anywhere you go. You have my word on that." I almost tack on, *I promise*. My word is probably shit to her. She'll soon find out I mean everything I say.

I release my hold on her wrists, slide my hand to her hip, expecting her to shove it away, flinch or reach for her phone. She doesn't. She stills, her shaking slows to barely there, breathing calming as she burrows her back into my front as close as she can get.

It's a relief to know she isn't recoiling away.

She isn't quite in my arms the way I want her to be. It won't be long until she is. I know it in my gut. She's the part of me that's been missing.

My only regret.

My life.

"I want to believe I'm safe. It's not easy. Nothing about this is. You don't know the man like I do. No one does. He's not who I'm thinking about at the moment. Your daughter. I can't meet her when I'm a mess." She blows the words out in panic, body going into a plank position.

I chuckle under my breath. I needed that to stop me from diving into questions. "Believe me, if Lexi were here, we'd know it. She won't be upset when you do meet, Sienna. She's like a tornado, a strong gust of wind that never winds down. Lexi is a breed of her own. You'll figure out what I mean in the best way. She's good for the soul." Call me biased, it wouldn't be a lie because I am. Sienna isn't going to know what hit her when she meets my baby girl. Even thinking about it sends warmth throughout me.

"I'm sure she's perfect. I can't wait to meet her."

I sense her hesitation in meeting Lexi along with disbelief in her parenting. Heard it when she said she was a good mother during her nightmare. She doubts herself.

I don't doubt her at all.

"She's everything, the same as Luca. He already has a place in my heart. I'd imagine he's a protector, like you." My heart wrenches. A tug so tight there's an emotional war happening inside of me. All are having to do with her screaming about rape.

"He is."

The seconds slowly tick by. Silence filling the air.

My heart and mind begin to battle.

Internal warfare. Pretty sure it's going to get a hell of a lot worse.

"I don't even know where to start."

"That's your choice." I might be eager to learn about Luca, but I'd rather hear her horror story so I can figure out how to help her.

"Funny, you put it that way. I haven't had a choice in so long it's still hard believing I do."

Christ, before she's finished talking, I'll be ratcheting up the need for vengeance and blood.

"I had my reasons for not telling you about Luca. I won't ask you to forgive me when I'd go through hell again to keep him safe."

I hadn't put all the pieces together until she screeched it. I'm not about to tell her that when I sense she wants to bring it up herself.

"I can't ease your pain, Lane. I wish I could. I need your forgiveness for keeping him from you. I can't make up for the lost time between you and Luca, but I know our son, he's a smart young man, like you. Luca is strong, independent, and a survivor. He's going to find a way to contact me.

I know he is. I'll get him back. When he does, you'll be proud of who he is. I can't think any other way than that. It's the only thing keeping me from going insane."

It might be the only thing when it comes to losing her mind. It's not what's pushing her forward in other ways. She's thriving at the restaurant, which seems to be her life right now. That's about to change right along with her having a choice in anything and everything.

Emotions I'm not used to having swell, filling the room, gathering those violent pangs in my chest of missing out years of my child's life.

"WE CAN'T REVERSE TIME. Don't beat yourself up when it comes to me. I forgive you for not telling me, Sienna. That guilt needs to end right here. That's a choice you don't get to make. Besides, you wouldn't have walked through hell if it weren't for me. If we don't drop the guilt, we'll never get past it." I'll carry that weight. It's on me. We both know it's the truth.

She lets out a sigh, and I swear I feel some of it slide right out of her.

"No, we can't go back. That's what guilt is all about. It likes to eat away at you until there's nothing left. I'm going to talk about Joseph. I want you to listen and not ask questions unless they have to do with Luca. I don't want to talk about the things Joseph did to me again unless I absolutely have to." I can already hear the humiliation in her voice.

It shouldn't be there, not with me.

I swallow hard. That barbed wire slinking its way right to my throat. By the time she's finished, it'll be in a gnarly knot.

Bleeding from the inside.

"Alright."

"The only secrets I ever kept from Luca was you and the things Joseph did to me. That's why, as Luca grew, Joseph would gag me when he beat and raped me, he left marks where no one could see. That night he didn't. He hit me several times in the face and choked me. That's why when I thought back while in the hospital, I knew his plan was to kill me. What I don't understand is he knew I'd take Luca when I left. Maybe he planned on us both dying. Maybe he hoped I'd be hurt, and he could take Luca. Maybe he figured he had me right where he wanted me, and I wouldn't go anywhere until the morning as we needed food for the week. I have a suspicion as to why, at this point, I don't care. I want our son back and Joseph to die." She says this with such fierce, confused reasoning as if she's already dealt with being raped and beaten. I suppose it's due to her having time to deal with it, knowing that was the price she had to pay to keep Luca safe.

It's fucked up. There's no better way to describe it.

I remain silent, hearing this woman strip herself bare is slowly cutting me wide open. It's pouring some toxic shit into my bloodstream, slamming at me left and right, beating the ever-loving hell out of me. I let it.

I deserve it.

She never did.

"I can't imagine this is easy for you to hear. I want you to know the one thing Joseph didn't touch was my heart. In the beginning, I led him to believe it was his. I couldn't give it to him when it belonged to you. My suspicion is that's why he finally took Luca. I think he got fed up with me. I don't know. I've wracked my brain, trying to figure out why it suddenly happened. Until I come face to face with Joseph again, I'll never know."

That could be. It'll be over my rotting dead body and many others before she'll see Joseph. Or him touching her again. She might be free to roam, but she won't be a victim to him ever again.

There's a lot more than the eye can see when it comes to Joseph. More than her suspicion. A missing link somewhere —something he's covered up well from Sienna and Lorenzo. A lot of people are looking for him. The man has scarce sources out there. If any at all. My gut tells me he's been planning to kill her for a while, working with someone we missed while researching everyone he's come in contact with, or it's someone we don't know at all.

Hell, even his whores don't know where he is. None of them have heard from him since before the accident.

My throat clamps shut, and I push past the lump to speak. "Sienna, I don't know what the hell to say to any of this. The first thing that comes to mind is you've been in my heart this entire time too."

Her constant sighing becomes heavier.

My heart aches over it.

"Yeah, well, the heart has to go through hell sometimes before it gets what it wants. We can talk about where you and I stand later. Right now, I need you to listen as I asked, please. This is hard to admit to you, Lane. So hard because I feel weak and exposed. I don't want to see pity in your eyes when I gather my strength to look at you. I did what I had to do."

"I can't keep quiet when you admit something like that. You are not weak. I don't pity you either, Sienna. I admire you." No words spoken by me in this conversation are truer. The ones inside my head, those are what I'm trying to contain. I'm barely holding them in. Little bastards are driving me to the brink of jumping off the bed and banging my head against the wall. Guilt clawing at my skull, regret growing deeper. Worry sucking me in.

"I can accept that as long as you don't ever show pity. At first, Joseph was sweet and kind. He said and did all the right things in the right way until a few weeks after we moved to New York, and I found out I was pregnant. We'd had sex before we were married, but I knew my baby wasn't his, so did he. Days after finding out was the first time he hit and threatened me. Joseph told me unborn or not; he'd kill the baby and me if I told anyone it wasn't his. He had people watching me on every corner. It was enough of a scare that I lied to my father and told him Luca was born prematurely. I lived with a monster who smiled while he had me in the palm of his greed, grabbing hands, and now he has our son." So much sadness bleeds through her words.

I squeeze my eyes shut like maybe it could block her words from tormenting me more. It doesn't help. Just beats me down at the same time it roars my rage Joseph could take a boy away from his mother. Everything he's done leaves an unsteady string of tension whipping through my body, stretching tight enough I could damn near snap in half. What the fuck is wrong with a man threatening an unborn child and their mother? Joseph isn't a man, though. He's a coward with sickness running through his veins. Any man who rapes and lays an unwanted hand on a woman is.

"Luca was a good baby. He rarely cried unless he was hungry. Then he wailed so loud until he latched hold of me. It sounds selfish when I say the first couple of years of his life were the times I cherished the most. Don't get me wrong, I bonded with our son, but that was the time Joseph stayed clear of me. There were no fists, no forced sex; he was barely home. I slept in Luca's nursery, watching over him every night out of fear that Joseph would smother Luca in his sleep."

I close my eyes, grasping for the bit of emotional energy I have left. For Sienna, I need to keep on shoving my rawness down, no matter how much I want to let it out.

"The night I left, he started arguing with me, and Luca came running. Joseph nailed him in the stomach. That's what made me see I had to leave after that." Her body begins to shake again. So hard you'd think she was convulsing.

My vision clouds in red. A slight blur around the edges as adrenaline spikes in my system. Joseph touched my son in anger. I will cut his limbs off and shove them down his throat for laying a finger on my son.

Those mental images of that bastard hurting her and our son will forever sludge through my mind. Living in those dark corners as a reminder of how badly I fucked up.

I can't handle it at the moment. It's too much for me to absorb.

"It's okay. I got you. We don't have to talk about it anymore." A hard breath leaves her, no doubt showing it guts and makes her feel better at the same time by letting some of her pain out.

"No. I want it all out of me. It's a poison that has been swimming in my veins for years." She sighs again, while my gaze transfixes on the patch of freckles that runs across her shoulder, most of them hidden by the strap of her tank top.

Jesus, she is brave. So much of her old self is waiting on the edge to leap out of their dark hiding spots.

"It had been a while since Joseph brought you up. That night he did. He used to threaten to kill you and my father, there were a few times he said he'd take your daughter and run away with both kids. I believed him and now look where we are. He took our son, and we have nothing. No way to contact Joseph because he left his phone at the house in Michigan. No way to know if Luca is alright. It's like they've vanished."

My chest stretches so tight at her admission. I had a feeling she was protecting me. Now I know, and it fucks with me all the more.

Revenge. I'll get it for her and Luca. I'll make Joseph pay for ever thinking he could talk about my daughter.

"Share a bit of Luca with me. What kind of things does he like to do?" I exhale through my nose. A level head is what I need. More importantly, it'll do Sienna good to end this conversation talking about Luca. If there's one thing that's deep-seated itself solidly in my chest, it's the love she has for him.

"That I can gladly do. Luca loves football and video games. He hates guns and loves math, like you. That young man is your son in every way, Lane. A Mitchell who will find a way to get what he wants. That is to stay alive until he comes home." A tremor rolls through her as she tenderly places our hands against her stomach. I can almost see it swelled with our son. Big and round and perfect.

"I don't know how to describe him other than to say he reminds me of you."

Every part of me seizes—emotion after emotion pounding its way inside of me.

Pain. Loss. Remorse. It's enough to fuck me right up.

Silence hangs in the air. I assume Sienna is trying to gather her thoughts while mine? They are about ready to erupt—ticking like a bomb set to go off at any time. What I don't expect after minutes drag on, is what she says to me next.

"You lied to me, Lane. You hurt me. You told me you loved me. You said we would be together forever."

I swallow, her words throwing another wrench my way. I guess when she said she wanted to get it all out, she meant everything.

"Yes, I'm well aware."

"I tried hating you. I tried forgetting you. I thought maybe I could until I found out I was pregnant. When I did, I wanted to tell you. I wanted to pick up the phone to let you know we made a baby. I wanted you there when Luca was born. I wanted you there for everything. Luca was supposed to come to you if anything happened that night. I told him to get to you. I knew you'd figure out he was yours."

A sense of calm falls over me. Or maybe it's the knowledge she wanted Luca to come to me. Hell, I don't know, all of this is as abrupt as it is heart-shattering and warming.

"Sienna," I whisper, not knowing what the hell to say.

My nerves catch fire, blazes spiking my pulse out of control with the blank moments in Luca's life I'd missed. I'll never have them, never be able to flip open the book of his life the way I do Lexi's. It hurts so deep that wetness gathers in my eyes. I'm not a crying type of man. I've had a lot of hardship happen in my life. Right now, I feel like I could fucking weep with emotions running so high over what I lost, what Joseph took from Sienna's body and mind, what I'll gain with having her in my life again, and what we could all lose if Luca isn't found.

I know she doesn't mean to rip my soul to shreds. Still, it does. It fucking kills me all over again that I was the man I was back then. It pours poison that stings the scars splitting wide open when she refused to listen to me when I tried talking to her after she caught me cheating. She ran out of her house and drove straight to Joseph's. I followed her there, parked my truck one block over, and hid. When they finally emerged, she kissed him before climbing into her car.

I hated her for that. I hated myself every goddamn day for driving her into another man's arms.

"I didn't lie about my feelings for you. I never stopped caring. Not for one second. I never forgot you either. Never forgot doing this, did you?" I slide a hand to one of hers, lift it to my lips, planting a kiss on the back of her palm. Funny how my brothers and I picked up that habit from Gabe of kissing a woman's hand we thought worthy. He used to do that to his wife every time he came home. He told us because he was a criminal, he would never be worthy of his queen.

"I remember everything, Lane. I don't understand how either of us can still care for one another after what we've done. We hurt each other, that's a lot to forgive."

My chest heaves, and I draw in a ragged breath. I wasn't a believer in fate, in all that bullshit that comes with destiny until Sienna came back into my life, but after these circumstances, that's the only way to explain it.

"I say it because it's true. I don't expect us to jump right back in where we left off. I'm not walking away from you. I wish I had answers to everything I did to hurt you. I'm not a liar or a cheater anymore, Sienna. The hurting part of our past needs to stay there right along with guilt and regret, or we can't move forward. I'm here, and so are you. You belong to me, and I belong to you. Together we are better. Together we will lean on each other until our family is whole. Let me take care of you. The rest will follow. I'm not living without you anymore." She doesn't get a choice in that either. I'd give her one if she didn't admit to still caring about me. I knew it when I went to her office. The proof is in her protecting Lexi and me right along with Luca.

She's a good woman. I was a fool once, not about to be one again.

My gut clenches so damn tight when she shifts away from me—a cold draft resting between us.

"I know you aren't a liar anymore. I'm not the messed up person you have in your head either. I'm broken. As soon as Luca comes back, I'll be repaired. I don't know how to trust you with my heart, but I want to. I want to so badly for Luca and me."

That's her fear of Joseph talking. It snuck up and laid itself right there in the spot she vacated.

"Never said you were. You say you don't trust me when you told Luca to come to me. If that's not trusting, then I don't know what is." I'll earn it ten times over by the end of our lifetime. I'll kick that fear to its death too.

"That's different than trusting you with my heart. You want to control me, Lane. Look at how you barged into my life, thinking you could tell me what to do. You showed up to talk to my father to protect me, you bought a house, gave me a job. I lived with a man who controlled my every move for far too long. My father tries to do the same, and by sitting in his office while he went crazy on you, I let him. I don't want a man to control me again. I have to stop letting it happen, or I'll never find out who I am. I want to earn my way through life instead of having things handed to me."

Curiosity rises in the blank space of my mind. My chest filling with love for a kid I hope has the strength his mother does to hold on for as long as it takes to find him.

"I'm not like them. I don't expect you to bend to my every will, but you will bend, and so will I. I want you just the way you are, expect you to take me the way I am. I won't change the man I am." She better get that through her head right now. I'm here and coming on like a hurricane as soon as I let all this sink in.

I refrain from whipping her onto her back and climbing on top of her. If only to plunder her mouth with my tongue and taste those delectable lips. Christ, I haven't kissed a woman in as many years as I haven't fucked. And yet, in the back of my mind, it doesn't matter because I know this woman and one taste of her was going to jar me back to life.

"You can run the restaurant any way you want. I'm not hovering over you. It's a gift, take it and make it your own, but you won't be sleeping anywhere except under the same roof as me. That is non-negotiable. You will let me protect you the way I should have."

I failed her. Broke promises, but I'll be damned if I do it again.

"God, your bossiness is going to be a pain in my ass."

She has no idea how much I want to be a pain in her ass. A pleasurable pain that has her begging for more. The thought has me gritting my teeth and tampering my cock to not grind up against her.

"I'm not sleeping at your house, Lane. Don't push me on that."

I huff out a breath, needing to remember what this woman has been through before I go dredging up the man I used to be again—the one who woke from the dead when he first saw her.

Silence takes over again. Makes an attentive man wonder what's running through her head. I always wondered what she was thinking. Sometimes I asked, and she'd share. Others? We'd sit, lay, stand in silence, and let our minds carry us away.

I chuckle when she starts yawning as the sun begins to rise. The light casting a vibrant hue across her hair spread out on the stark white pillow. I can't wait to touch it and fist it in my needy hands.

"I'm going to take a shower. I'll use one of the guest bathrooms, so I don't keep you up. It's your day off, get some sleep. I have a few errands to run. I'll be back before you wake. If not, the house you've been living in is two blocks over. Security will be outside to take you home." I don't bother mentioning that Gabe texted a few hours ago to let me know Aidan had flown in from New York sometime in the night with valuable information about Joseph. He was tight-lipped when I asked what it was. He responded with an address and a time for me to meet him.

Whatever Aidan found out is what had Lorenzo acting the way he did last night. I'm sure of it.

Shockingly, yet like music to my soul, Sienna laughs, wrapping that sound around me, making me want to draw it out of her every chance I can.

With a slight tremble to her shoulders, she turns to face me and lifts her head, giving me a view of that perfect face free of makeup. The same freckles still pepper across her nose. I used to run my fingers across them, could even outline them in my sleep. I remember how self-aware she was of them. While me? I told her they are her signature trademark for her arousing, exotic beauty.

Looking at her is like staring at an angel. One that is still holding so much pain behind those stunning eyes. I'd do anything to draw it out of her if I could.

"You've been two blocks over this entire time?" Her lips twist into a sad smile, eyes filled with uncertainty. I'll take that look over fear any damn day.

It takes every ounce of the willpower I have not to give in to the pull between us and kiss her.

Tear right through those shields guarding her heart.

"I'd do anything for you. Anything. All you have to do is trust me."

CHAPTER SEVEN

Sienna

I burrow myself back into the warm, soft sheets after using the bathroom, wishing I could fall back to sleep. How can I when my ears are ringing with a frightening alarm that Joseph could come after Lane and Lexi?

No one understands what being terrified of someone does unless they've walked in your shoes. It's expected when Joseph embedded it into my brain, especially when he followed through by taking Luca.

My grief is so deep. There are days I don't know if I'm coming or going. One day I can tuck away my pain for a while and look at the beauty of the world around me, the next, I'm questioning life's meaning, and no longer see the world in color.

I let my guard down with Lane this morning, which I haven't done with anyone except Victoria in so long, and it felt like the most natural thing in the world to open the door to my walled up heart and let him in. I can already feel myself letting loose of the binds that man has always had wrapped around me.

I ached to press my face into Lane's chest and breathe him in while I shed those few layers of my dead skin that had been itching to peel away, but I didn't, and now I wish I would have come out and told him there was no chance of a future for him and me.

Hostility, anger, and hurt vibrated through him. I felt it, and yet I still let so much pour out of me. I feel like I've broken a man who, in less than twenty-four hours, has proven how much he still cares. Stabbed him unintentionally in the heart and managed to twist the knife.

I should have gotten up and walked away. I shouldn't have told Lane anything, and now I feel no better than I did.

The last thing I ever want to do is hurt Lane. No matter how much of a bitch I was to him in my office. I don't want the man suffering because of me, and now I feel his pain seeping underneath those fresh layers of skin.

When will it go away? When will I rid myself entirely of guilt? When will I not fear a man I know can't touch me again? When will I get my son back?

I should feel better that I let some of it out.

"Damn you, Joseph. Get out of my head," I whisper.

I swallow against my dry throat, against the heat burning through me still from laying close to the man who always gave me this sensation to come alive when he was near. He's somewhere in this house, naked and wet.

The images of Lane's muscled body all suds up flit through my mind, warming everything inside me in ways that haven't since the last time he touched me. God, I can almost feel his hands on me.

I need to get out of here and stop thinking about him sexually before my mind carries me away. I'm not clear-headed. I'm as vulnerable as he is right now in ways that make us both dangerous to each other's hearts.

Instead of doing what I should, I reach for my phone, slide it open and go to my photos, and find the one of Luca and my father I'd taken the last time he'd come to visit. My father is sitting across from Luca on the floor, both engrossed in trying to put together a two-thousand piece Lego rocket Father bought him.

I have picture after picture of the two of them, and it breaks my heart that it's killing my father too, no matter how angry I am with him right now.

I'm not sure if I can forgive him yet for what he did. The man sat there on his throne, tossing out his power and worrying about what others will think of him instead of looking at the big picture—putting Luca first. I despise him for that more than him ignoring the chills running through my veins and how he tossed me right into my past after telling me how guilty he felt. He needs to wallow in the level of despair he brought on himself and put this family and the men that have proven their loyalty time and time again above anything else.

I've no doubt Lane and him will work out their differences, but there's a part of me that's deservingly angry at my father.

I should've never allowed him to think he could play God right in front of me when he knew I wasn't going to leave his office. I tried to detach the way I did when Joseph would force himself on me. It did me no good when all I could vision was Luca never getting to meet the man who gave him life.

Luca and I come above his organization right now. Let his men take the rules and use them by killing Joseph, and whoever else helped him escape. Joseph might be a devious man, but he didn't disappear without help.

Confusion. It warps my mind. I want to be free of it all

and live a life surrounded by love. "Why is that so hard to achieve?" I look toward the ceiling as if God would drop from the sky and answer me.

Exhaling, I push to sit, lean back against the headboard, and run a hand through my hair, nearly climbing right up the wall when I hear someone doing their best to tiptoe as quietly as they can into the room.

"Hi. My aunt is waiting in the car to take me swimming, so I only have a minute to talk. I forgot my bathing suit. I went to put it on, and it had the tags on it still, but I pulled them off all by myself without ripping it. My daddy is going to be so proud I didn't get the scissors out and use them. He doesn't let me touch sharp things without a big person helping. I sure hope I didn't wake you. My dad would be mad if I did. I didn't want to leave without kissing him. You aren't him. You're prettier than he is but not as handsome. He's the handsomest of all the men in the whole wide world."

My heart squeezes tight. It cries out this mushy sensation as I stare at the cheerful little girl with a smile so bright it fills me with joy when I should be embarrassed—when I shouldn't be feeling anything close to happy.

"Hello. You're right. I'm not your daddy. He's taking a shower." I beam at her. She generates that kind of sunshine right off a person. How I can tell that with a look is beyond me. She's perfect though, like I knew she would be. A handful, I bet.

Freckles scatter across her cheeks. Her curly hair is up in a ponytail, and she has on a pink one-piece bathing suit with white polka dots. By far, the cutest little girl I've ever seen.

"Do you think he's handsome too?" She lets out a giggle that pings off my chest, tilts her head to the side, eyes curious—that smile like a bright ray of light.

"Oh, I think he's the most handsome." I'm confident I'm turning fifty shades of red right now. Somehow though, I find it comforting, maybe a little easier meeting Lexi this way than worrying and wondering about how she'll be when the time comes to yank her perfect world from under her feet.

I can only grasp onto hope as tight as I can that it doesn't. That she remains safe throughout this and comes out on top of the world when it's over.

"Well, then we're going to be the best of friends. Don't tell my aunt Ellie that. She's my best friend too. I don't want her to hurt if she knew I had another best friend. We could all three be best of friends. That would be so cool. Woah, you have the prettiest hair. It's even prettier than my aunt Ellie's. Don't tell her that either, it will hurt her feelings all the more, and I love my aunt so much."

There went my heart. It puddles in a pool at her feet.

Lexi is a tough little thing with a heart bigger than she is.

"Your secret is safe with me. I promise. And, friends it is," I say on a nervous laugh. If she only knew how much I could keep a secret.

"Well, maybe I'll tell you another one then and see if you can keep that one too, this isn't the secret, but my dad promised to take me on a date soon at his new restaurant. I haven't been to The Grill House yet. That's the name of it. It has twinkling lights, and you can see the city. And did you know people can grill their own steaks and burgers if they want or they can have the chef do it for them? I'm going to work there when I get big. Wear a big white hat and make all the food. Have you been there? Maybe you can go with us. I already know I'm having French fries and chicken nuggets. Man, they better have chicken nuggets. I better ask my daddy to put them on the menu if they don't." She crosses her arms over her chest, lips going into a pout.

I understand what Lane means about his adorable little girl. She's a warm whirlwind—a ball of delight.

Awkwardly, I sit here, having no idea what to say or do. For many reasons, I want to pull the covers over my head and hide. Mostly because I never thought I'd feel a pull to a child that wasn't mine as I do this little girl. I want to bring her into my arms and tell her I'm sorry. That sometimes people make mistakes.

Maybe someday I can. Perhaps she'll understand, and her along with Luca, will forgive me for every wrong I've done.

"I have heard of it. I work there. The Grill House has the best French fries, and they have nuggets. I bet he put them on the menu just for you. Your daddy must love you a lot to take you there. Do you think we should ask him if I can go with you? I mean, I'd feel bad intruding on a date." My heart thrums erratically imagining Lane on a date with his daughter.

I bet women drool seeing them together. I know I would even if I didn't know him. It's adorable when a father comes in with his kids. I've caught myself staring at them many times, pretending it was Lane. It's ridiculous, but when you robotically act as if everything is alright in front of your son, it's things like that I wish would come true.

"Yup. Daddy loves me to the moon and back, and that's a long way, so it's a lot of love. I love him to infinity. Probably farther. He's the best dad ever in the ever of dads. He sometimes swears, though, but not as much as my uncle Seth. We have a swear jar, and Daddy took me to Disney and gave me all the money from the jar. He let me buy whatever I wanted. And you know what? Uncle Seth and

Uncle Logan gave me secret money I bought my dad a shirt with it. It says World's Best Dad. Did you see it on him, he wears it every night unless it's in the laundry. If you slept in his bed, you must be his girlfriend. I'm so mad at him about that because he says I can never have a boyfriend, and that's not fair." She rattles off her words quicker than I can catch hold of them, lifts her shoulders as if this isn't the first time she's talked to me.

"Um, well. I've known your dad for a long time." Shit, I have no idea how to answer the rest of her questions.

"Well, you can tell me later 'cause I have to tell you more things and then I better go before my little cousin wakes and starts crying. He's a baby and falls asleep in the car every time we go somewhere. My uncle Seth says my cousin falls asleep because I talk too much. He's such a big dorky tease. Guess what? We have other jars on our counter now. Want to know what they are? I'll tell you because they are so cool. We have a new bike jar where I put all the change I find and my allowance in it. Daddy says he thinks there might be fifty whole dollars in there. That's a lot of money toward my new bike, and I have a cooking class jar too. The class cost five hundred dollars. Daddy says I'm not old enough to take the class yet, but by the time I get big, I'll have enough money so I can. I have to do my homework every day before I play and not argue with my babysitter or Aunt Ellie to get money for that jar. Sometimes I want to play. Daddy doesn't get mad, he won't give me my money, but he helps me with my homework. Phew, I have to rest my mouth. It hurts from talking." She lets out a big puff of air. I can see why. That's an awful lot of words coming out of a teeny thing like her.

My stomach takes in a ton of guilt when I think about

the affection shining from her eyes when she talks about Lane.

Suddenly everything constricts—pressure building on my insides. I'm starting to suffocate over taking away years from Lane, Luca, and this little girl.

If I thought I was a horrible person before, I undeniably do after meeting Lexi.

"Wow. You are so lucky."

Her eyes light up, and she plops down at the end of the bed. Mouth hurting, aunt waiting or not. She isn't going to stop talking. I'm not sure if I want her to or if I want to run.

"I know. Daddy reminds me every day he's lucky to have me too. I don't know what the word lucky means. Something special, I think, and you must be special like me because I've never seen a lady in my dad's bed before. Did you and my dad go on a date? He doesn't go on dates with anyone but me. At least that's what he said. Hey, I was wondering, maybe I can come to work with you one day. You must like to cook if you work there. We could make something together for my daddy. Do you like to swim? It's my favorite of favorites, and I have a lot of favorites."

It's hard to grab hold of anything else she's said except the part of Lane not dating. He doesn't strike me as the type of father to bring home random women and let them meet Lexi but not to date? That can't be possible.

"No, we didn't. I was so tired I fell asleep. Your dad brought me in here. I'll tell you what, if your dad says you can, then I'll cook with you. I haven't been swimming for a long time. I like your bathing suit. Pink is my favorite color." My lips spread open in a smile as she jumps right back off the bed and moves closer, stretching her arms above her head and twirls. I don't recall when the last time was a genuine smile crept up on me in surprise.

I shouldn't be smiling at all, but I can't help myself.

It's hard to believe this ball of energy is Lane's adorable daughter. She is a tiny bundle of inquisitiveness and radiates light like an angel—medicine to cure a broken soul. She'll be what Luca needs to bring lightness back into his world. She's undoubtedly bringing it into mine in a matter of minutes. But it can't stay there. I have to keep her safe from Joseph. The same as I do Lane. It breaks my heart all over again.

I hope she and Luca get along as well as Lane does with his brothers. I hope they bond and protect each other forever. Even if I'm not around, that's all I want.

"My name is Lexi Mae Mitchell. Daddy calls me his princess. I'm seven now. When school starts again, I'll be in the second grade. Oh, look, you have freckles like me. May I touch your hair, pretty please?"

Oh, God. School. Luca is going to be so far behind. He loved school as much as football.

My guilt. It's beginning to choke me now.

"Only if I can touch yours. My name is Sienna. I have lots of freckles." I scrunch my nose. I'm not a fan of my freckles. I'm peppered with them. Lane loved them, though.

Lexi beams at me, her little lips lifting upward—a giggle slipping out of her mouth. I want to giggle too.

"For real, your name is Sienna? You're the Sienna! The Sienna! Oh, gosh. I knew you would come back one day. You're the lady Daddy talks about sometimes when he reads all the books I have about *The Little Mermaid* and Merida from The *Brave*. They both have red hair. Daddy said yours was the color of Merida's but smooth like Ariel. He said you were the prettiest lady in the whole wide world. I'm the prettiest girl. Well, at least Daddy, my uncles, and Grandpa Gabe and Uncle Lorenzo say I am. I love everyone in my family so, so much. I think you're going to be family too. That means I'm going to love you."

Every part of me feels the impact of Lexi's words as they smash against the wall in my chest, putting a giant crack down the middle. He told his daughter about me. Dear Lord, this man is barging right into my life and blowing me away. I don't deserve it.

I've got to figure out a way only to see him as Luca's dad. I can't allow him to slip any further into my life than he already has. There will never be a man like Lane again in my life. I'm okay with that.

I have to be.

"I've never watched *Brave*. I've seen *The Little Mermaid*. I think your daddy is right about you being a princess. Do you have a crown?" Please, God, give me this. Don't let her little mind go back to love and family.

She nods her head. An even bigger smile slides across her mouth and reaches her eyes.

There isn't a hint of fear in this little girl. Her inquisitive eyes go wide as she jumps right onto the bed next to me. Lays her head on the pillow and reaches out to touch my hair. She strokes and strokes. I'd imagine it's a mess. It usually is when I don't put it up on top of my head before I go to bed.

"Your hair is so, so soft. Mine is too. Aunt Ellie buys me this clear stuff to put in it once it dries. I'm big now so I can smooth it in my hair all by myself." She pulls her hand away and tucks it under her cheek.

"Ohhh, your hair is soft and pretty," I say as I run my fingers through her curls.

"You look sad. Uncle Logan says his house is his happy place. Daddy says I'm his. Did you fall asleep here to make you happy?" Her forehead creases with a frown.

"Well, I..." ...am thankfully saved by your dad. I swallow when I hear Lane coming down the hall, a second later he's rounding the bed.

His hair is still wet from his shower. The jeans he grabbed out of his closet sitting low on his hips where he plants his hands, lifts his brows, and stares down at Lexi. The corners of his lips twitch, the man trying hard not to let a smile stretch across his handsome face.

My eyes roam everywhere, up and down that remarkable body stopping at the V dipping down into the waistband. My core clenches, mouth waters as my gaze travels upward, admiring the way the muscles flex in his arms. And his naked chest is a work of carved perfected art. The man is a god.

I gasp when I notice a tattoo of a red rose across his heart dripping with teardrop shapes of blood. He talked about getting a rose inked on him one day due to him loving the smell of the lotion I still use to this day.

He did that for me and because of me—those tears. I hate them.

"You'll always be in my heart. I'm going to put a bright red one inked with the color of your hair over mine." He said that several times when we'd sneak out to lay and talk under the stars.

"Daddy, you were in the shower for a long, long time. I forgot my suit, but I didn't wake Sienna. We're going to be the best of friends. I knew she'd come back to you. I just knew it."

My mind scrambles in disbelief as I watch him look at her. There is so much adoration in that man's eyes. It's the best look I've ever seen on his face. It makes me want to reach out and be a part of it. For the life of me, though, I can't believe Lane would tell her about me.

"Come hug me, princess." His Adam's apple bobs as he swallows hard and pulls Lexi into his arms, mouthing he's sorry, and he'll be right back as he searches my face to see if I'm okay.

I'm far from it. I slip my mask I wore for years in place. I won't let Lane see I'm teetering on edge.

"He'll say yes to you going on a date with us, Sienna. All you have to do is ask," Lexi hollers as I swoon when he flips her around, her little squeal contagious as he plants her on his shoulders, and she bends to kiss him on his forehead.

I can't ask for what I want. I can't take a chance of stepping out of the box because what will happen to Lane, to me, to Lexi if Joseph were to call and demand I come to him if I want Luca? I'd go without any hesitation on my part.

What would happen if Joseph found a way to snatch Lexi? No one is safe from the evil of my husband. My heart can't go through losing people I care about all over again.

The minute they are out of sight, I slip out of bed, dart out the slider, gather my sense of direction, and run the two blocks home, completely aware of the two members of security swiftly jogging after me. All the while knowing besides locking myself away in a white padded room, there's no escaping Lane Mitchell.

Not this time.

CHAPTER EIGHT

LANE

Most big cities had neighborhoods with dilapidated houses that can barely stand. Broken and boarded windows. Homeless people on every corner. Drug dealers. Hookers, you name it.

The outskirts of Houston I was driving in was no different than some I'd seen in New Orleans, New York, and most big cities. It reeks of horrific crimes. Shit, I can't wrap my head around.

I wasn't prepared for this part of town, much like I wasn't when Sienna told me she'd been beaten and raped. How could anyone be for unimaginable words like that?

It hit me hard. A punch in the gut, and honestly, I've no idea what direction I should go when it comes to her from here. Do I leave her alone? Do I come on full-force to remind her she's not a lost lamb waiting for the big bad wolf to grip her by the neck anymore?

Sienna said she believed she was safe, and I think she does. However, there's more to it. I bet some of it has to do with me. The rest is the fear Joseph trenched a hole, covered it in cement inside of her.

Can't blame her one bit. It lives inside me too. Mine is fresh, this open festering wound. Insides being crushed and pulled apart.

My blood simmers, that's for damn sure. Joseph has crossed too many lines. I won't rest until he's beaten—and I don't mean just beaten with my fists. I mean dead as Sienna wants. There isn't a place he'll be able to hide that'll keep me from finding him. I don't care how it happens or who finds him. I don't need him to suffer; I only want to distinguish him from her life.

For now, I stuff it down, needing to focus on the reason why I'm driving through what seems to be the pit of Houston.

The entire hour drive from one side of town to the other, I tried convincing myself I wasn't scared out of my goddamn mind.

I couldn't.

I'm terrified of what Aidan found out about Luca and why the hell we're meeting at some warehouse in the worst part of the city. I'm about to see just how far I'll go to save my son with a glimpse into the underworld. One I haven't shed light on years.

Death.

I'm getting a stealthy whiff of it, and it stinks like a rotten sewer.

Rattling me to the bone.

I'd killed a few people before. In my eyes, they were undeserving to breathe any longer. All before Lexi was born. Of course, I'd helped Logan kill a few years back. I just wasn't the one who drew their last breath. Now that I can smell death, the thought Joseph has my son tangled up in some corrupt danger has me wanting to blow someone's head off.

I'm about to go from a devoted father who sits and plays dolls with his daughter, to a blood starving monster to save his son, I know it.

The thought of Lexi ever knowing I have, and undoubtedly will, take lives if needed, leaves a foul taste in my mouth. It's ten times worse than the day I looked into her eyes hours after she was born and made a promise that I'd never walk back into Behind Closed Doors again. That I'd do everything in my power that she'd never find out the type of man I used to be.

Lexi was so damn happy earlier as I carried her down the stairs and out to Ellie. Her arms were waving in the air as she whooped it up that she finally met Sienna. If that kind of smile ever left her face because of me, I'd hang my head in shame.

"Jesus, the thought of my little girl someday finding out anything about my past or this fucked up situation would surely kill her," I mutter to myself, lean over to grab my .38 out of the glovebox. I still hate guns, haven't touched this thing in years either.

I force down the thoughts of my daughter, letting it rest in the corner with Sienna until I find out what I'm about to learn regarding my son.

But as I pull into the warehouse parking lot, drive around back as Gabe instructed and park, it might not be long before I shoot someone.

That someone happens to be my older brother, Logan. Gabe and Seth stand alongside him, all three leaning against the building.

I ignore the shake of Seth's head as I climb out and make my way toward them. My eyes on Logan. The three of them might be here to jump my shit before we attend this meeting, I expected it. The problem at the moment is if Logan thinks he's going anywhere near danger, he can think again. It worries me enough Seth is involved.

"The fuck you doing here, Logan? I don't want you anywhere near this mess. Does Ellie even know you're here?" God forbid if anything were to happen to Seth or me, Logan needs to take care of Lexi. Not to mention, he now has a child of his own.

"You don't have a say in what I do. I answer to my wife and no one else. I'm here for the same reason you are, to get answers. That, plus, make sure you don't go off and do something stupid like sneak away to save my nephew." He slaps a hand on my shoulder before drawing me in for a hug. "Take it easy, alright? Don't blow off steam wasting energy you need to use, Lane. I'm here to have your back. Nothing more, nothing less."

My body is tightly coiled. I can't ease up. Not even if I tried.

The sneaking around, though. I'll leave that to Sienna. The woman sent me in an uproar when I fished my phone out of my pocket to retrieve a text from security, letting me know she'd snuck out. I'm a little pissed at her for that. No matter what made her tear out of there, she will under no circumstance ditch them again. She knows better.

I sigh in relief that my family is here, giving the support we all need instead of reaming me a new asshole for keeping this from them. I wrap my arms around my older brother and hold on for a moment. It's hard, so damn hard not to let the tears itching to break fall. Instead, I think of how damn angry I am that people without reason can go about destroying others.

Protectiveness shines in his eyes as he draws back, and I

have to turn away. I recognize that look—the yearning to keep your family safe. It dangled like a dagger over my heart as I left Sienna in bed this morning. I saw it in my reflection when I stepped out of the shower, felt it when I picked Lexi up from Ellie and dropped her off with the sitter. It took over me when I'd taken charge after Ellie was kidnapped, and Logan had been shot, and I feel it in my bones over my son.

"I'm not going to do anything stupid, not like this asshole here." I chuck my thumb in Seth's direction.

"Fuck off, pretty boy, or I'll deck you in the face again." The reckless little shit laughs.

I don't as I recall how Seth knocked me out a few years back, thinking he and Logan's best friend Rocco were going to take it upon themselves to save Ellie from the man who kidnapped her. I had to lie to Lexi. I told her I tripped and smacked my face into the side of a table. She cried her eyes out, worrying about me. Cute little thing going to the kitchen and somehow finagling a chair to the freezer to grab a frozen bag of peas. She sat on my lap, holding the bag to my face for a minute before pulling it away so she could splatter my owie as she called it with kisses and asking if it felt better. It felt better with every wet sloppy kiss.

More knives stab at my heart as I think about my innocent little girl again. If I don't stop thinking about her, I'll butcher myself before I know what's going on.

"You can try. Just know if you do, I'll break both your hands. That way, you won't be out there having me worry about you."

Seth's grinning now, pulling his long hair he's been growing out for a while back into a ponytail as he gives me a full-on pearly white smile. I should deck him for it. The thing is, Seth is the biggest protector of us all. He doesn't think I know he is, but I do.

"You'd do the same for me. Besides, Luca is my nephew too. He's going to need someone he knows to bring him back here once we find him."

That's right, Seth and Logan have met Luca. Through all I've learned in the past few days, I'd forgotten that.

It makes me thankful as well as places a twinge of jealousy in my chest. It also has me on edge as to what lengths everyone will go through to save Luca. Mostly Gabe. He might be a natural born killer, to me, he's my father. The man took on a role he didn't have to, turning us into men and setting us straight while letting us make mistakes when it came to the club. He hated that place more than I did.

I can see out of the corner of my eye, Gabe is staring at me to make sure I'm alright. I'm not, and he knows it. All three of them do. They aren't either. I will be as soon as I take the time to catalog everything in my head before it explodes. Even then, I doubt I'll be the man I once was. I'm okay with that as long as Luca comes out of this alive and well.

"I think we can all agree that when someone fucks with our family, they live to see very few days. I want to tell you something, Lane, the few times I talked to Luca, I knew straight away he was a smart kid. A couple of times, I thought 'shit, this kid would get along well with Lane.' The boy can solve an equation that looks foreign as fuck to me. He's a Mitchell; he's his mother's son. That sums up to a survivor. We'll find him, Lane. You get your shit together and take care of Lexi and Sienna, but if you keep another secret from me, I'm going to bust you in the face for real." I'd do the same for Seth in a heartbeat.

"As I said, I'd like to see you try, you little shit. I'm not apologizing for not telling you. I still care about Sienna. More now, after learning what she went through to save Luca." I'm not about to elaborate or tell stories that aren't mine to tell. Not that my brothers or Gabe would expect me to. They never would.

"I don't want no damn apology, asshole. I want you happy instead of infested with guilt. Look at things this way. If things had worked out with you and Sienna, you wouldn't have Lexi."

I nearly stumble back at Seth's words. I don't know where I'd be today if it weren't for Lexi, but fuck, Sienna paid for our love while I was burying myself in women, making money hand over fist while all the while trying to forget she ever existed.

It's a rocky road trip to Hell with me as the driver.

Guilt. Yeah, I'm letting it consume me.

Seth wraps his arms around me, lifts me off the ground, and bear hugs me until I grunt. Placing me back down, he offers me his hand, which I take.

I feel it. Those sibling binds wrapping around me—the way my brothers are trying to ease my mind. If only it would work.

"You don't owe us an apology, Lane. You are my son. We were waiting for you so we could walk into this meeting as a family. To show everyone, including my brother, that we have your back." Gabe's voice is thick with emotion. Felt like shit, causing a rift between Lorenzo and Gabe. They are as close as I am with my brothers.

"You want to tell me what it is we're walking into?" My voice rasps with the dread curling through my muscles.

"I don't know everything, Aidan found out, he came straight here before he called Lorenzo, which was before I contacted you. Whatever went down is my guess as to why

Lorenzo acted the way he did toward you. I'm telling you three right now to let me handle what you're about to see. If I had it my way, none of you would be here. Then again, I wouldn't be able to stop the three of you if I tried." Gabe's body doesn't shift with discomfort as mine is, nor does he swing his gaze from me as his face morphs into one I've seen many times. The guy is turning dark.

Ominous. A killer I wouldn't want to be on the wrong side of.

Sweat begins to slide down my temples. The edge I'm on, the death I smelled giving way under my feet. My body goes cold, back rigid when Gabe opens the door, and we step inside to Lorenzo and Aidan, glancing up from a table covered in what looks like maps.

That's not what catches my eye and holds it. It's the man strapped down in a chair, his body lurching forward as he tries wiggling out of the rope around his wrists and ankles. Matteo stands behind him with a layer of madness clouding his eyes, and a bloodied knife in his hand.

Blood drips down the guy's face in the chair and his hands. There are gouges of flesh cut out of his cheeks, the crimson color dripping splotches on his white dress shirt.

What the hell is happening here?

A dreaded vibe creeps up my neck, the floor trembling under my feet with every step. Or, maybe it's me shaking as I catch a dead cold, uncaring glare from the man's in the chair eyes.

Five different ways to kill whoever this guy is in a minute play through my mind. There'd be no stopping me from finishing that piece of white trash off if he's involved. I will wrap my hands around his neck and choke the life out of him.

The stranger's brows shoot up when he notices us. He's

dressed in an expensive wrinkled suit. His mouth is pressed in a firm line as his stare tightens on me.

His devious smirk holds me captive as I follow Gabe and take a seat. There's not a chance in this lifetime I'll be able to sit long and let someone handle it as Gabe said, not when that fucker is trying to corner me with a baited hook I'm too smart to nibble on.

He keeps it up, and he'll have a shattered skull.

"Over the past few days, while I've been searching for the whereabouts of that slimeball over there, he was sitting inside Joseph's house torturing, then killing my men I had camped out there in case Joseph showed." Aidan pulls out his gun, turns around, points the trigger, and clips the guy in his kneecap.

Sprays of blood shoot in every direction, dripping down his leg and dotting the floor, a howl of pain rips from his mouth, bouncing off the walls.

"That's for killing my men. Consider yourself lucky your death belongs to Lorenzo and not me. I'm known to burn off people's flesh and shove it down their throats when someone fucks with what's mine. Then again, fire is your thing, so maybe they should burn you alive." Aidan shakes his head, shifts back around, and nods at Lorenzo.

Lorenzo clears his throat, drawing my attention to him.

"Over the past year, someone has been setting fire to buildings in New York owned by me and The Diamonds. At first, we thought it was the Mexican cartel seeking retaliation over a disagreement that happened years ago. Come to find out; it's an act of revenge of a different sort—an action brought on by Joseph. Where Joseph is, we still don't know, but our guest here was spotted by Aiden last night outside of Sienna's house. Caught him as he was pouring gasoline all over the house to set it on fire."

I couldn't care less about fires to their warehouses. That is not my concern, what is, is what has Lorenzo so agitated.

When Lorenzo's eyes lock with Gabe's, I damn near break. I'd never seen so much pain coming off him as that which I'm witnessing.

If there's such a thing deeper than desperation, he's jampacked with it.

"Sienna didn't take anything with her when she escaped except her purse. When Gabe and I flew to New York to get her, I told her to leave everything behind, and once I knew it was safe for her to go back, we'd get the things she wanted. Luca's baby pictures and things he made in school was all she wanted. The gasoline destroyed them. Irreplaceable things ruined. Unsalvageable. Sienna has nothing but memories and the few pictures I have of when Luca was a baby."

Bowing my head, I pinch the bridge of my nose.

"Goddamn it. Why? Who the fuck is this guy, Lorenzo?" Seth yells from beside me, while I struggle with wondering not only that, also what this is going to do to Sienna when she finds out. "Someone better start talking before we draw our own conclusions here. Is Luca dead?"

Shit, he better not be. Sienna will be lost forever if he is.

God, how much more can a person take before they break beyond repair?

Lifting my head to take a look at my younger brother, I catch Gabe place his hand on Seth's shoulder to calm him down. That's probably a damn good idea. Seth has admitted several times over these past months that Luca's disappearance has his taste buds craving a drink. Knowing he's his nephew now has tripled it, I'm sure. It makes me worry all the more about him.

"No," Aidan answers with a tone that says, 'don't doubt me.'

That boy cannot be dead. Life is cruel, but not like this. Fuck no, not like this.

"No, as in your positive or no, as in you aren't sure?" I slam my fists on the table. Ready to cold-cock someone. Not giving a shit if I'm stepping out of line. On someone's toes or what the hell ever else code the mafia lives by. I need a straight-up answer. Proof? Something?

Lorenzo clears his throat again, my eyes observing his every move. His hands are shaking, lips quivering. He's on the verge of losing his shit.

Whatever he's holding back is going to rip my guts out.

I rake my hands through my hair, grip the back of my neck, squeezing until I feel pain.

"No, as in we're positive. At least from what Aidan and Matteo were able to beat out of this guy." I growl at Lorenzo's response.

"You're going to trust the word of some guy you have strapped to a chair?" I throw my arm out in the direction of the guy since someone seems to be stalling by not giving us his name. That, plus, if I look at him, I'll fly over this table and kill him.

"Lane, listen to me. I might be a hard son of a bitch. If my grandson, your son, was dead. I would have told Sienna first. Give me some credit."

Staring back at him, I try to remind myself I trust Lorenzo and that he is undeniably going through as much torment as everyone else. If anything, Lorenzo isn't a liar. Not with his family.

We have a staredown. For now, we draw a truce.

At my silence, he continues.

"I'm only going to say this once. Joseph has gotten

himself tangled with three men calling themselves XYZ. These men are like phantoms. So undercover that someone could be sitting across from them at dinner and not know it. They came out of the womb with debauchery already bleeding in their blood. Government officials, the NYPD, FBI, no one has been able to find them." He chokes on his words.

I've heard of them. Dangerous to college girls in New York City. The last I'd heard, they kidnapped a half dozen young women in one day in broad daylight. They snatch them off the streets, their homes, college campuses. It doesn't matter. If they have an eye on you, then you are theirs. Taken and never seen again, unless you're a sick fuck, who can finagle yourself into the dark web and pay a hefty price to watch a faceless man rape a woman. Or so the news says.

And these people might have their hands on my son? Jesus Christ, no wonder Lorenzo is cracking.

Acid bubbles in my throat. I swallow that nasty taste down before I upchuck all over the place.

"Xander York. Yves Julien and Zackery Hanson are three men kicked out of Columbia University fifteen years ago for filming students having sex. Up till Aiden found this one, no one knew their names or where they were. This guy here is Xander. He claims Luca is in good health."

My jaw unhinges as I wait for him to say more.

Like maybe give me an update on my son's mind.

Revenge.

That word is going to simmer inside me until the day every ounce of blood drains out of Joseph.

I will gut him.

My heart hesitates to beat for a second while my brain struggles to catch up. I knew that son of a bitch was untrustworthy. Still, how the hell could Joseph keep this a secret, and for how damn long? How the hell could a man take a child and throw him into a wolf's den as prey?

And the thought of Joseph tearing through an innocent person then going home and doing vile things to Sienna is like a thousand knives slicing me wide open.

"Aidan followed him to his vehicle before he could set fire to the house. He grabbed him from behind. I wish I could say I find it inspiring how quickly Xander talked. You know what they say, though, people behind the screen have no goddamn balls once they are caught. They run and hide, seek out shelter while shitting their pants. He gave Aidan a location, but by the time he and his men got to the house, it was wiped clean. No sign of any woman. No sign of Luca."

Terror grips onto the fringes of my mind, as my concern leaps between Aidan to Lorenzo and back again. I'm not sure if I'm ready to let my thoughts infect my brain about what they could be doing to Luca. There's too much rattling around up there.

The unthinkable. They could be forcing my child to do things that could fuck him up for life.

And those girls. However many they had, are they dead? Jesus, we'll likely never know.

Sickness.

I will never be able to wrap my mind around it.

Lorenzo takes a seat, his shoulders slump. Forehead wrinkles. Body folds. His whole being appears exhausted from the earth before resting his head in his palms.

I lock stares with Aidan. I don't know him all that well, not like Seth does and not as well as I used to know his daughter Victoria. When I called her a few months ago, I was surprised she spoke to me since we haven't talked in years, but she did, and I couldn't be more thankful Sienna had someone to talk to, I only wish that someone would have been me.

He's rough around the edges, big, burly, and in great shape, for someone, I'd guess to be in his late fifties. He's trustworthy, I sense it. Knows his shit, no doubt been around the block a time or two.

"Joseph is one of XYZ's clients. He showed for a taping with Luca in hand claiming he'd bargain Luca's life with our families by asking for protection to expand into other cities if they'd let him be their number four. He told them he'd been setting fires to the warehouses to let us know when the time came for him to negotiate, we'd know he wasn't fucking around. That he'd continue to destroy us if need be until we caved. The information I've gathered wasn't easy to dig up, but,"

Again, I don't care about these fires.

"But what?" My patience dwindles with every passing second as I wait for Aidan to speak. Swear to God there's a pain in my chest so severe if it keeps up, I'll have a heart attack. I'm thirty-years-old for shit's sake, way too young, unlike Lorenzo, who needs to take a back seat and let someone else drive.

"Tell us, damn it." Seth stands, hands gripping the edge of the table, limbs shaking. He wants confirmation of what my instincts already know.

On the other side of me, Logan lets out a pain-filled growl, and I glance down to see his hands balled into fists resting on the table.

Aidan closes his eyes briefly, and when he opens them, I see the answer, the defeat in his eyes, the devastating pain— the words no father wants to tell another. He doesn't want to say it because if my son doesn't find a way to escape or isn't found, he'll always be the man who delivered the news that stole my soul.

"We might be criminals, but we can't offer protection no matter how much we want to. That would be like us committing the crimes. It would start a war amongst other families. I don't know if or when Joseph and the remaining two will reach out to us. Honestly, I don't think they will. I can only promise that I'll take my last breath before I give up searching for Luca, Joseph, and the other two men."

What he means is they could kill Luca if he isn't found. Use him in ways I can't think about, in ways that have me crawling out of my skin. My son will disappear just like all those young girls, and I'll never meet him. Sienna will never hold him again, Lexi will never know she had an older brother.

Our family will never be the same again.

It could take days, weeks, years even to find Luca. Those men could be anywhere by now. The only hope we have is that the sick sons of bitches surface. Even then, it makes me think about the victims they'll take.

It's a no-win fucked up game to the innocent, and it makes me feel as if I'm losing my mind.

I can't take anymore, the desire to kill, the need to get out of this suffocating building is driving me insane.

"That's my son. If you've laid a finger on him, you will beg on deaf ears for mercy." I point my finger at Xander, yelling so loud at the smirky asshole staring me down, I wouldn't be surprised if the windows in this place aren't shaking.

Screw letting anyone handle this. Screw standing down.

"They haven't. I've been doing this long enough to know when someone lies to me. I wouldn't give you my word if I didn't mean it. You have it, Lane. My word as a man who would have already cut that scum wide open if I thought he was lying. Let me keep digging. There is more going on than what any of us know. You have to trust me."

"Trust is all I've got. Just find my son."

"I will, Lane. We will." He lifts his chin to either Gabe or Seth. The hell if I know who is where anymore. All I see as I divert my eyes toward Xander is someone who needs to fucking die.

I grind my teeth, adrenaline coursing through my legs. I want to jump up and snap the neck right off Xander. The weasely vile son of a bitch.

I want blood. I want to take off to New York with Aidan, Seth, and Gabe and whoever else. It Goddamn fucking sucks knowing they'd tie me up before they'd let me go.

I'd never wanted to kill someone so badly in my life. Before I knew Luca was my son, my dark side had awoken thinking about Sienna. Now, it's more sinister than any amount of viciousness I'd ever known before.

"Are you sure he's done talking? Sure he doesn't have the missing pieces you're looking for?" I ask Aidan while keeping my eyes on Xander.

"Yes, he's given up all he knows."

My head starts swimming just as quickly as I am out of my chair. With every step I take, revenge licks at my fingers.

A roaring fire to kill.

All I can think about is what Luca has to be going through. How scared he is, how he's probably screaming and begging and crying for his mom.

"Not so fucking smirky now, are you? You don't hide my kid from his mother and live, asshole." I snarl. My body begins to shake, just staring at a man such as him burns my eyes.

A plea to spare his life comes as he struggles against the ropes to get himself free. The one wrapped around his neck turns his skin red and raw. He has nowhere to go, but like the dumbass he is, he continues to try to free himself. In a way, I want to help him along so I can slice him from sternum to scalp.

I shake my head when Matteo offers me his knife. I want this man's blood to stain my hands.

"You are certain he has no idea where his revolting friends are?" I look over my shoulder for confirmation at the same time I grip hold of his throat. Pain radiates up my arm as I squeeze until my muscles jump.

"Yes, but Lane, I asked you."

"I know what you asked, Gabe, and you know I would let go if any of you can honestly tell me you wouldn't do the same." My vision blurs as I swerve my head back around and squeeze harder.

The silence behind me settles my argument.

"You'll never find them before they sneak up on the rich bitches who think they are better than everyone else. They will play and taunt and tease. They will rip women apart. They will kill your son." He coughs out. Bloody spit dribbling down his chin. Eyes about ready to pop out of his head.

I flinch at his words. Could swear Matteo lets out a hiss.

"Well, it's too fucking bad you'll never know, will you?" My fist connects with his jaw, then another into his stomach. Every time his head drops, Matteo is there to lift it back up so I can deliver more. The blood from his face soaks into my hands and clothes, and still, I don't stop pummeling his face, not even when his flesh tears away more than it was. I don't stop until I'm satisfied no other young woman will ever have to breathe his toxic air.

CHAPTER NINE

Sienna

"Please tell me you'll be home tonight. I'm cooking. I know it doesn't make up for the way I acted the other night. There is no excuse, Sienna. I was wrong. I won't admit it to anyone except you." My father expresses in an uncomfortable, out of character sentiment for him in my ear. He's never like that. In my opinion, it serves him right to be uneasy.

On the other hand, he is wrong about admitting it to no one besides me. He owes it to Lane and his brothers. That's not my worry, not when I need a moment in the spot where I come to feel close to my son.

Adjusting my phone, I stare into the light blue cloudless sky, thankful for the most part he isn't trying to make up an excuse. If he did, it would add to my frantic thoughts and anger me more than I already am. Being that he wasn't at the house this morning after I ran through the neighborhood like a crazed idiot, we'll talk about it tonight.

"I'll be there. Just don't put too much garlic on the French bread." My voice remains steady, a light laugh tumbling out—the opposite of the mixed myriad of emotions inside of me.

It's a good thing, I suppose, if he suspects I'm overly emotional, he'd only get further upset.

"Ah, you wound me. What is garlic bread if you can't taste the flavor? I'll see you this evening. I love you, Bell' Angelo. Enjoy your view, sweetheart."

I grunt. Whether security told him where I was or not, he knows where I go on the days where I miss my son so much, my heart threatens to stop beating.

"I love you," I whisper back, hang up, clutch my phone to my chest, and turn toward the view I was admiring before he called.

Sighing, I take the city of Houston in. If anything had the power to have me pause for a moment and consider that even though my heart is full of indescribable pain, it's the panoramic view of the skyline lit up accompanied by the white lights weaving through the rafters surrounding the rooftop of The Grill House.

I can't get enough of this spot. It reminds me of all the times Luca and I would stare at the New York skyline. The kid was struck with wonder with questions as to how someone could design a structure that went into the sky. As strange as it might seem, this is the one spot that I feel closest to Luca, and today I need it more than ever before.

It scares me that there might come a time where I won't sense my son is beside me. That time will slip away like the tiny grains in an hourglass, and that he'll forget about me. That his brain will become stained in so much poison that he'll forget the things I taught him.

To be kind to others, respect an adult. Brush his teeth. To smile and be happy.

Then as quick as his presence envelops me, my thoughts

dim to a dull aching torment that he's locked in a dank and dark basement sleeping on a mattress in the corner of a cement floor where Joseph is treating him worse than a prisoner and Luca doesn't understand why. He could be starving, freezing, thirsty. He could be lost in this world somewhere and not remember anything.

Despite how cruel Joseph was to me, he never was toward Luca until that horrible night, and every time I think about the fear, the anger, the worry he has to be feeling, it scares me all the more. Luca isn't one to hold his mouth. That was one of the things I'd been working on with him. I couldn't get it across that back talking does him no good. He might be a kid, but he's a Mitchell, and he won't shut up unless someone forces him.

"Your dad should be able to answer any questions you have about buildings. He owns an architect firm with your uncles," I say, wishing both were here next to me so I could see Luca's face when Lane explains.

At the moment, there are no lights across the skyline. No strung lighting draped across the wooden beams above me. No couples or friends out having dinner and laughing as the city is as quiet as it can get on a hotter than Hades Sunday afternoon.

Many times I've come out here and stared at the bright lights while wondering if Luca was still in New York where he was able to enjoy the skyline that goes on for miles. The absolute beauty and amazement of what it has to offer. There's nothing quite like it. Although Houston's is much smaller, Luca will love it here, especially with the football stadium a few blocks over from the restaurant.

"Luca, God, sweetheart, I miss you so much. I have things to tell you. There's a man you need to meet, he's your real dad, and he loves you already. You have a little sister who is the sweetest girl. You are going to adore her, Luca, and Lexi is going to be honored, having you as her big protective brother. Please do as you're told and hold on. I know you'll find your way back to me." The words tremble as they come out of my mouth, my brain switching to the man that took me to his home where he held me all through the night.

I wanted to tell Lane more about Luca. Not only because he deserves to know everything, but also, when I shared things about our son with him, it didn't feel like the air in my lungs was stale and still.

I'm sure it's partly due to Lane being his dad. The other is what scares me when it comes to Lane Mitchell.

I crave him. I always have, always will and here we are only a few days back into one another's lives, and the signs are all pointing to the fact that no matter how much time has past, no matter how much we've hurt each other, no matter if I'm frightened right out of my skull of Joseph, my body, my heart, my mind, they miss Lane.

The man is bossy, no doubt still possessive. And now, it seems like he's taken the upper hand when it comes to taking control of everything in my life.

And I don't think he's doing it to control me. At least that's what hope is telling me.

Lane is still as bold as he was—the kind of man who doesn't take shit from anyone. There's something else different about him, though—something deep within that I've tried putting my finger on all morning.

It's kindness. That's what lays beneath the intimidating man. He's soft and sweet at the appropriate time. He always had it with me. It's different than before. It's the kind of compassion that has me wanting to grasp onto him. To change my ways and to take hold of the second chance he's offering.

I'm not ready to let him in as far as he wants to go, and it's not that I don't want to. It's that damn fright I still have when it comes to Joseph. He's not as stupid as people might think he is. He catches wind of me with Lane and Lexi, and God help, our son.

I'm worried Lane will want to go in search of our son too. If he does and something happened to him, guilt would kill me more than it already is.

God, I hate being this woman. Insecure and mixed up. My world has been turned upside down, stomped on, flattened, and here I am, thinking about the man I've always loved.

It's not right.

My phone buzzes in my hand, stealing away my thoughts. How I wish it would be Luca, but it's not. It's my assistant manager, Bella, letting me know she's here looking for me.

Frowning with wonder as to why she's here, I type out a reply telling her to meet me in my office.

I adore Bella. She's smart, witty, and I found it odd she was already hired as the assistant manager before I arrived when the woman has more experience than me. I didn't ask her why. Butting into other people's business has never been my thing. Regardless, she's helped me adjust to becoming a genuine people person without wearing my mask, without knowing the background of my life.

My bare feet sting from the heat as I quickly cross the wooden floor, wiping the beads of sweat off the back of my neck, and make my way into the restaurant. The coolness of the air conditioning blasting me in the face when I descend the stairs and slip into my office only to jump right out of my skin when Bella is standing in the middle of the room holding the most adorable baby in her arms—nervousness coming off her thick and heavy as she chews on her bottom lip.

I part my lips, attempting to speak. I'm speechless as memories of Luca being an infant assault me. All I can do is stare at the baby. His resemblance to Luca is strikingly similar. So much so it has me closing my eyes briefly only to open them and avoid looking into his eyes.

Bella huffs out a breath before rattling off words that make sense; at the same time, they don't. "There's no better way to tell you than to be honest. I'm Ellie Mitchell, Logan's wife. I'm sorry I lied to you about my identity. Lane and I couldn't think of another way to draw suspicion off him then for me to be your assistant manager." She pauses, takes a deep breath, and continues before giving me a chance to grasp hold of what she said.

"There are a few more things you should know too. The woman that pretended to be the owner is Renita. She's like a mother to me. Renita took me in after my parents died. We don't normally go around scheming behind someone's back, not unless it's to protect those we care about, and we care about you, Sienna." She exhales, a slightly weary smile lifting her mouth.

I'm a little stunned and not surprised one bit. I'm amused more than anything. Impressed, and honestly, tripping all over the place in my mind about how this fairy tale life Lane is giving me makes no sense.

Goosebumps scatter across my skin. Lane meant it when he said no chances would be taken when it came to me; he's had me covered with someone he trusts wherever I go.

He can't protect my heart from breaking over and over

with so much worry that there are times I don't think I'll survive. No matter how much Lane or anyone tries, they can't.

The man has me so spun up, if I'm not careful, it won't be long before I'm unable to recognize reality from fantasy. Because the truth is, I'd walk away and go right back to living in hell if it meant I was able to be with Luca.

A frown pulls at Ellie's forehead, dragging me out of my thoughts. "I know you're upset. All I have is an honest apology. I'll answer any questions you have. I'll help in any way I can. So will Renita and once you meet her daughter Norah, she will too. If you need space we'll give it, need a shoulder we have that too. Just know we are here and aren't going anywhere."

Right. I doubt I'll open to any of them about my past anytime soon, but to know the opportunity is there is enough for me right now.

With all that's happened in the last few days, I'm sad to say I never even gave Renita a thought. Since the weeks it took her to train me, I've only seen her three times. She's come in to check on things. She spent most of her time in the kitchen, her hands in the chef's business, helping and telling them how to cook.

The last time I spoke with her, she was leaving on a month-long vacation to Europe with her sister and daughter.

"Does Renita live here?" I don't know why that's the first thing that pops out of my mouth, maybe because I felt this motherly protectiveness coming off the woman whenever she came around. Now I understand why.

A mother's love has no boundaries. That phrase holds so much truth. I fell head over heels for Lexi within minutes. I wish more than anything I could get to know her better.

"No, she lives in New Orleans. Although she is in Europe having the time of her life. Once you become a member of Renita's family, you're one for life, beware though, she'll offer her advice whether you want it or not. She'll drive you nuts while at it too, but her heart is as big as anyone I've met." Respect gleams in her eyes. A tinge of jealousy rocking under my feet. Ellie looks so happy and content.

I can't believe this black-haired beauty is her. Uncle Gabe talked about her all the time. He thinks the world of Ellie.

I'm not sure what to say as I'm so overwhelmed—reeling that Lane is going to yank those binds right out of my hands and sweep me off my feet no matter if I try pushing him away or not.

The room turns quiet except for the sound of her son cooing away to himself as I attempt to process this information down.

"And from now on, your paychecks will be coming from Mitchell Holdings and not Wynn Industries. Wynn is my maiden name. We can talk about all that another time." Her words come out a tad clumsy and awkward. I suppose mine would too if I were staring at a woman who can't seem to form a sentence other than the one I did.

Speak, Sienna. You have a voice to use now. You had no problem using it with Lane, no problem talking business with Ellie before.

Lane. He's my problem. Well, not so much a problem as a constant in my mind. He just crept right in like I knew he would.

Sneaky with his perfect face, his muscular body, his kindness. All that soft mixed in with his hard. I could go on and on.

"Well, that explains why you said you'd take care of payroll when we were delving out who would do what. Here I thought it was because I had no idea how to punch a timecard until you and Renita showed me. It was to hide Lane from me. That man is as sly as he ever was." We both laugh slightly, a welcome break in the tension.

"You know as well as I do, how sneaky, devious and not to mention utterly handsome all three of those Mitchell men are. Lexi is like them in the sneaky department. She slides right under your skin with just one word. That girl..." She takes another deep breath and glances down at her baby. "That girl is wiser than her years. She's a gift."

I swallow, give her a slight nod in agreement. Lexi is precious too. As far as the three brothers, if Lane hasn't changed in that way, I doubt Logan and Seth have either.

"Anyway, I didn't know you were inside Lane's house earlier. I'm sure Lexi shocked the hell out of you. I don't mean for this to sound heartless, you meeting her was what made me tell Lane I was coming to you. I'm sorry for everything life has thrown at you." Tears form in her eyes. There's more to her sorry than the deceit and what I'm going through. Ellie feels terrible for bringing her son.

It makes me feel like a horrible person. Especially after all she's done for me.

She lifts the baby's tiny little hand from his mouth and starts to turn away from me. I stop her by placing mine on her arm.

"Don't do that to me, please. Don't treat me any differently now that I know who you are. I have to continue with my life, whether my heart is breaking or not. It has nothing to do with you and your son. I'd be showing him off to everyone if I were you. He's a handsome boy. I love the name, Braxton Gabriel. My uncle had tears in his eyes when he told me you named your son after him." I've rarely seen my uncle show emotion like that. It was heartwarming.

The last thing I want is for someone to feel like they can't show off their happiness around me. I might be splintering a little more with each passing day. Entirely confused and being tugged in every direction, but I'm not heartless.

"Naming him after Gabe was the only thing Logan asked. He let me choose the first name. The two together fit. You're a lot stronger than you give yourself credit for, Sienna. I admire your strength. If you feel the need to let go of it, come to me, please. I can't understand what you're going through. I do know how there are days when you feel weak, how there are times when you want the world to swallow you whole. How you feel like an alien has taken over your body because nothing around you seems right. You can give in to your weaknesses, Sienna. You have to forgive yourself, and it's the hardest thing to do when it isn't your fault in the first place."

I draw in a sharp breath like I could suck some of Ellie's strength into my lungs and store it there.

Forgiving myself seems so far out of my reach. At the moment, I can't even see it.

"I couldn't have described my life better. Thank you, Ellie. It's strange hearing it from someone else." A knot forms in my throat, hot and anchored down with a tangled web of emotions.

Finally, finding some courage with my heart rate speeding, I slide my index finger down her son's chubby cheek, admiring everything cute about the little man.

Wide eyes stare up at me, sweet rolls of baby fat on his legs. He does remind me of when Luca was a baby, except his eyes, are as blue as the sky outside.

"They look alike. My son and yours. Little Mitchell

boys. He's what, three or four months old?" Luca has a little cousin. He has so much family to come home to. He's going to be surrounded by love.

"Almost four, and yes, they do."

"You gave up a moment of your life you can never get back for a stranger, Ellie. I don't know what to say, except thank you again." This woman is more incredible than I imagined her to be by giving up a lot of time with her baby for me. It shows how deep the bond of the Mitchell family is. They'll sacrifice anything for each other.

"That's all you need to say. It was my husband, his brothers, and Gabe, who taught me the meaning of sacrifice. Even more, you did too. I didn't miss anything I wouldn't have if I'd worked anywhere else. What's done is done. I won't turn away from family, and to me, you are. After getting to know you, I know you'd do the same for me."

It's strange how she feels like family to me too. As far as sacrificing goes, my little boy, the one I did it for, is now paying the price.

"I would in a heartbeat, Ellie."

A warm wave fills my chest when we both smile at the same time.

"Now that you know, once we find a replacement for me. That is if once everything we're throwing at you settles and you aren't angry, I'm going back to my store. I own a consignment shop. Even though this place means a lot to me, and I care about you, I miss my store."

"Of course. No one told me you owned a store. I can't wait to shop there. I look forward to swinging by and letting you show me the heels you have on hand. They're a secret favorite." I own one pair of heels now. Before, I had many. I wore them when Joseph and I would go out to make me appear to be the confident daughter and wife.

On the outside, I was. The inside was a tattered and battered woman.

"I have plenty of everything. Thank you for not being angry. Lane told me to stop worrying. I was a wreck. Nothing's changed between you and me, Sienna, except we won't have to open up to one another because we know each other's stories. Gabe told me you asked how I was doing whenever you saw him. I liked you before I knew you."

As uneasy as it should be learning this new information, it's refreshing that Ellie and I already know each other. We don't have to talk about the ugly scars of our past.

I couldn't be more thankful for that.

All I can do is smile at her. A barely-there uplift at the corners of my mouth, but it's genuine, not fake like I've been giving her for months. Self-consciously, I tuck a lock of hair behind my ear.

"The Mitchell brothers can be the biggest assholes at times; they are protectors at heart. They've instilled that in me. Don't be angry with Lane, please."

"I'm not angry with anyone. Confused, frightened, and weak, never angry, not anymore." At least, not with Lane.

A look of understanding glides across her face.

"Survivors aren't weak, Sienna. We are strong. No matter what happens, don't give up fighting those demons. Don't let them win, no matter what." Her tone is believable, but her words hit me hard. Especially those last few.

No matter what is a scary phrase when you have no idea where your child is. Or if you'll ever see him again.

CHAPTER TEN

Lane

I wake to a tiny foot in my face. The other resting at an angle where I'm able to see the bright pink sparkly polish I painted on her toenails last night. I did that, plus her fingernails, wiped the spaghetti off her face the other night, pressed my palm to her forehead to see if her fever rose at least a hundred times, held her while she cried because her tummy hurt and tucked her into bed this past week with hands that killed a man.

I never blinked an eye at it. You mess with my kids, it might cost you your life.

My mind conjures a quick flash of squeezing the life out of Xander, and I feel nothing. No remorse, no guilt, no shame. Just bitterness and hate that gave me all the more motive to ask that, if given the opportunity, I want to be the one to kill Joseph.

If I needed a reason to kill him other than hating his fucking guts when he married Sienna, it would be having my son around barbaric perverted monsters of their own making.

Carnage. I can't get it out of my head.

Above killing Joseph myself, is making sure Luca is safe and getting him to Sienna. Nothing is more important to me than that. But Joseph will die. If not by my hand, then by Gabe's. That was an order from Lorenzo I'm okay with keeping.

I knew Gabe wanted to stop me from killing Xander because he was afraid guilt would hit the minute I looked into Lexi's sparkling eyes. It did the opposite. It made me realize once again how quickly my mind was overtaken by rage to seek justice for Luca along with every woman Xander has ever touched without permission.

It made me think of how the parents of the young women taken have to live the rest of their lives not knowing if they'll ever see the person they love again.

I hardly gave cleansing the earth of that man a second thought until now, but every time I looked at my daughter this week, I had to look away before she saw the pain from the bone-chilling disaster building inside me like a rumble of an avalanche.

It's coming, and I'm unable to get the hell out of its destructive way. It's in my chest building inside of me, and before long, I'm going to slide right down that slippery slope heading straight for a cliff.

Meaning, I'm about ready to lose my shit.

I screw my eyes shut, hoping like hell to simmer the violent rage in my body. Revulsion and misery and regret are swirling through my blood.

It's uncharted territory for me dealing with more than I can handle when I have to remain normal around Lexi. The girl can pick up when something is troubling me. If she hadn't been climbing the walls with excitement the first few days after meeting Sienna, she would have caught on to the pressure ready to break free and erupt, and none of what I'm feeling has anything to do with Sienna walking out on me.

That's an entirely different issue. One I told myself I'd give her some space while I weeded through my thoughts as I sat on pins and needles waiting to hear from Gabe, Aidan, or Seth. They went back to New York. They have nothing as of last night—no clue, no word, no bogus sighting.

A mystery that has to be solved.

I can now understand why Sienna is holding in her tears. It's a lot harder to let it out than one would think. With her holding all that agony inside, it has me worrying what her reaction will be when Lorenzo figures out a way to tell her about Luca. As of this morning, when I called him, he hadn't yet.

Brave. I need to remember Sienna is a lot stronger than any person I've known.

Careful not to wake Lexi, I roll onto my side to stare down at her peaceful sleeping form. My thoughts drift to the information I found while searching the web, trying to find out any information I could on XYZ. I knew evil existed, but the articles I read about women, young girls, and even boys sold at auctions to become slaves hit close to home.

They could be ruining Luca's innocent life the same way. It leaves a gaping wound of regret inside me that won't ever go away.

Fuck, I'm dying here drowning in my thoughts—an uncomfortable strange place for me to be.

Lexi's sweet little face from the other night when all she wanted was for me to hold her while she cut a fever whirl behind my eyelids.

While I watched her when she finally dozed in my

arms, I'd imagined those young girls stolen being like her, always needing to be on the move—wanting to dance and sing—wanting their moms or dads when they are sick. Mouths are firing off chatter a mile a minute, giggles and jokes, and when one question brews in their curious minds, ten more follow before you have the chance to answer the first.

And then they bloom into young women with years of dreams ahead of them. Only to have those dreams ripped away and in their place an unforgettable nightmare.

I'd die a thousand deaths if anyone dared lay a finger on Lexi. I'm dying inside now as I wish I were able to save every person XYZ and criminals alike prey upon. It is slowly dragging misery along my spine as I envision Luca waking and curling into a ball of terror, and I get it, that guilt living inside Sienna. It's right there ready to eat me alive. Her pain is mine because of how we're deeply connected in more ways than having a child together.

Shoving thoughts of all that's gnawing away at me except Lexi, I glance down, shaking my head as I watch her sleep on her stomach. Body sprawled sideways across my bed, hair a disaster of tangled curls that will take me forever to comb out.

And the hell if I care that she'll wail and screech that it hurts. Hell, if I even care, she'll stomp her feet when I tell her we'll cut it off if it hurts that bad. That remark usually shuts her up for about ten seconds before she starts chattering about how princesses have long hair.

This morning, I don't care that she climbed in bed with me when she knows not to. Usually, I put her back in hers and remind her that for whatever reason brought her in here, she's to wake me so I can lay beside her until she falls back to sleep.

Today though, I need my sweet girl as much as she needs me.

"Hi, Daddy, you let me sleep here all night," she says softly as her eyes flutter open. That precious morning voice brings a smile to my face. I give her two-minutes tops before the grogginess wears off, and she'll start talking my head off.

I crave it.

"I did. Don't make it a habit, okay? Did you have a bad dream?" I hate it when she has one. She can never remember what they are half the time. Her little mind only aware it made her wake.

"I won't. No, I didn't have one. I think Ariel did 'cause she fell out of bed and broke her arm. She didn't even cry. Can you fix her? Uncle Seth bought her for me. He's going to be so sad when he comes back from his vacation that she's hurting. He's been on vacation for a long time. Can I call him? I miss him so, so much." Unhappiness filters through her usual first thing in the morning chit-chat. Little lips quivering as she rubs the sleep out of her eyes and holds the limited edition doll out for me to see.

One of the plastic arms is missing. For five hundred bucks, you'd think they'd make the things better. Then again, the way Lexi carries the doll with her everywhere she goes except to school, I'm not surprised.

It's a damn good thing Seth bought three of them. It might be hard to dirty the new one up to match this one, but if it puts a smile on my baby's face, then I'll stay up all night until I get it right.

"Well, we can't have Uncle Seth sad now, can we?" I give my best impression of Seth by pouting my lower lip and crossing my arms. Big ass dork has his pretend sad face perfected. He should as many times as Lexi serves me first whenever we've sat down to have a tea party.

"He doesn't do it like that, Daddy. He does it like this." She places the doll on the bed and tugs her lips down, flashing me her bottom teeth. She's lost several already. "He's such a grouchy butt when he's sad too." She giggles, giving me all her uncontaminated sweetness.

That's more like my girl, hate to have her starting the day bummed out over her doll.

"I think Uncle Seth and Grandpa misses me 'cause I miss them all the way to the stars. Please, can I call? I want to talk to both of them."

God, this kid, she's my brothers', Gabe's, mine. Hell, even Lorenzo's ray of sunshine. They'll be happy to hear from Lexi. It'll light them up hearing her voice.

"I'll let you if you get up here and give me a kiss, hug, and a secret unless you're going to keep your foot in my face all day. If that's the case, I'll have to eat it. I'm starving. It stinks, though. Are you sure you washed it?"

She scrunches her nose, a shriek coming out of her tiny little mouth as she scrapes it across my scruff.

"No freaking way. I'm Princess Lexi. Don't you forget that, buster. Yes, I washed it. Even between my toes. You can't eat my leg. If you do, I won't be able to dance with you later. Remember, you said we could dance to whatever I wanted tonight. It's going to be so much fun. I'm going to laugh so, so hard when you do the low. The last time you fell over." She breaks out in howls of laughter, clutching her stomach like it's the funniest thing she'd ever seen. It probably was. I can't dance worth shit.

For her, though, I'd do anything as long as it makes her happy.

"I don't think you're funny, little girl."

"I'm not, but you are. Oh, it's Saturday. My favorite day. It's do-anything-Lexi-wants day. We missed doing whatever

I wanted last Saturday 'cause you had grown-up stuff to do. I want to go to the park. You know the one with the fountains, Dalton said they let you play in them. I don't want to play. I want to dance like that one time me and you did in the rain. Do you remember that day, Daddy? It was the best of days. The best of the best just like you." She giggles again. I can't help to soak it in and relish in it.

Lexi and I have been doing whatever she wants within reason on Saturdays for a few years now. Last Saturday was when I went to see Sienna at the restaurant. I picked Lexi up from Ellie and Logan's only to turn around and take her back. All hell broke loose after that.

"I remember, princess. You mind telling me who this Dalton is?" I frown, eyes squinting. Giving her a pretend angry stare. I know who the kid is. He has the hots for mine. Dalton best back off now, or I'll be scowling at him when I drop Lexi off at school in a few months.

"Seriously, Daddy. You do this every time I bring him up. Don't you worry none, he isn't my boyfriend. Boys are gross. Someday when I'm big, I'll have a boyfriend, but only if he knows how to swim and dance. It's a deal-breaker if he doesn't. And I can have one 'cause you have a girlfriend and you're big."

My eyes go round, heart-stopping, then taking off in a sprint. I've no idea where Sienna and I stand. I suppose it's time to figure it out.

"You can quit growing up on me now, Little Miss Sassy Pants. If these boys don't know how to swim, I'll teach them. Now let's talk about how I'm the best. If I am, that makes you the best daughter."

I won't be teaching anyone how to swim. I'll quietly tell them to stay away from my daughter and dunk them under a few times for good measure.

"Like father, like daughter. Only I can't be the best dad when I grow up. I'll be the best mommy. So much better than my mommy was, but now she's in Heaven like all dogs go to Heaven, right?" she asks more out of curiosity than sadness.

I'm not about to let thoughts of Lexi's mother, Stephanie, ruin my day with her. She doesn't bring her up that often but when she does, it pisses me off that my kid is missing out on a bond with her mother. Stephanie wouldn't have bonded with her, though. She would have waltzed in and out of her life if I had let her. That was something I didn't want for Lexi. Either you're in forever or out for good. Plain and simple.

"Exactly like that. Now back to Lexi day. If my girl wants to play in the fountains, then that's what we'll do, but first, I need breakfast." I gently grab her ankle. Open my mouth, snap my teeth together, growling as I attack her foot with soft little bites, acting as if I'll chew away at it.

Loud laughter rings through the air, the sound of it slamming into me as she wiggles and kicks and screams with excitement for me to stop. I don't until she manages to get herself free, pushes up and slides right into my side, kisses my cheek, hugs me and whispers what she calls a secret by telling me she loves me before resting the doll on my shirt-covered chest.

Where she got this hug, kiss and secret from I'll never know. It's something I'll cherish till the day I die. Something that came out of the blue when she was three, it's been our thing since.

"Your heart is beating way fast, Daddy. We better have cereal so you can drink all the milk to keep your heart beating strong. I love you so, so much."

I chuckle. Shit, this kid has been my world for so long. A

blessing I never knew I needed. I'm always waking up wondering if I'm raising her right, doing what I'm supposed to be doing by teaching right from wrong.

"I love you more."

"No way, Jose. I even told Sienna I loved you the mostest. We should call her to see if she wants to come with us. I like her, Daddy. She likes me too, I know it. Her hair is so pretty, just like you said. Is she for real your girlfriend now? Are you going to kiss her every chance you get? That's what Uncle Logan said he does to Aunt Ellie when I told him kissing was, crap on a cracker, what's that word, Daddy? I can't think of it." She places her hands over her mouth, wrinkles her forehead in concentration.

I internally bust a gut over her crap on a cracker remark. At least I'm doing something right using that phrase instead of swearing half the time like I want to in front of her.

I have no words to describe what Sienna is to me. Not any that Lexi would understand. She's the other half of my soul. The missing piece that I should have protected. She's mine, and I need to make her realize that before I lose her to that fear.

I peer down at my princess to see a grin so bright on her face that laughter tumbles out of my mouth.

"Disgusting."

"Oh, yeah, that's it. You told me to tell boys kissing is disgusting, and if they try again, I can kick them in their privates."

Her shoulders lift to her ears, that grin firm in place. "But you can kiss Sienna if you want. I think she needs hugs and kisses and secrets. She was super duper nice, but she was sad, Daddy. We need to make her all better."

There goes my girl, temporarily flushing the poison out of my mind with that big caring heart.

No one wants to kiss another as severely as I do Sienna. I need to so I can breathe again. I want to get to know the woman she's hidden away. I want to give her the life she's always deserved.

"She's all better, baby. Let's spend the day just me and you okay? I'll ask her when I talk to her tomorrow."

"Okay, Daddy. I'm going to leave Ariel right here while I pee and get our cereal. I love you forever and ever and ever." My girl throws her open arms around me, kissing me on the cheek before placing the doll next to me and hopping off the bed.

"Wash your hands and let me pour the milk."

"I will. Don't forget your phone. I have to talk to Uncle Seth and Grandpa. I'm going to tell them all about Sienna." I shake my head as her voice sings out from down the hall.

Running my hands through my hair, I grab the doll, push to sit, slide open the drawer of my nightstand and take a moment to collect myself as I stare at the picture of Luca.

Can't help to wonder what it would be like for me and Sienna to walk into the kitchen to hear laughter from Luca and Lexi. We'd be a family. Something I never thought I'd want until I held Lexi for the first time.

"I'll do everything I can, son, to bring you back safe. Once I do, the agony, the regrets living inside of me will be as free as you and your mom will be."

That's a promise I'll die trying to keep.

CHAPTER ELEVEN

Sienna

"What are you doing here, Lane?" His name slips out of my mouth with ease. If only he knew over the years, this past week, it's sat there on the tip of my tongue just waiting to slip free while I imagined his fingers were caressing my skin.

I tried edging him out of my head as I went through the busy days and lonely nights. It's impossible. He's so much more than that to my bleeding heart, so much more than repairing it.

Seeing him here dressed in a black suit and pink tie that if I placed a bet, Lexi picked out is adding to all the turmoil having him back in my life is creating.

God, the man is too gorgeous that it's difficult to look away. It was always like that. He'd catch me staring in the high school hallways. Just the smallest glimpse was enough to get me through the rough days of keeping him a secret.

My legs tremble as I advance into my office and shut the door behind me. My hand refusing to let go of the firm grip on the doorknob to avoid the temptation of reaching out and touching his skin. To plant my face into his chest, inhale his scent, and have him hold me.

I don't want him to tell me everything is alright. It might never be again. I could be one of those mothers who live the rest of her life, not knowing if her child is dead or alive. I'm not that far down the rabbit hole to hell to realize that. I just refuse to say it out loud.

Comfort. That's all I want—someone to ease the pain even if we're both feeling it.

I'd take all Lane's away if I could. Bottle and store it in a place inside of me where it would never touch him, but I can't.

"Lane, is everything okay? Look, I know running out was wrong, I..." can't seem to form the rest of the sentence. I was never this way. I used to be quick with my words, say whatever was on my mind, whether someone wanted to hear it or not. It goes to show how much I missed the woman I was. How much Joseph dragged her out of me.

God, I hate him.

"You what?" There's so much affection and hurt, and hope and frustration in his gaze when he glances my way that I'm thankful I'm hanging onto something, or my wobbly legs would give out.

"I'm sorry."

The man says nothing more as he continues to stare. Taking in every inch of my face.

Needing to sit, I release my grip on the door as well as holding onto his gaze. I move past him to take a seat in my chair behind my desk.

The sight a minute ago when I noticed him standing in the middle of the room unmoving as he stared down at the photo of Luca he'd taken, rooted me to my spot. I wasn't sure if I couldn't move out of fear that something happened to Luca or because a spark has been flickering in my mind since I saw him last as I laid in bed thinking of no one else, but this beautiful, protective man with a side order of danger and seeing him here again sends that ember with one look, one touch from him will throw my body up in flames if I let it.

My throat dries, nerves rapidly firing when he lets out a breath and looks back at the photo. He's aching.

"That was taken on his birthday last year. He was born on September 10th." He'll be ten. His Golden birthday is less than a few months away. To some, that means nothing. To me, it's everything now that Lane knows. Hope has to pull through and bring Luca back before then. Missing holidays are one thing. Missing his birthday will have me hitting rock bottom. And I've tried so hard not to fall into the depressed state I'll never recover from.

"He'll be home by then." There's not much hope behind his words. Par for the course, I suppose when the man is right there beside me now—going through the worst nightmare of a parent's life.

That's what this is. It's a recurring daily nightmare you can't escape from, no matter what.

There's more to Lane's pain than Luca. It's his pain when it comes to me. It's inside of me too. I wish that spark would burn it away. I've hoped and wished for a lot of things when it comes to the mistakes I've made.

Concern sets in when he still hasn't told me why he's here, so I go with what I planned on telling him the next time we saw each other.

"Ellie came to see me the other day. She told me everything. I don't deserve what you're doing for me. In a matter of days, you made me feel like I'm worth something. You make me want to try to live again." I know if I want to feel and breathe and live a life filled with happy emotions, I have to work for them. Without Luca, I don't know if I have it in me to try, but I want to.

I told my father the same thing last night while we cleaned the kitchen after dinner and got onto Lane as our subject. I'd been waiting for him to ask me about Lane and me. When he didn't, I brought him up to clear the last bit of polluted air between us. I nearly stumbled when a smile lit up my father's face. It wasn't one of his best smiles, but it was much better than the spitting anger from the night in his office.

He did wise me up as well as shock me with his sudden change of heart by placing his finger under my chin to force me to look at him. He apologized once again, before telling me true love has a way of finding its way back home. And when it does, it's worth the fight to knock down the past that tore you apart.

I do love Lane. I'm nowhere ready to fall head over heels into it. Someday I might. I have to work on letting go of my fear before anything else. I won't drag him into my hole any farther than he is.

"You deserve everything, Sienna. I'll prove it to you if you let me. That's all I ever wanted was to give you everything. I'm not talking materialistically. I mean a lifetime of happiness. To give you all of me and to get all of you in return." Lifting his head, he studies me for a moment, with a determined stare, then expels a breath before looking away.

Need twists in my stomach. My pulse is picking up speed, heart back to fluttering again. I have a feeling that the organ wants to kick-start back to life quicker than my mind does.

Luca's face flashes in front of my eyes. It blots me with

reminders of guilt. No matter how much I try pushing it aside, it's going to be there. It can't be helped.

"I'm starving for you. A hunger that won't subside until I taste every inch of you. Even then, it won't be enough. It'll never be enough. Not with you, La Mia Vita. Not with you." The last comes off his lips on a whisper as his firm, pain-filled gaze lifts to mine.

"You scare me, Lane."

"I don't scare you. Your guilty-fear-filled conscience does. You won't shove it aside enough to let yourself feel, that's why you ran out of my house. You are hanging on by a fine-thread. I understand that more than you think. I'm barely hanging on too, Sienna. While I'm happy to be stuck here with you, my mind wants to be searching for our son." His throat bobs, words gruff.

I'm glad he isn't. There's nothing more to say about that.

"You want to protect Lexi and me from Joseph. I couldn't care for you more because of it. I wasn't born yesterday. I know if that rotten asshole called you right now, tomorrow, ten years from now, you'd do what he asks. No one would blame you for that, but I'm standing before you now telling you it won't come to that. I won't let it. Do you hear me? He doesn't get to touch, come near or breathe your air again. You are not alone in this anymore. I mean that in every aspect of the word. I won't give up on you and me. You get all that straight right now." He punches those words out as if he'd been waiting to say them. As if he knew what I was going to say. He probably did as I'm sure it's written all over my face.

And it angers me.

"I have a right to be scared of everything when it comes to Joseph. I have a right not to want to hurt you or Lexi." Fear and frustration build. My voice is getting stronger by the second. "I have a right to be scared of losing someone else! I have a right to be terrified of putting someone else in danger!" Sorrow takes the driver's seat. "Lane, he's out there somewhere. He won't let me be happy if he finds out I am." I trip over my words because I want to take that leap and everything that comes with still caring about this man.

"Joseph won't have a goddamn choice. He comes within a mile of you, or he breathes too fucking loud in your general direction, we'll know. If he shows in this city without Luca, his welcome committee will serve the kind of pain that would make the Devil himself confess. You are surrounded twenty-four hours of the day. You told me you knew you were safe. You weren't born yesterday, Sienna. The men watching you, me, Lexi, and my family are professionals, and you know it. Be fearful all you want, but be it with me."

His words collide head-on, knocking the wind out of me in every sense to every word.

Long gone is the controlling tone from Lane, this plea to let him in is bordering on sweetness. A different man than the one who will turn into a wild animal if he crosses paths with Joseph. That's what petrifies me. Two crazed men protecting what's theirs. One has a right and has always owned my heart. The other is so demonically possessed that he thinks he does. Joseph is like a shark to blood. A psychopath with deadly, destructive intentions.

"I would never take your rights away from you. You deserve to have a voice. You also have the right to live and love. I want you to share those with me. You deserve to have the man who goes through life with you worship the ground you walk on. I'm not the perfect man. I am the one for you." He burrows one hand into his hair, long fingers tugging at the strands.

God, everything that's coming out of his beautiful mouth I've longed to hear.

"I've always known you were the man for me, Lane, but—"

"No. There are no more buts. Let go of them and the voice filling you with the ways you shouldn't be happy. You've been beaten down, but you aren't fractured, broken, or crushed. If you believe you are, then Joseph wins, and I'll be damned if I let him take anything more from you than he already has. I want back the woman who wasn't afraid to step out and take a chance, the woman who I promised to love until the day I die. The woman who I want to fall in love with all over again. The woman I want to hold and love and cherish. The woman I can kiss and fuck until all she sees is me. I want you, and by God, I'm going to have you. You can let that frightened voice try to convince you all it wants that you shouldn't want me. It will never defeat me." There's his demanding tone, bigger, stronger, and willing to do anything to prove that it's true. The one that's going to control certain things in my life no matter how much I try to fight it.

He's like a light switch—just a flick, and it's on or off. I wouldn't want him any other way.

My heart pounds, my breathing becomes ragged as I sweep my eyes to the floor. Everything in the name of love is standing close. All I'd have to do is walk into those arms and take it. It's Joseph's consequences that are stopping me from moving forward.

Being frightened of one man, wanting to fall into life with another, is a toxic combination, I know, yet that part of me who has always loved Lane is begging to give in and say yes. By all he's said, the way I can still feel he's looking at me as if I were the most sought out woman in the world, and he's the lucky man who has my heart, he's going to bulldoze my walls and take back my soul that has always belonged to him.

"Don't do that. Don't look away from me. This conversation needs to happen. I'm not about to let you go through life without me being the one to give you everything you deserve."

On a hard swallow, I meet his gaze, those deep green eyes that used to steal my breath trace every inch of my face, again lingering on the spots where my freckles are. I've never seen him look at me this way. As if he'd treasure me, love me, and fuck my brains out all at once.

"You don't think you have a right to be happy, and you do. I felt that way once. It was the day Lexi's mother walked away. I peered down at my girl in my arms and made a promise that no woman would come between her and me. No woman would ever walk into my daughter's life to where Lexi would become attached and then for whatever reason turn and walk away and leave Lexi broken-hearted. You are the only woman I'd break that promise for, and do you know why?"

My heart stops beating as my brain tries to take in what he's saying. I have a feeling there's a lot more to what he means—answers to what had been driving me crazy as to what Lexi meant about him not dating.

I'm at a loss for words. To try to construct a sentence would be hopeless when the only thing running through my head at this very moment is how much love Lane has for his daughter. How he put her first the way, a parent should their child, how he'd do the same for Luca. It places respect and admiration in my chest for the man who is catching me off guard in a way that hurts and heals.

I knew he wouldn't listen when I asked not to push me.

What I didn't expect was for him to tighten those binds, to let him pull me a little closer by confessing something that has my brain in a frenzy.

"I don't know how to answer you, Lane," I whisper, searching for hope—wishing for strength to take hold of what he's offering.

"Well, I do. You are the only woman who would never walk away from my daughter if things went south between you and me. You are the only woman I ever talked to her about. I told her I knew this girl once. She was the prettiest redhead in New Orleans. One day she asked me if I loved this girl. I told her, yes, and I hoped one day you'd come back so I could prove it to you." Pinching the bridge of his nose, he closes his eyes. All I can do is stare in shock, feeling his words down to the core of my soul.

"I would never walk away from Lexi if you gave me the chance to get to know her, but Lane, I don't know how to be happy without our son. I don't know how to stop feeling guilty for wanting to be. I can't stop it from spinning. It consumes me."

The same emotion stares back at me when he opens those mesmerizing eyes. They hold so much of it. It festers mine all the more, squeezing my lungs and tugging at my heart.

"Guilt isn't going to go away until you have Luca in your arms again. We can share our guilt by building on what we mean to each other. Luca needs stability when he comes back, and I want him to have it. I want to give him the whole damn world along with giving it to you and Lexi. Let me in so I can walk beside you. Let me take your hand when you need it. Let me hold you when your mind fills with too much. Let me share the pain and love you the way I messed up the chance to do years ago. Let me make you smile. Seeing one on you will put one on me."

Energy flies through the room. Surging and uncontrollable.

"Lane, there are years between us."

"Fuck the years between us. I said before I didn't expect us to start where we left off. I'm asking for a chance to show you I'm the man for you. Do I want to touch you, kiss you, fuck you? Yes. With every fiber in my body, I want to bend you over, place your palms on that desk, and slide inside of you. You can make all the excuses you want. I won't buy any of them because that scared woman inside of you wants me as badly as I do her. Did you not listen when I said I want back what's mine. Tell me you haven't thought about me holding you this past week while you fall apart. Tell me you haven't thought about me kissing you, touching you. I've thought about your arms wrapped around me so we could fall apart, try to cope, adjust, survive together. I thought about your lips, your body. You, I've thought about *you*."

I suck in a breath, mind entranced from his words.

Overwhelmed and dazed.

My chest heaves when he advances toward me, igniting his power as he places the picture down on my desk, adjusting it on an angle to face my chair.

The chair that in a few quick strides he's leaning into, gripping the sides, his hot, warm breath skimming my ear and sending a shiver down my spine. His scent is enveloping me in promises to make me happy. He smells like home—a unique combination of fresh soap, dominance, and man.

"For now, the emotional part of our conversation is over. I want you to feel me, Sienna. Feel the presence of me over those heartbreaking emotions. Let me hold on to half of them. Every part of you deserves to feel. That includes your body and your heart," he whispers—a heady threat and a beautiful promise.

I whimper.

He's going to devour me like I knew he would.

I clench my thighs together—the move has him drawing back with a seductive smirk on his face.

"Do you still feel it, that connection between us, the heat on your skin whenever I'm near, that shockwave of desperation? The desire to be fucked until you go out of your mind? When I do fuck you, all you're going to feel is me when you stand on shaky legs, and I drip out of you. I have felt you in the middle of my chest every damn day for ten years. I missed you, and I am so damn sorry for hurting you. I'm going to push you whether you want me to or not. Don't deny me to slide into your tight body, don't deny me to grab hold of your beautiful heart and hold it in my palms. Don't deny me what has been mine since the day I met you. You, Sienna, every part of you belongs to me the same as all of me is yours."

Need. It trembles through me.

My breathing hitches as he moves his hands up to my face. I expect him to cup my cheeks the way he would when he'd kiss me. Instead, both hover close to my skin, ghosting around my neck, my shoulders, my breasts, and down my stomach.

His tongue sweeping out to wet his lips as he watches himself.

"You are stunning. I want to touch you, but I won't place my hands on you until you ask me."

He drops his gaze to my lips, and I swear on the holy

God I nearly come right here when he grips himself, unashamed to show his want.

"That mouth of yours. I missed it, missed that wicked little tongue that fought for dominance when it tangled with mine." When he brings his mouth toward mine, I part my lips. But his linger as he stares at my mouth for the longest time.

"I won't kiss you until you ask me. Trust me when I do, that tongue better be prepared to duel with mine until we have to stop to fill our lungs with air, and then I'm diving right back in."

His words hang in the thick air, his lips twitching as if he were waiting, daring me to deny it so he could prove it.

This man is going to seduce me without laying a finger on me. It is the most erotic form of foreplay he has ever done to me.

A tease that will have me begging.

"This neck, fuck, La Mia Vita. I look forward to trailing kisses on every inch. I'd start here." He blows out a hot tingling breath at the base of my ear. "Then here." He blows out another and another as he moves down the slope of my neck. "I'd end here before moving along too." Another one sweeps across my collarbone.

I swallow, center clenching and pulsing as his body bends slightly at the waist, he dips his head, hands coming up, fingers bending slightly as they cup the swells of my breasts without touching.

I'm mesmerized in his trance, my nipples aching—pussy on fire.

"These amazing breasts. Tell me; Sienna, are your nipples as pink as they were? Do they remember how I used to suck on them until you'd arch your back and tell me the other one needs the same amount of attention? Do your breasts scream to be pushed together while I slide my dick in between them? Goddamn, I can't wait to fuck them and come all over that elegant neck." He leans in a little closer, slamming me with a gust of his intoxicating power.

I've no doubt the way I'm flushed, my body temperature is about to hit the ceiling, my skin likely his favorite color—pink with a tinge of red.

I'm about a second away from passing out due to the dizziness in my head.

"How about your heart? Did it miss me as much as mine missed yours? Did it pound so hard you couldn't breathe whenever you thought about me? Mine did when I thought about you. I don't want to breathe anymore without you. You've always owned my heart, Sienna. There isn't another woman who will."

With the slightest movement of his head, his eyes meet mine. My breath catches in my throat when I see so much longing and desire that I almost beg him to touch me, but I'm held captive in his seductive spell that all I can do is nod.

And then the man pulls a gasp out of me when he drops to his knees. His mouth is less than an inch away from the spot aching for his touch. I want to lift my skirt, grab the hair on his head, and shove myself into his face.

"This pussy, I missed it. Missed the taste, the way it would clench tightly around my cock and milk me dry. When I fuck you, you will feel me when you sit, stand, walk, because I'll have taken back what belongs to me. I want all of you, your mind, body, heart, your life. You are my life, and once you are ready for me. Once you stop believing you don't deserve to be happy, I swear to you as a man on his knees. A man who doesn't deserve your forgiveness that there won't be a day gone by that I prove you do. I will give you the life you have always wanted—a life with me. You are worth everything. Everything, Sienna."

I swallow hard. I want to drop to my knees too and promise forever. Still, that part of my heart filled with emotions I can't sweep away, it screams I don't deserve to be happy. I know that is why Lane is pushing me with words instead of touching me. Why he said, he won't until I'm ready. He's reminding me what it's like to be valued.

"I'll wait for you, Sienna. If you don't want me to touch you, all you have to do is tell me. If you want to talk, walk, be together, then I'm okay with that. I am okay with waiting as long as you need. I want you to be clear on that. There's one more thing about the promise I made to Lexi that you need to know. When I said I wasn't letting a woman in, I meant it in every way. I haven't had sex since before Lexi was born. With you coming back into my life, I've never been more grateful for sticking to that promise."

"What?" I've found my voice. It's not the one Lane stated I have. I thought I had that voice a few days ago when I told myself I would use it with Ellie because I could. No, that one sucked right back into my lungs by Lane forgiving, wanting, and offering me things I've dreamed of when he should hate me.

"I didn't stutter. You heard me."

I did, and I can't believe my ears.

He brings a hand up to my cheek but quickly retreats by dropping it to his side. I can see the indecision torturing him, a strained temptation he's choosing to ignore.

"We loved each other once. We can get there again. Let me fix your broken wings so you can fly. I promise I won't let you fall without catching you. You don't have to be alone anymore. Not when you have me to take it away. Not when what we had, what will have again is a second chance to fall deeper in love. It's there, Sienna. An unbreakable love."

Pushing to stand, he walks to the door, each step away from me leaves footprints on my heart. Prints that belong to a man I have many questions to ask and so much submission to give.

He pauses after swinging open the door and glances over his shoulder.

"I've missed everything about you, Sienna Ricci. Mostly, your heart. Don't make me wait much longer to take care of it. I could live without everything else except that."

CHAPTER TWELVE

LANE

"You've always carried this fucked-up world on your shoulders, Lane. Well, goddamn it, sometimes in life we need to ask for help. Even though you didn't, you sure as fuck are getting it. I live in New York half the time anyway. I know first-hand how that knife cuts so deep into your gut, twisting the shit out of it until you're bleeding to death. It can possess your every thought. The more people looking, the better." I prop my phone up to my ear with my shoulder, hit send on the final bill for a customer to my assistant, and shut down my laptop.

I should have never answered my phone when Rocco called. Wouldn't have mattered though, he'd be out there hounding like a dog regardless.

The guy went through hell several years back. He still hasn't found his way out. He dropped right down that hole from rawness, suffering and witnessing his fiancée murdered. It was a horrendous act of jealousy that messed him and Seth up.

Both witnessed his woman getting shot to death. That,

plus Seth losing the girl he cared for over it, started his spiral into drinking. Seth fell for Rocco's younger sister. She moved after the murder. Just up and left without a goodbye.

My brother recovered from his addiction, Rocco didn't. I'm not sure if he ever will. The guy doesn't care about anyone except for my family and fucking away his feelings. It's a damn shame. He'd make a great life partner for someone with as big of a heart as he has.

"How's business?" I ask, changing the subject. I'd forgotten Rocco took ownership of the building, and Logan bought and turned it into another club right in the heart of Manhattan. Legit dance club with an underground sex organization I'm sure puts the one he owns in Georgia to shame.

My mouth dries, nausea roiling in the pit of my gut when I think back to the days I was as rooted in the sex world as he is.

I let it digest me. Swallow me whole.

A piss poor excuse for not being man enough back then to fight for Sienna. Look what it cost her?

Guttural agony.

I'm deflating because of it.

I swallow the reality. It'll come right back up, stirring those emotions, yanking on my gut to let it out as soon as we hang up.

"It's going good, asshole. Don't try averting on me. I'm no fool, man. You best let that shit out, it'll poison you if you don't. Do you get me? Listen up. I know more about computers than all you pretty Mitchell brothers put together. I wish I were calling with news that I found XYZ. They vanished, man. I couldn't find a thing on the dark web about them except a few videos floating around. That is some messed up shit to watch. I scrolled through, hoping there'd be a contact or some shit, hell I don't know. Shit will bleed out of my brain. That's for sure." The disgust and aggravation in his voice carry through the line.

Dark fury clutches hold of the back of my skull. That ache deep inside my chest, ready to burst. Hell would have to freeze over before I ever watch one of those videos. How Rocco did it beats the fuck out of me.

XYZ up and deleting themselves off the web only brings the sparks under my ass a little closer to the roaring fire. I'm about ready to go up in flames—nerves fraying with nothing to snag hold of to keep me from falling face first, submitting to my guilt, letting it out.

Wonder if it'll do me any good.

Doubt it.

"That doesn't surprise me. I appreciate you stepping in to help, I do. The dark web isn't a place I want you to be." I don't know jack shit about it except for bits and pieces. That place is a community of its own. Dangerous. Even though Rocco is a junkie for danger, that doesn't mean I want another person I care about getting messed up in this.

With my luck, someone would track his ass down and come after him—someone as screwed up as Joseph.

"Yeah, well, I'm damn good at what I do. I guarantee nothing will get traced back to me. I'm almost to my destination. I'm going to scour the streets with your brother. I have to keep that little shit in line, and don't you go messing up Logan's face. He isn't the one who told me. Take care of yourself and that woman. You got a second chance, man, and a son I'll kill every rotten motherfucker in my way to get him to you and his mom."

The line goes dead at his last word, and I throw my phone on my desk instead of chucking it at the wall that is shrinking in on me with each breath I take.

How the hell am I supposed to take care of a woman

when it's going on a week since I filleted myself wide open in her office? I obviously went about it the wrong way when it comes to Sienna. I'm not giving up by any means, just going out of my mind all the more.

Agitation starts to weave its way through my veins. Fueled by the desperation to get Sienna back and try to find my son. The only thing keeping me stable right now is Lexi, and even when I'm with her, I'm having a hard time focusing.

Desperate.

I hated that word.

For some reason, it reminds me of my mother. The woman was so anxious to do whatever it took to mourn the sudden death of our dad that before his body was even in the ground, she'd forgot her sons were standing next to her grieving themselves if it weren't for Gabe, who knows what would have happened to us.

"Someone needs to throw my kid and Sienna a bone here, damn it." Screw me and the future I want to create when the love of my life needs it.

A lifeline. A reason for her to keep on hoping.

I wasn't a desperate man any more than I was one to walk a tightrope when it came to every aspect of my life. With every step I've taken since finding out that young boy has my blood running through his veins, that rope is getting thinner. I can already feel it wobbling underneath my unsteady feet. It won't be long before it snaps.

It's enough to drive the sanest of men insane. And I consider myself pretty damn balanced.

"The hell with it, Rocco's right." I need some air, need to get this out of me before I rip my office apart. My rationality is slipping with all that's prodding away at my skull.

I'm starting to feel sorry for myself—this helpless man who doesn't know which way to turn.

Pressure. I knew the time would come where I'd buckle underneath that avalanche roaring on a mission to bury me alive.

I'm spiraling. Heart strung between heaven and hell.

Flying to my feet, I tear down the hallway, pull open the door to the back of the building, and bend at the waist. I could puke, I could cry, I could ram my fist into the brick wall of Mitchell Holdings, I could yell until my throat bleeds raw. It still won't expel this strange feeling coursing through me.

I am ready to destruct—that ticking time bomb on the final countdown.

I whirl around, chest heaving when the door flies open to Logan, staring at me with dark circles under his eyes, brows pinching together.

I hate that for him. It riles my ass that my older brother is stricken with another Mitchell curse. Swear to God; we were born with them hanging over our heads. Now, one has cast my son.

"The fuck? Jesus, why the hell are you even here? I can run Mitchell Holdings on my own." My head jerks back. I don't like his tone. It's bordering on pissed off.

He best not be taking his lack of control out on me.

"We're already missing Seth, not about to dump my workload on you. Besides, you wouldn't know how to do my job to save your life. What's your problem anyway?" I stiffen my jaw, grinding my teeth.

Logan is as shit with numbers as he is an asshole right now. I draw up the bids after the clients okay the blueprints. He'd scratch his head, trying to add everything up.

"You are my problem. I expect you to do your job if you insist on being here. I don't need you sitting in a meeting with clients, not paying attention to questions about where they can or can't cut corners to stay within budget. You've been doing that for days. Look, I could handle working when things got rough with Ellie. The way I see it, you can't."

He takes a step closer, asshole having the nerve to chuckle.

I clench my fists.

"I've done my job. Don't come out here accusing me of slacking off. Not today." For Christ's sake. The client he's referring to had to ask me twice. "We got the job. You, on the other hand, can get out of my space."

The blood drains from my face. I guess if I'd looked a little closer, I would have noticed the fury buried underneath his tiredness.

Still, who gives a rat's ass about this company at the moment. He just compared my son missing to the secrets and lies he kept from his wife.

That remark is as much heartbreaking as it is a low blow.

If he takes another step toward me, I'll come unhinged.

"I don't think I will. I'll do whatever I have to do to get you to open up. You've ignored me when I've asked if you want to talk. You don't give me a clue as to what you're thinking, how I can help, you give me nothing. You hole yourself up in your office and then leave without saying a word. Do you want our employees to catch onto what's going on? If so, let's call a meeting."

"Call one, see if I give a shit. If I want to stay in my office, then I'll stay in my office. If I want to go home, then I'll leave whenever I damn want."

Both of us cock our heads to the side, staring one

another down. I have no idea where this sudden attitude is coming from other than my older brother must be losing his mind the same as me. If so, he might want to rein it in before I drive my fist into his mouth.

I'll use him as the outlet to beat these feelings I can't restrain out of my system.

My mind is out of control, his words are unexpected, but I'll be damned if the thing that pops into my head right now is how much we resemble one another as I glare at him. It's damn near scary. We have our differences; that's for sure, but when it comes to our looks, all three of us look a lot like one another. If it weren't for Seth being covered from neck to ankles in tattoos along with his long hair, we could stand side by side by side in a lineup, and no one could tell us apart unless they knew who was who.

"Excuse me? My son is missing, Logan. A son I didn't know I had until weeks ago. Sienna is drowning in grief. I have regrets flying around in my skull. Blame and shame. Helplessness and fear as I've never felt before. I'm torn apart between leaving my daughter with you and Ellie to go search for Luca, and you, the brother I've always looked up to is going to come out here when I need a minute to clear my head and fill it with bullshit." I don't think so. I will take the anchor tied around me and take him down with me.

"You're right. What happened to Ellie and me isn't the same. Someone needs to open your eyes. Since I'm the one here with you, it's me."

I cringe as the puncture of his words pierces through my flesh.

"My eyes are wide open. Luca is with a man he thinks is his father. I can't begin to conceive what that must be like for him. He's not quite ten years old, Logan. He could come back to his mother damaged for life. He could not come back to her at all." I all but growl the words to get them past the tears clogging my throat.

I'm not afraid to break down and cry. I prefer to do it without my older brother being a self-centered prick all of a sudden.

Something close to the way I'm feeling flashes across his face. That shuts those tears right down and fuels my wrath like there's no tomorrow. He does not get to feel sorry for me. He does not get to come out here, invading my space with demands and comparison. He does not get to tell me what to do. He does not get to do a damn thing except shut the hell up and stay out of this and let me be.

There is nothing he can do. Not a damn thing except keeping the love I have for Lexi alive inside of her, so she never forgets how difficult this was for me if I choose to look for Luca and end up dead.

This is the worst curse ever to be cast on my family. It is unfair.

"You son of a bitch," I bark at the top of my lungs. "I don't need you to look at me like that! Like you, fucking feel *sorry* for me. I don't need you to act like my father. I don't need you to tell me how to do my job. I need pulling out of this nightmare. I need the woman I care about to come out of her shell. I need her to know what's going on with Luca so I can pick up the pieces. I need to find Luca before I lose my fucking mind. I need a little goddamn space when I ask for space, and if you weren't my brother, I'd pound you into the pavement for not giving it to me." I scoff, all the bitterness inside of me along with that bomb explodes when he smirks.

There's no escape route for the shards of pain that shatter right through me. It propels me into an open space filled with more.

It's everywhere.

Pain.

Motherfucking agony. I can only take so much of it.

I grab him by the collar, shoving him against the wall of our building. The place the three of us put everything we had into by taking a chance it could grow into a legit business we could be proud of. And it has.

"Fuck you, Lane," he rasps as he reaches out and grips hold of my shoulders.

I jolt back, dropping my hands and shrugging out of his clasp as if he'd punched me in the gut. Not in a million years would I expect the man who has watched over me and Seth most of our lives to follow me out here and spew this kind of crap in my face.

I snap, shaking my head as I get within an inch of his face. Evidently, something crawled up Logan's ass and died. Not once has he talked to me this way.

You'd think he'd be as miserable as I am. You'd think he'd be scratching at his skin not to be in Seth's position right now. For some goddamn reason, he's not.

"Fuck me? My life has abruptly come to a stop, and you of all people say fuck you, Lane! I took care of you when you needed me the most, and you say fuck you, Lane! You have a good life now, the wife, the kid, the love I've always thought you deserved, and you say fuck you, Lane! No. Fuck you, Logan. You can take this business, our brotherhood, and shove it up your righteous ass!"

The force of my wrath bangs on my ribs to unleash. I want to kill someone again. Beat them until they are unrecognizable.

"That's right, I said it. I'll repeat it. Fuck you, Lane." His voice cracks, eyes peering at me intently.

A low growl rumbles in my chest, shooting straight out

of my mouth. I'm a second away from punching him in the chest so he can feel how it is to have someone talk enough bullshit that it yanks out your heart.

Instantly, my fist flies with all the rage boiling over. I clock him in the cheek just as he turns his head. He stumbles backward, shakes his head, and smiles.

The asshole smiles.

"There he is, my brother who would beat a man's ass if he so much as looked at a woman at the club after she'd say no. There he is, the man I have more respect for than anyone else. Get pissed off, hit me, beat my ass, but don't you dare hold that shit inside."

I blink—the confusion as to where Logan all of a sudden attacked me flaps in the air like a surrendering white flag.

His reason.

It's not funny. There's not one damn thing to laugh at, but yet I feel like I could. Logan knows me well enough to push my buttons better than anyone.

This is where not only our looks are alike, so are we. When someone you care about traps inside themselves. You'll push until they break free.

That's what I hope Sienna soon realizes I was trying to do for her. That's what Logan is doing for me.

I should deck him in the face again and laugh while doing it.

He moves his jaw back and forth, eyes digging deep into mine.

"You're not quite back to yourself, yet are you? Where's my brother who killed a man the other day? My brother, who gave up everything for his daughter? The same man who helped me put Seth to sleep while he cried for our mother? Where is he? He's in there hiding underneath guilt. I'm pulling him out before that poison eats him from the inside out. You want to cry, then right here is a shoulder. I know this is gutting you. I'm so damn sorry you are going through hell."

Something black rises inside of me, circulating with the range of emotions I can't contain. That's when I break. I sag into Logan. His arms circle me, and I cry. Fuck, I cry until I'm ripping at my hair and seeing red.

"I'm torn apart, Logan. Luca is my son. My flesh and blood. Half of Sienna and me. What do I do if he never comes home? What do I do?" My voice drops into a suffocating whisper.

A beg.

A plea.

"You fight. You fight through every emotion. You beat those bad ones down before they pull you under. If they are more than you can take, then you come to me, and I will battle with you. You stay strong for a woman who needs it. I'm here. I'm right fucking here, brother. Do you hear me?"

I hear him loud and clear.

I cave to the agony, balling my fists into his shirt, taking that shoulder, and I weep.

I surrender to the guilt, the shame, and everything I can't do to bring Luca back and make Sienna's pain go away.

CHAPTER THIRTEEN

Sienna

My hand pauses above the waistband of my panties as the hero in the book I'm reading grabs hold of his cock and thrusts into the heroine. It's been a long time since I've become this wired with an out of control need to touch myself. And honestly, it doesn't have a thing to do with how hot this book is.

Desire. It's slipping right through me, hitting those spots that have been dead for years.

The passion of wanting Lane winds around my legs and up my spine when I remember the way he used to touch me everywhere. We might have been young, but that man knew how to work my body. His hands and fingers, his tongue, worshipped me with purpose, with one mission in mind. To draw as many orgasms out of me as he could before he'd fuck me like an uncaged animal.

My body felt like it was the torch to his striking match.

The things he'd whisper he wanted to do to me, then ask me to voice when we were younger I had no problem slipping them right off my tongue.

Now the man has me rattled. Shaken my world, knocking my knees and rocking the ground every time I try to stand.

"Damn it," I yell, chest alive with a surge of lust.

Holding the book close to my face, I grip the sheet with the other, refusing to touch myself as I focus on the words, letting them sink into me. Nothing I do will satisfy me except the man I want badly anyway.

God, please don't let this come back and hurt me. I've let him strip me completely bare. Not just for sex. My heart. I've opened it wide for him once again. Allowed it to be gutted open. I won't survive the pain this time. I know I won't. He's come on strong. Like a hurricane barreling through my body. Full force and weighing me down.

I've grieved for this man for far too long. The heartache over losing him has followed me through the years. I might have tried to convince myself that I didn't love him, might have tried pushing thoughts of him away. The truth is, he's a part of me. Always has been, forever will be ingrained in my soul.

"Fuck me, please."

His eyes snap to mine. With an underlying possessiveness scattering across his face, he pulls out and plows back in. Pleasure spears through my veins, thrumming my heart and pulling at those strings that have been strung taut and tight between us. I want them to break.

To set us free from our pasts, pushing forward with a hefty shove.

"Fuck, you feel good." His tone is hard and worshipful. It sets me soaring.

Freedom to love him, to finally be with him within my reach, I'm grasping onto it and never letting go.

My body goes languid, succumbing to him as he slams into me over and over with raw, unbridled recklessness. Primal and fierce, his hands digging into my thighs, eyes never straying from mine as he takes complete control and loves me as he promised.

"Fucking Christ, you are perfect. Years. So many years I've waited for this. I've wanted you so fucking bad. Swear to God, it's always been you."

THE PROBLEM between my thighs intensifies as the lines in the book become blurry. I could easily take care of it for now. It would come back the minute my thoughts drift to Lane again and how good it would feel to have him touch me with those big hands. To remind me of the pleasurable wicked things he used to do.

I want Lane to rip me apart. Drive me to the brink again and again before he plunges inside and fucks me in more ways than one.

I want to run to him and grasp hold to every word he's said. To start over.

I slam the book closed, climb out of bed, so confused—that intensity between right and wrong swelling.

Grabbing my phone from my pillow, I call Victoria, clutching the phone to my ear. I should have never called to tell her what a mess I was after Lane left my office. Then two days later, I receive a delivery from her containing a box of books, telling me they'll not only help me pass the time of my lonely nights but getting lost in a book is good for the soul.

So like the lonely woman I am. More so now that my father left the other day to God knows where, I pulled one out, shook my head when I saw the sexy muscular man on the cover, and without reading the blurb, I went in blind knowing full well there'd be sex.

"God, how could I think I could handle reading something like that when the man has me riled up." I can't continue like this.

I pace as I listen to the line ring and ring. I'm preparing to ream her butt out over voicemail when she answers.

"Sienna, is everything okay?" she asks worriedly.

"Not by a long shot. Should I thank you for the books or clobber you over the head with one the next time I see you? If I look at the rest of them, are they going to be second chance emotional romances too? You are a traitor friend," I say, not taking a breath before continuing. "You of all people know I'm barely holding it together. When Joseph calls—"

"Woah. Slow down and shut it, Sienna," she cuts me off, anger bristling from her high pitch. "I sent them to make you realize it's okay to hold on to what you're feeling and grab onto something else. You have to stop agonizing over when Joseph calls or when Joseph does this or that. Listen to me for once, please. I'm begging you to open both your mind and heart and not only hear me. Hear Lane too."

I pinch the bridge of my nose, drawing in a deep breath.

Lane's not even here, and I can hear him. His deep voice laced with so much compassion, so much heartache. So much assurance that I can't think straight. I know he cares about me. I could see it in the way he was watching me, with those parting words of wanting my heart more than anything else. I can hear the wheels in Victoria's head spinning too.

Maybe reading that book was what I needed to kick my ass in gear. To step over the line and give my all to the man who won't stop convincing me, he'll do whatever it takes to bring me back to life.

"I'll listen, you have to listen to me too. I'll run back to Joseph if he calls. I will sneak away if that's what it takes. It will break my heart into a million pieces if I get attached to Lexi and her to me. The mere thought of hurting that little girl."

"If anyone faults you for that then they aren't worthy of your spit. If you let go and give into Lane, the two of you can figure things out together. You can't go on living like this. You have to trust your family that they will find Joseph. If he calls, then you tell someone. Trust someone other than me, Sienna. You say you do, but do you really?"

My heart thunders in a faltering ache.

"I do trust them. It's me, I don't."

"Why? You give me a good reason why you don't trust yourself? Using the excuse you'd go back to Joseph isn't good enough anymore. We'd all do it if that we're the only choice we had."

Chaos rages through me like a blistering fire.

Silence fills my bedroom—cat grasping hold of my tongue.

"That's what I thought. You can't. Stop being afraid of that man who abused you for years. He might have Luca, but he will be found. I've never been thankful my father is a killer until Joseph took Luca. That prick will get what's coming to him. You have to let go."

I start shaking, searching deep inside for the lost woman I used to be. My chest goes tight. Darkness arrives leaving me dangling somewhere between the woman who was hanging on for her and her son's lives, and the real me—the one who would fight for her freedom and do everything to get her son back with the man she wants by her side.

"I'm not going to say you deserve to be happy, not when deep down, you know you do. What is it *you* want, Sienna? What is your heart telling you to do? If you tell me you're worried about Lexi and Lane again, I'll be on a plane to set you straight. Stop with the excuses." I can hear how determined she is for me to find happiness flooding from her pores.

"While I'm on a roll, I may as well plant the same bug in your ear as I did the other day when you went on about only spending hours with Lane in the last decade. So damn what. You owe no one an explanation for anything you do. Not anymore. Get to know Lane again. Have the best sex of your life while doing it. You are doing nothing wrong. Don't you dare go into how unfair it would be for you to be happy, not when I know for a fact that man cares for you more than you realize. More than I ever thought a Mitchell could." She speaks so calmly and quietly, which shocks me as I compare it to her hard, truthful words.

Victoria and I have been there for one another through thick and thin. She's my rock and knows me better than anyone else. We've cried so many tears on one another's shoulders over me as well as her. Years ago, I tried to convince her to go to her parents after being bullied in school. She laughed through self-conscious tears when she'd answer that her dad would probably kill them if she did, and her mom would screech at the top of her lungs that he would not.

She's a beautiful woman on the inside and out. She's slightly on the curvy side and let me tell you, some of the things she repeated back to me those mean teenagers said were worse than cruel.

We'd cry and cry when she'd help me cover up my bruises, begging me to let her tell Aidan what was going on in my home. I didn't listen then, but I hear now. It's blaring in my ears.

I love Victoria. Right here, though, I wish she was standing in front of me so I could yell and scream at her for keeping a secret from me.

"You know, only my best friend would tell me to pull my head out of my ass without coming out and saying it. Only my best friend would keep something she thought was too hard for me to handle. What do you mean by fact? How long have you been talking to Lane?" I blurt, knowing full well she has.

"Right, and only your best friend would say, I'm not telling you a thing until you answer me."

I inhale and exhale deeply. Not because I'm hesitating —but once I say it out loud, there'd be no turning back. I'll jump in my car and admit it to Lane, and he'll never let me go.

"I'm going to say what you don't want to hear. There's not just me to consider anymore. That's what I'm more afraid of than anything else."

"And you have every reason to be. The crazy son of a bitch tried to break you, but he didn't. You are still standing, and let me say this. You say you trust Lane. Why aren't you acting on that trust and let yourself go to him? The man isn't going to let anyone near Lexi or anyone he cares about, including you. He told you as much. Quit trying to convince yourself you don't deserve that man." God, she sounds like Lane.

I squeeze the phone as if it could relieve some of the stress out of me and replace it with belief.

"I'm conflicted, confused. I have all these feelings swinging back and forth. I'm nervous and unprepared."

I'm still trying to wrap my head around him, not being with a woman in years. Lane is an attractive man, he probably had women throw themselves at him, and the fact he didn't even give them a thought further proves how devoted he can be.

I didn't share that with Victoria. It made me realize how loyal and faithful to his word he is. It has me wanting him all the more.

"Most of those feelings are nothing new to you. They are enhanced for valuable reasons by Lane as they should be. I'd think Joseph would have broken you if you stopped caring about others, Sienna. As far as confused, I can't help you there. You need to jump into what Lane is offering to rid yourself of it. Loving the man is nothing new to you either. It might not be as strong as it was. It's there, though, and by the sounds of it, he's right there with you. You might have abruptly walked into Joseph's arms, Sienna. You never walked away from loving Lane. It makes no sense, but when has anything when it comes to love."

"When did you become so wise with relationships?" She hasn't dated in years. She claims not to have the time. There's more to it, but whenever we'd get on the subject, she'd tell me how busy she's been trying to make it on her own as a designer. She refuses to borrow what she calls blood money from her parents. If there ever was a person to love their family with her whole heart and hate what they do, it's Victoria Hughes.

"It's my turn to tell you something you don't want to hear. If you hang up on me, I'll drop everything I'm doing and be down there before the sun rises." I'm uncomfortable with that opening sentence. It stirs flapping wings of frantic low in my stomach.

"You've told me plenty that I didn't want to hear. I needed it, though." Sinking onto my bed, I lean against the headboard, drawing my knees to my chest.

"Yeah, well, a little nudge now and then doesn't hurt anyone. Listen to me good, Sienna. Take this straight to your heart and keep it tucked in there. Until Luca comes home, there won't be a day where you won't think of him. I'm not telling you to give up on hope. It could be years before he comes back. I believe he will. No matter what is happening to him right now, that boy has been raised by you. He's going to need his strong, loving mother when he comes home. Let him come home to the woman you were the night you left."

She's right. I've known it all along. To admit it could be a day, a year, or more before I have Luca back is something I've shoved so far back in my mind. I have to leave it there, or I'll never take a step forward again.

"I love you, Sienna, and no one on this earth, in my opinion, deserves to be treated like a queen than you. You are royalty in your own right, but if you don't climb out of the grave Joseph tried burying you in, there will be nothing left of you when Luca does come home. Is that what you want for him? Is that what Luca would wish for you? After all these years separating you and Lane, that man left his heart at your feet. Give him yours and have him fight through this with you. Now, yes, I've talked to Lane. He's been calling to ask how you are."

My entire body breaks out in goosebumps, all my dreams of being with Lane again float to the surface of the murky waters in my mind, ready to drown my fears.

To battle and win until the end.

"I'm going to ask you one more time, Sienna, and your ass better be honest with me. What. Do. You. Want?"

"I want Lane."

CHAPTER FOURTEEN

Lane

At the cutting of headlights, I swing open the front door to a stunning vision I knew was heading my way after security informed me a minute ago. As I watch her round the front of her car, biting that plump bottom lip, creamy white skin glowing from the lights lining my driveway, each step she takes sends a current through the air.

It strikes me in the chest.

The woman is a fantasy come to life in silk sleep pants, a plain white t-shirt with no bra—those mouth-watering nipples on full display.

There is no mistaking how badly I want her, my cock throbs, my hands itch, and my mouth waters to quench that craving to taste this woman I've had for far too long.

Still a few feet away from me, she tilts her head ever so slightly and chews on her bottom lip. I want that lip. Want it touching my own. Want it wrapped around my dick, licking a hot blaze up my shaft.

"Your house looks like a tiny castle. I didn't pay attention when I left here before. I find it sexy, heartwarming, and quite possibly the sweetest thing that you'd buy a house fit for your princess." Her lips stretch into a smile that doesn't quite reach her sorrowful eyes. I can't blame her as they mirror my own.

A gasp tumbles out of her mouth when she looks up to the tiny tower higher above the rest of the house. That tower is what sold me when I searched for the right home for Lexi and me. The top is her bedroom. The bottom is her playroom. Of course, it was a surprise to my princess. One that had her so damn excited she didn't shut up for weeks after we moved in.

But I don't want to talk about my house, my daughter or anything else except the reason Sienna is here.

Her eyes dart to where I'm rubbing my thumb over the tips of my fingers. I used to do that whenever we'd be in a room full of people, and I was dying to touch her. There's no one stopping me now. All she has to do is spit those words out I want to hear.

Those light green eyes meet mine, flowing with hundreds of questions. I can see them as clear as day. Hear them turning in her head.

It guts me for not telling her about Luca before I claim her, but once I do, Lorenzo will come clean with her because I won't keep secrets from Sienna ever again.

"I'm nervous," she admits, swiping her tongue across her lip again. That move is straight up making me lose my mind.

I want to kiss this woman so damn bad. Swipe her bad memories away with my tongue. That regret at putting them there will live inside of me for the rest of my life. I'll be damned if I'll let it rule me any longer once I have her again.

"That makes two of us. It won't stop me from kissing

you, won't stop me from cupping those full tits in my hands, pinching those nipples until you arch your back, and I take them in my mouth. It won't stop me from tasting your pussy until you come all over my face. It sure as hell won't stop me from fucking you over and over. Above all that, Sienna, I want you to give me your broken heart and let me heal it." I lift my chin in a challenge, tone like gravel due to wanting her to trust me completely. For her to know, she is worth more than the way Joseph made her believe.

I want, and I'm going to get back the woman I once knew, and together we will deal with the heartache laid at our feet.

I place my hands above the frame of the door, lean in until I'm close enough to follow the path of her tongue. Our chemistry ricochets off each other, sparks getting higher by the second.

She looks up at me, that sorrow clouding over with burning desire.

Fuck, there she is, the girl that was wild and ferocious and blew my mind in bed so much that I couldn't get enough.

The mistakes I made back then not to tell anyone I was in love with Sienna gut me all over again. Yet, with our raw emotions flying all over the place, the way our heartbreaking situation has drawn us back to one another, I forget about how I fucked up.

My soul's purpose, along with it belonging to Lexi and my son, is for Sienna to live again.

"Say it," I demand. Tone rough and jagged. "Tell me what you want. Tell me you're mine." My nose barely grazes the side of hers. I inhale her sharp intake of breath. If she doesn't hurry, I'm going to lose the last bit of restraint I have left and take her against the side of my house.

Fuck the fact that I bought a house in a friendly watch neighborhood. They'll get an eyeful of me thrusting into her tight little body that's begging to be devoured.

A moan that shoots straight to my dick escapes her mouth when she lifts her hands. One brushes over my bottom lip, the other flat on my bare chest, right over the tattoo I had etched into my skin. A reminder of what I'd lost. Her touch as much welcome as it is torture, knowing how much I missed her.

My body jolts with vibrations that have me struggling like a barbarian not to tug that shirt down and expose those breasts.

"I want you to kiss me. Touch me everywhere. Take me to your bed and give me your all. In other words, I want you to fuck me, Lane."

She doesn't have to ask me twice. I'm burning with a roaring flame for this woman.

I yank her into me, wrap my arms around her, and slam my mouth down on hers at the same time my hands dive into all that blazing hair, palming her head.

When her plump lips part, my mind lights on fire, and the warmth of her mouth spreads throughout my entire body. Sienna is a necessity I will no longer go without.

Swear on my life, this kiss is my salvation.

Our tongues collide. Slow and seductive. I can't recall the last time I kissed a woman. I know not one of them had my heart pounding so damn hard that I'd gladly let it smash right through my chest.

Sparks fly. Flames ignite.

Fire and ice.

Sliding my hands down to grip her ass, I yank her off her feet, getting those long legs to wrap around my waist. Without losing her mouth, I kick the door shut and twist the lock. With long strides, a throbbing cock, and having her close to me, I make it to my bedroom where I shut the door, lock it, and pray Lexi doesn't wake.

"La Mia Vita," I groan, slipping my hands underneath her sleep pants to grab her ass only to find her bare.

Jesus Christ.

I squeeze as she takes advantage and slides up and down my length.

My chest heaves when I drop her to my bed—the outdoor lights shadow the outline of the woman who has starred in every one of my fantasies, her lips swollen, eyes drifting south to my dick.

"Are you sure you want me to touch you?" I want the reassurance one more time to know she's here with me and not thinking about the ways Joseph defiled her all these years.

"Yes, I want you, Lane." She moans, making it damn hard not to strip her down and fuck her right here.

I place a knee to the bed, hook a hand around her neck, tilting it back for the assault I crave on her skin as I drag her to the edge. My other hand trails up to palm a breast, and her tiny sighs of submission drive me insane.

My entire body throbs with such potent need for this woman that when my lips hit the flesh at her neck, my balls pull tight. I'm not sure I can be gentle with her.

As if she can read my mind, her hands grab my ass, tugging me on top of her, nails digging in through the thin fabric of my shorts.

I groan.

"Touch me," she pants as I drag my teeth down over her neck. Hearing her ask, those noises escaping her mouth winds up.

As if I could be wound any tighter.

I force myself to stand and drop my shorts. I'm planning on taking my time getting reacquainted with that tight little body, not about to have a barrier between us when my dick yells he needs to slip inside.

I grip my shaft, hard tugs up and down.

Sienna squirms, that damn tongue darting out again as her heady gaze locks on my hand.

Goddamn, I love it when she looks at me like that. Can't stop visualizing the young girl who in front of everyone acted innocent. She was until I got my greedy hands on her, drawing her untamed side out. It turned me on like nothing else.

"Take your clothes off if you want me to touch you." I release my cock. The veins are throbbing in anger, on the verge of bursting as he points toward the ceiling. Fuck me; I'm aching.

My brain struggles to get oxygen into my lungs when her hands go to the waistband of her pants. Eyes still on mine, she slowly slides them down her trembling legs, tosses them onto the floor and arches her back in a tease as she inches the shirt over her head. Her pussy, tits, and delectable mouth all waiting for my hands, mouth, and cock.

Nervous, my ass. This woman is a bottle of sin and seduction. She hasn't forgotten how to taunt me to please.

I don't give myself the privilege to study her body. Not yet. I want that face etched into my memory when I touch her.

"You're mine, Sienna. We will start over. We will fight together. However long it takes us, we will make it through every damn thing in life that tries to drag us down." I punctuate my words that wrench on my heartstrings. Our son has to come back. I refuse to believe life can be so damn cruel any more to a woman that's lived ten years in the pits of hell protecting her child.

"I believe you. Tonight, I need you to fuck me. Tomorrow we can talk." Something more noticeable than her carnal plea splinters through her eyes. Whatever it is, doesn't belong in this bed—not tonight.

Once again, I drop to my knees, hands going to her thighs and I spread her wide. Her pussy is pink and bare and glistening with arousal. Parting her with my fingers, I watch her expression as I plunge two fingers inside, thumb locking on her clit. Her head thrashes back and forth, hips buck into my hand. Her glazed-over eyes roll when I thrust in and out of her tight little channel.

"Over the decade, did you wish it was me finger fucking you when you touched yourself? Did you want my cock stretching you, filling you? Did you want my tongue tasting how sweet you are?" I want that mouth to continue using her voice. I want her to tell me exactly what she wants.

I ruthlessly drive my fingers in and out of her drenched desire, my cock like granite as I watch her start to fall apart. She is so damn tight, so fucking perfect; I'm going to be straining not to come within seconds once I'm inside.

I groan when she plants her feet on the bed, pushes to sit, fingertips glide down my stomach that spasms under her touch. She wraps her hand around the base of my cock. One hundred percent the Sienna I remember as she pumps me in her hand, thumb running around my throbbing head. Gathering the pearl-colored bead glistening at my slit and bringing it up to her mouth.

And she sucks.

"Yes, I did. It's always been you, Lane." When my name rolls off her tongue, I feel the power of it wrap tightly around the organ, pounding hard in my chest.

"Fuck, Sienna." That's what I want to do is fuck as much as I want to make her come until she screams she can't anymore.

Hand going to my dick again, she grabs the back of my neck, tugging me forward to kiss the ever-loving hell out of me while I finger fuck her hard and deep. Ripples of pleasure shake through her body as she trembles and clamps down on my finger, riding out her orgasm all over my hand.

She cries out when I press her onto her back, slip my finger out of her and press it into her mouth. "Taste yourself." She moans around her tongue, sending the vibration right up my arm.

I'd love nothing more than to wedge my face between her legs. At the moment, I want to swipe her flavor off her tongue.

I hunch over her, hook one leg over my shoulder and push us into the center of the bed, planting myself in between those spread thighs. My cock is soaking up her dampness as I grind. I latch onto a nipple that is begging for attention. Sucking until I've left a mark, and I groan as she draws my finger in and out of the warm well of her mouth.

"Can't wait to have my cock between those tits. My cum marking what's mine."

Licking up her neck, I collide my mouth with hers, run my hand down the curves of her body until I've hit my target, dipping two fingers inside and fuck her with my tongue and fingers in sync with each other. Neither of us comes up for air until she screams my name into my mouth through another orgasm.

"I want your sweet little cunt. Want it like never before. You ready for me?" I wind my hand around her jaw, sweeping it over the soft skin of her cheek. Thumb pressed to her fluttering pulse.

"Yes—" floats assuredly out of her.

Keeping my hand on her face, my eyes on her, I lift my hips, grip my dick, and slowly push inside.

Shit. It's been a long time since I've felt this sweet pussy—fucking hell.

I snap my eyes closed, hated taking them off her beautiful face, but I need a minute to collect myself. Can't seem to help it.

Feeling her heat bursts forth and enthralls me. I brace my hands at the sides of her head; with every inch, I memorize the feel of her tightness expanding around me as she adjusts to my size. It's indescribable. Silk wrapping around me. Warmth like I've never imagined.

"Give me a minute. You feel too good." Heaven. The sweetest torture.

"You feel good, too. Better than good, Lane." I let her words sink into my skin. My breathing picks up, heartbeat racing against my ribs.

I release a feral groan when the urge to move pinches my balls. I pull out and slam back inside hard enough that a growl of pleasure rips from my throat.

When her pussy clamps down in a vise-like grip, the scent of her filling my nose, I lose my goddamn mind. Insanity devours my vision, and I fuck her—driving my dick to power faster into her slick, wet heat.

My hips thrust harder than ever before, hers rolling, teeth sinking into my shoulder. I bury myself inside of her with every deep push. My cock is screaming out to blow. She feels too damn good for me to let go just yet.

A smirk tilts the corners of my lips as my eyes take in the sheer bliss carved all over her face.

While my length pushes in and out of her pussy, my

mouth takes hold of hers. I don't think I'll ever be tired of kissing her.

My cock pulses, her pussy tightens. I devour the loud, satisfying noises escaping her mouth with mine as she grips so hard—her mouth as thirsty for mine as I am for hers.

"Come for me."

It takes little time for her to clamp back down on me. Her cries of passion, her release all over me, hits deep. I come on a roar, my entire body twitching, shaking with spasms as my cum coats her sweet, sweet walls.

"La Via Mita," I whisper, dropping my forehead to hers. For a few minutes, we got lost in each other's eyes. In the depths of our pain. In the past. In the calm before the eye of the storm.

"You okay?"

She nods, her expression changes to admiration as if she still can't make sense of the connection we share.

I sure the hell don't understand after all this time either. But I know what I want. Know what I need.

And it's *her*.

CHAPTER FIFTEEN

Sienna

Life is short, they say, don't waste it dwelling over what is out of your control. When a person lives a normal, healthy, happy one, I agree. When you live in a toxic environment, the days seem like they will never end. However, if you pursue a goal in trying to achieve happiness, then time flies by in a blink of an eye. It's a crazy notion, but it's true.

Spending these past few weeks with Lane and Lexi has flown fast. My happiness has come and gone. Worse, with each passing day, my guilt and grief build. It's horrible and overpowering, and no matter how hard I try to shake them away, they have an iron-clad grip on my soul.

I've found myself laughing more times than I have in ten years, but when everything around me is silent, that's when my thoughts carry me away. Hearing that strange sound known as deep laughter coming out of me is as foreign as sleeping without a nightmare.

Or, knowing I won't ever have to lay my head on a

pillow after a day in Hell only to wake before the Devil and prepare myself to walk through the fire all over again.

It's as abnormal as falling asleep and waking up with safe arms wrapped around me.

Lane has drawn the woman I once was sexually right out of me with a simple touch. Kissing me until we had to break for air, then he was right back, working my mouth with harsh lashes of his tongue—teeth nipping at my neck, down my chest, where he feasted on my breasts—his fingers and cock taking ownership of my body, driving me clear out of my mind.

I missed living in a world where I feel like I can breathe again.

I missed me, but until Luca is in my arms, the best part of me will always be missing.

Lane has tried everything to show me it's okay to move forward. Not only in bed, but with getting to know each other, and every time I try to take a step, I glance down to find I'm still standing on a dividing line between what my head is telling me is right, and my heart it's wrong.

I'm at war with myself.

The sad part is I know Lane is too. I mean, our companionship, our caring for one another. Our relationship growth is moving forward, but our spirits, our lack of true happiness is far behind.

There's one thing I've noticed with Lane, and it is the best part of him. He's not once let his grief show with Lexi, except for today, which should have been the perfect day at the Galveston Pier with Logan, Ellie, and Braxton, and then following them back to their place to sit on the beach.

I have a feeling whatever has made him draw into himself is going to cause me to lose the little happiness I've found.

Lane is hiding something from me. My heart has been pounding like a jackhammer all day with the possibilities of what it could be. I can't explain it, call it intuition, call it a woman who wore a mask for years is usually the first to pick up when someone else is. Call it the same strange vibes I felt vibrate through me with my father when I went to tell him Lane is Luca's dad. Or, hell, maybe it's Lane's heart calling out to me to save it from drowning in misery.

But something is going on. Something I have a feeling the man has been holding onto for a while, and it's eating him alive. He's wound up. Muscles are continually twitching in his jaw and nerves on edge.

And the weird thing is, there isn't a doubt in my mind whatever he's hiding, my father told Lane to keep it from me.

I know it has to do with Luca. There's nothing else it could be.

During breakfast was when I first noticed a change in Lane. His mood never faltered from the attentive father he is. Or, the way he's been treating me as if I were the queen living in his remarkable castle with its homely lived-in vibe. A cherry wood grained kitchen that Lexi and I have spent so much time in, an Olympic-sized pool and his bedroom done in tones of gray and black. I could go on and on about how much I love his house.

Everything inside of me tenses. Knots tangle my stomach. The hollow space inside me fills with anger. It skates under my skin, traveling through every cell as I glance over at Lane. Whatever is bothering him, it's eating him more and more the longer we sit in the sand.

Although I should be mad at him, I'm not. I'm angry at my father because Lord knows if anyone steps on his toes and tells me a damn thing concerning my son without his permission, he will fly off the handle. Well, screw that. He's going to learn a lesson if he's behind the downfall of Lane. The man I'd clarify as sinful, sexy and oozes seduction appears to be on the edge of ruin.

His head tilts, our eyes lock, and I search through the depths of those green eyes for an answer. Quickly I become lost in the sea where I'd drown trying to find it. He's buried it under the debris of his raw emotional pain.

God, what is he hiding that is gutting him right down to the bone? I'm about to excuse myself to call my father and demand he get his ass home right now when Lane's gaze changes, devouring me with a potency that would sweep me off my feet if I wasn't sitting down.

"You look beautiful with the wind blowing your hair. I'm dying to fist it while I take your ass. I own every part of you except that. I'd make you come so hard you'd beg me to make you do it again. You going to give it to me, Sienna?" he asks, roughly. A challenge. Not a request. An if and when.

His words catch me by surprise, sending a tremble through my body, coating me with as much anticipation as I can fit inside me after today has overloaded my mind.

He just lured me right in.

A long, slow roll of his throat catches my eye. I'm unsure if I can go there just yet. That's a part of me Joseph would shackle my hands to the bed, threaten to cut out my tongue if I screamed, and he took from me until I felt like I was tearing in two. I told this to Lane the other night when I felt brave to share some of the horrid things done to me.

"You're awful sure of yourself." I tease as my eyes wander over the arc of his shoulders, down the vein that pops at the side of his neck, the muscles in his arms flexing like he's fighting his urge not to pluck me right up from my spot.

"Sienna, my hands, my fingers, not a part of me will ever hurt you. When you're ready, I'm erasing the last piece of that son of a bitch from you." He already has, by the way, he's taken care of me in all ways possible.

I'm not humiliated, ashamed, nor do I feel dirty anymore over Lane knowing what Joseph did to me. All it took was one touch from him to obliterate Joseph's filth.

It's not the same, yet it runs alongside us talking about taking it slow when it comes to how we feel for one another. We might be having sex, but like Victoria said, Lane and I do need to get to know each other again. And we are. We've talked, asked, answered so many questions, and I want that stability. I feel my own getting stronger every day. The solid foundation Lane talked about when it comes to him and me is solid. I want Luca to see that when he comes home.

I'm just not ready to give him that part of me. And again, I didn't want to be afraid, but I am.

Lane's eyes shutter closed, pinching tight, and when they open, it's as if the earth shifts. The wind coming off the ocean dies down, the air becomes still. His eyes change color from the calmness before a tornado to hurling you into the eye of its devastating storm.

Destruction.

Terror shoots through my spirit, this sixth sense ringing in my ears like a warning. Telling me Lane isn't going to be able to protect me from whatever is weighing him down.

"You've been sitting next to me, deep in thought. Don't retreat on me now. I love hearing your voice even if some of the things you say cut me deep and bleed me dry. We've opened up to each other these past few weeks. Tell me what's running through your mind." He leans forward, grasps my chin between his thumb and forefinger, tilting my head enough to stare deep into my eyes. He's begging me to open up, to share the burden dragging me down. I see him too, though. Whatever he's hiding is whipping him in every direction.

I'm trying to figure out what's running through yours. Of course, I don't ask that. For my peace of mind, I wish I could. I know Lane would tell me if I asked. I won't put him in a situation to have to deal with my father again. I'll deal with him, and this time, no matter what's being hidden from me, I won't be so easy to forgive.

It kills me to keep my mouth shut, not to beg him to tell me what's going through his mind. But I can't. It infuriates me to the point I could combust. It makes me want to slap my father across his face with all I have in me that he thinks he has a right to put Lane in a position to hurt over keeping something from me. I thought Lane, me, my uncle made my father clear that I was to be in the know of everything. I guess I was wrong.

No matter what my father's excuse will be this time, he has crossed his own sacred line.

Betrayal. Loyalty. Deceit.

How dare he make Lane go through more hell than he already is? He's taken advantage of him.

"The same thing as always. I want Luca here to live the life he deserves, for you to get to know him. To watch you and him do things together. Every day that passes, my hope dwindles." I'm not lying. I've thought about those things so many times these past weeks. My hope seems to be fading.

Missing years and millions of unspoken words pass in a frenzy across his face. The heartache that will never leave, mistakes he learned are slipping from his softening gaze. I focus on him as my own mistakes assault my brain. Nightmares and demons who always sound like Joseph bare their fangs and claws, biting and scratching to tear through the happiness and take ownership of my mind.

Tears instantly well in my eyes. I struggle hard to keep them in check as I always do, but a few leak out of the corners, and he's right there to wipe them away.

Sorrow eats at my chest again for hiding Luca from Lane. That'll never go away, but somehow, someway, I have to live with the pain and carry on. And I can. I can do it whether by myself or with the guiding hand that Lane, Ellie, and his family have extended toward me.

"Let go of the rest of those tears, Sienna. If you don't, I'll fuck them out of you later. Only they won't be sad ones. They'll be tears from coming over and over because your sweet pussy won't be able to take my tongue buried inside of you for hours." He grins, it doesn't reach his eyes, yet I'm caught in the trance by the promises I know he'll keep.

My heart clenches. I can feel those assurances in the crackling air around us, stirring up in the wind. Twisting and imploring me to let go and cry those tears.

"It's a lot easier said than done, Lane. I cried so much in the first few months that up till you brought it up, I didn't understand why I held them back. I'm afraid if I let go and cry, I'm letting defeat win. I can't let go of hoping Luca won't come home. It probably makes no sense to anyone except me, but when the only person I've lived my entire adult life for is missing and knowing all it would have taken was for me to be brave enough to call my father, I can't let go of them. They are stuck the same way I am. I'm angry, Lane, so mad I allowed this to happen. You blame yourself.

I blame me for marrying a man who would hurt a little boy. The only way I'll cry is when I have Luca in my arms. I'm trying so hard to get through every day. I know you are too." I choke on my words—the admission falling freely from my mouth.

I hated Joseph before. I can't describe what I feel for him now. It's a loathing that I honestly believe if someone placed a gun in my hand, I would beat him with it before shooting him through the black void where his heart should be.

That is how angry I've become. How bitter with every single day that devil's spawn of a man keeps me away from Luca.

He's baiting me with silent torture. And I hope. God, do I ever grasp hold that I get the chance to stare that bastard in the eye and witness him take his last breath. But I know I won't. Lane and my father have made it perfectly clear that no matter what, I will not be going anywhere near Joseph.

"It makes sense to me. One second, minute, hour, a day at a time is all we can continue to do. If I could crawl inside your heart and mind and burn the pain to ashes, I would. If I could bottle those tears up and toss them in the ocean, I would. I can't do that anymore than I can turn back time."

God, he's a damn good man. Spinning me up, hands ready to catch me when I come tumbling down.

"I'll take one minute at a time." That's all I can give anyone. That's all I've been doing for months. All I've been doing since Lane is back in my life.

One minute. Sixty seconds. It feels like an eternity when you sit here, adding up how many there are in a day. One thousand four hundred and forty minutes. Eighty-six thousand four hundred seconds.

It's tragic. Just like our love story, and it might not be a happy ending.

Lane knows it, and so do I.

This urge to do something to comfort him wraps around me. The next thing I know, I'm gripping the back of his neck, and I kiss him. Deep and long and satisfying. It takes all my willpower not to push him onto his back and straddle his waist.

That wouldn't be a wise thing to do when Lexi and Ellie should be back from using the bathroom any minute.

A minute. There it is again.

Despair takes over one of us, maybe both when I place my hands on his shoulders, his cupping my face. We kiss with more passion, a higher degree of longing than any other before this. I wish we could stay in this moment forever.

Forever.

That word sticks when I think of Lane—crashing through me. A white-knuckling head-on avoidable collision. It could mean a long time. It could be short-lived.

It could be that minute.

"I..." His voice cracks when he pulls away, grinds his teeth, and his face pinches in sorrow.

"I'll always take care of you, Sienna. No matter what happens. No matter where tomorrow brings us the next day or the next. You've grown stronger. I can't allow you to get lost to where I can't find you. That said, I know you, the you that wants to protect me. The you that's figured out." He stops, doesn't finish what he was going to say. My eyes follow his to where Lexi runs our way. Her pigtails are swishing behind her. The Ariel doll I helped Lane replicate last week, in one hand, her bag of cotton candy she talked Lane into buying her today in the other.

Even though a smile lights up his face when Lexi reaches us and sits her doll next to me, Lane's expression doesn't change. It says what he didn't finish. For me to let him talk to my father because whatever information awaits me, is worse than I could ever imagine.

I don't think so.

Lane has underestimated me if he thinks that will happen. This is between my father and me.

"Look, Daddy. Aunt Ellie, let me bring down my cotton candy from the house. You break off a piece, and it melts in your mouth. It's the best thing I've eaten in a long time. Well, it's a tie with the waffles, whip cream, and chocolate chips Sienna made this morning. They were so good. She's a better cook than you." Lexi giggles through her words as Lane positions her on his lap.

"That so? I guess I won't have to cook anymore then." And just like that, this little girl is the clear blue sky before the dark clouds come rolling in.

My lips tremble, and I look away toward the ocean. Beyond the waves, the breath-taking sun begins to set. Beautiful smudges of coral, violet, turquoise, and a fiery orange blend together to create a sight so astonishing it sweeps me away from all of my worries, replacing them, momentarily with the warmth of safety and security.

The other day when Ellie and I took a walk on the beach, it became one of my favorite places. So peaceful and uplifting. I can see why they chose to move here, although I love Lane's neighborhood too.

"Fine with me. I'll go to The Grill House every night. Sienna and I will make chicken nuggets, mac and cheese, and share a skillet cookie. Now, open wide and take a bite. I'll start calling you a chicken if you don't try it."

I smile through my sorrow. The other night the two of

them came into the restaurant for dinner. She hasn't stopped talking about the skillet cookie since. I wasn't able to eat with them as I was finishing my last interview for an assistant, but I did catch dessert.

I turn my attention back to Lexi and Lane just in time to catch her clucking like a chicken, her arms flapping, hands shoved up in her armpits.

"Bwak Bwak Bwaaak, chicken. Sienna, my daddy, is a chicken." Amusement dances across her face. Where she gets her wild spirit and lively energy from beats me. It's contagious, though.

"You best knock it off, or I'll start calling you Ursula, the sea witch or Cruella Deville. How about Maleficent?"

God, my brain freezes, I couldn't concentrate on the Disney movies we watched this week. I sat staring at Lane, snuggling with Lexi. He was completely engrossed in the stories even though he's probably watched them over and over. It was the sexiest thing I've ever seen.

"Stick and stones can break my bones. Wait, I don't want to break any bones, that would hurt. They'd have to stick a needle in me like that time I had my tonsils out. Nope, no broken bones for me ever. Try a piece, please."

I try not to laugh, but Lexi is the type that draws one out of you. Not realizing she's doing it at a time when you need it the most.

A surrendering grin slides across Lane's handsome face, he doesn't take his gaze full of love off of her. His shoulders shake as he barks out one too. Not Lexi, though, she's as serious as a heart attack. More so than when she tried getting him to eat a piece earlier today.

"I don't want you breaking any bones either." He reaches up and tucks a piece of hair behind her ear.

That loving move is almost too much for me to handle. I'd give anything to run mine through Luca's. I've said that also.

I've shared and talked so much about our son that Lane knows him inside and out. It'll make things less awkward when they meet.

My heart thuds against my ribcage when Lexi shoves her hand into the bag and rips off a big piece before pushing the sticky sweetness between his lips. He opens his mouth and takes it.

"It's delicious, huh?" She beams at him, this knowing gleam that he doesn't like it at all. It melts and breaks my heart how well she knows him.

Luca baby, please come home. Please.

"No, it tastes like shit." He fakes a gag, scrunching his nose. "No more of that tonight for you."

The sour way he puckers his lips has me laughing again.

"Okay," she says without throwing a fit, wraps the twisty around the bag and places it next to them.

"I knew you were going to say a bad word, Daddy. You owe me five dollars. I should double it because sugar does not taste yucky. You better get used to it 'cause when I take my cooking class, I'm baking a big cake, lots of cupcakes and cookies for your birthday and all my school parties. You won't have to buy them at the store anymore. You will have to keep making the Christmas bags with candy. Those are the best, like you. Did you know I have the best dad in the whole wide world, Sienna? My teacher, last year, said he was the greatest."

My heart flips on itself.

Lane Mitchell is in a category of his own.

"Believe me, I do know." I think he has the best

daughter in the world too. A daughter I will take care of. A daughter I will love as my own. A daughter who isn't replacing my son, but healing me in a way I never thought possible.

"Five times two equals ten. Ten whole dollars. Yes, you owe me ten bucks." She lets out a whoop, pumps her fists, jumps off his lap, and holds out her hand—the prankster doing her best not to laugh.

Even though I'm enjoying their interaction, my heart crumbles that she figured that number out effortlessly. Luca would have done the same. He would have added those minutes and seconds up so quickly too.

"Good job with the math, princess. However, I believe my daughter just tricked me. It's five or nothing."

Gently tackling her to the sand, he tickles her until she's squirming and squealing.

The girl has him wrapped around his finger. He also lets her take it so far. Lane has done an excellent job raising her. She's respectful when he tells her no. She listens, asks questions, and observes—a lot like Lane.

It's endearing.

"Stop, Daddy, or I'll have to pee again, and yes, I washed my hands after. You will give me all of my money, or no more Lexi kisses for you. Want a piece, Sienna? It's our favorite color. Did you know that pink is Sienna's favorite color too, Daddy?" She grabs the bag, her doll, and places them on her lap.

God, the way she says daddy is so hard to describe. It's like the sun, the moon, the stars all rise in her voice when that word comes out of her mouth. She worships him.

"No, thanks. I'm still full from dinner. Maybe tomorrow."

Lane looks over at me, holding me in the grips of his

stare. Silently telling me there will be a tomorrow and many more to follow. He shoots me a wink before turning his attention back to Lexi. I'm confident I turn as pink as the cotton candy because I know what he's thinking.

I woke this morning in a panic, eyes blinking several times to get used to the morning light. My heart was twisting when I realized I left my phone in my car last night.

I kept thinking about what if I missed a call from Luca. What if he's been trying and trying to get a hold of me? What if I'm the only number he can remember and he's hurt?

Lane calmed me down when he pulled me into his arms and told me he slipped out of bed after I fell asleep, and my phone was on the nightstand where I've been putting it. Then he went on to tell me to relax, told me I was taking the day off from work.

I opened my mouth to argue about not working, snapping it right back closed when a big hand glided up my stomach, traveling to my breast, leaving a trail of chills in its wake.

I felt my face flush pink to which drew a sly quirk of his brow.

A shiver ran through me when he pressed his nose into my hair, rocking his erection into me. When he gripped a handful, tilted my head back, and sucked lightly on the pounding pulse at my neck, I let out a whimper of pleasure, and the pull between my legs increased to a pulsating craving for him to put his mouth right where I ached.

And he did. He flipped me onto my back, slipped under the covers, spread my legs, dragged his tongue from my clit to my ass, and went on to make me relax.

I was floating on a cloud by the time Lexi came charging

into the bedroom, plopped herself in between us, and asked if I was spending the day with them. When I told her yes, she jumped up and down on the bed—hooting and hollering and shaking her cute little bottom. We then made breakfast together while Lane showered and made a few phone calls.

Calls that I know had to do with our son.

"I did know that. Pink looks pretty on you both." He grins again, his innuendo toward me makes me squirm in the sand.

Every part of me is battling inside, this sudden happiness—this strange feeling of belonging. It, in truth, is too much.

I've lived inside my mind for far too long. And I've leaped right into being touched, loved, and adored.

"I'll be back. I'm going down by the water with Aunt Ellie, Uncle Logan, and Braxton. I love you, Daddy. You too, Sienna. Thank you for today."

Right, Ellie and Logan. I forgot they were down here.

My heart stutters, opening as wide as my arms when Lexi hops off Lane's lap and onto mine. I hold on to this precious girl—affection weaving throughout me, the booming exposure of my ability to love another child trying to wedge in between. I won't allow that to happen any more than I'll let my fear of Joseph drag me back down.

"I love you too, Lexi." Then she kisses me on the cheek, walks away, not having a clue she's taken me out of my element, breathing a little more life back into me.

Glancing back at Lane, my chest trembles when I notice he's not looking at Lexi or me.

He's eyeing the man I catch out of the corner of my eye, standing on top of the cliff.

My father.

Suddenly, my stomach flips as the hairs on the back of

my neck stand on end. I swallow around the giant ball of panic, making it hard to breathe. It grows, and the minute it reaches my heart, it's going to explode.

What if Luca is dead? What if that's what they are hiding from me.

CHAPTER SIXTEEN

Lane

"I told you to go home, Sienna. What I have to discuss is not something you need to hear." The non-negotiable tone of Lorenzo's voice claws at my skin, and my muscles tense with the anger rolling through me.

"I'm not leaving. Everyone here knows what's going on with my son, but me. I'm a grown woman, Luca's mother, in case you forgot, and you are way out of line when it comes to me. Discussing my son is not a subject you hide from me. You lied to me that night in your office. Here you are lying and hiding again. You don't stand for people lying to you, so why should I?" Sienna's voice brims with resentment and anger. The complete opposite of her posture and begging eyes.

Swear to God watching her try to remain as tough as nails is a hundred times more painful than when I had to shove my finger into one of Logan's bullet holes a few years ago to stop the rush of blood gushing from his shoulder.

That was a nightmare I stumbled upon. This one is happening right before my eyes, and no matter who tells her, it's going to end with an endless amount of gut-clenching pain.

I do my best to keep my ass planted in the chair off to the side from where Sienna sits at the edge of the leather couch. Her body bent forward, hands pressed together, resting under her chin as if she were saying a prayer. Lorenzo sits on the wooden coffee table across from her. His appearance is much better than when he broke at the warehouse. It won't be if the man doesn't put her out of misery. He'll be wiring his jaw back together.

"I didn't lie to you. I saved you from witnessing something I don't want you to be a part of. You are disrespecting me, Sienna. I don't take kindly to it. When I say enough, I mean enough."

Sienna's head kicks back, her chin trembles, and damn her. She still refuses to cry. Maybe if she did, Lorenzo would see just how shitty of a thing that was for him to say. An uncalled for slap to her face.

Then again, crying in front of him is likely the last she wants to do. It would show him she can't handle it. And she can, no matter how much it hurts, she can handle it.

"I was taught to respect people from you. Take a look in the mirror right now, and I guarantee you won't like the man you see because the man I see isn't respecting me, he's condemning me to more hell. You want my respect; then you are going about it all wrong. I've bled plenty of blood. I can handle anything you throw my way except you treating me the way you are right now. I don't need you or anyone else to spare me from watching you torment someone if that's why you're afraid. If they had anything to do with this, you can trust I'd gladly kill them myself." Yeah, no. That'll happen over any man in this room's dead body, that I'm positive.

Especially mine.

I grip the back of my head, sliding my hands together to hold back the frustration slamming against my skull. Why the hell won't he tell her?

I should have told him to fuck off when he made it clear he'd be the one to inform her. It was a command I didn't take kindly to have to obey. Even though it crushed my heart into a million pieces, I knew then I was in no position to disagree. I didn't like it one bit that until Sienna was mine in every way, that he held that kind of power over me. He doesn't anymore. She's mine to protect, even from him.

"What part of me wanting to shield you when we're trying to put the pieces together, don't you understand?" Lorenzo's back goes straight. He's on the verge of breaking. I feel for him. I honestly do, but he has blinders on when it comes to looking past the daughter he wants to save to a woman who has a right to know even if it does throw her into a pool of tears.

My gaze shoots between the two, and Sienna narrows her eyes, chin inclined in defiance like she has no intention of backing down. Well, good. She has five more minutes to strengthen that backbone of hers before I intervene.

"You aren't protecting me. You are breaking my heart. You have me leaning toward holding a heavy grudge against you. Lane should not have to bear the weight of the agony you've put him through alone. We've grown closer these past few weeks. Don't make me turn to him for answers. I demand to know what is going on right now. No more excuses. No more bullshit. It is not up to you to decide what I should and shouldn't know." Her face turns red with anger.

Beautiful and strong.

I glance at the clock. Four minutes before I come unhinged.

It isn't the time for my dick to twitch, watching her face off with Lorenzo in the middle of Ellie and Logan's living room with grit, determination, and a steel spine. Liquid fire shooting out of her eyes. This side of her is what I've been waiting on. And, goddamn, does it turn me on.

Sienna's temper shot up when she saw Lorenzo on the cliff. He gestured with his hand for her to come to him, looking down at us with a glare that would have shot me dead if he could have. He hasn't spoken a word to me yet. Whatever I've done to piss him off between the last time we talked and now, he'll have to wait to piss his ring of authority around me another time.

Thank God, Sienna lowered her anger to a simmer until Ellie had Lexi in the car. I fell for her a little more after that. At first, Lexi didn't want to remove herself from Seth's lap. It wasn't until I told her Logan and Ellie were going to the airport in Houston to pick up someone. A surprise for Sienna that she jumped down, clapping her hands in excitement.

I'd called Victoria to be here for Sienna in a way I can't. I knew once she found out about Luca, she'd either break, making it impossible for me to glue her back together. Or, she'd rage on the outside while slowly dying more on the inside.

I'm hoping for the last.

Hope. Like Sienna's, mine in finding Luca is fading with every breath I take.

"Well, that's good to know that my daughter wants to resent me when I'm doing all I can to save you from more pain. You need to calm down. You know nothing about how we handle things." With the cruelness in Lorenzo's voice, the skin on my knuckles turns white as I tighten my fingers until the muscles in my arms shake.

"You're damn right, I resent you. I have every right to. Again, you are condemning me to more hell. I find it funny that you only hear what you want and then turn around and say what you want. This isn't about what you want. It's about Lane and me and our son. Get it through your head that I don't care how you do things. I am not a weak person, but you sure make me feel like one." She pushes out a frustrated breath, and her entire demeanor softens when she turns and looks at me.

"I'm as calm as I can be, Father. I know you are stalling because you are scared to tell me. I know you did wrong by expecting Lane to keep something about our son from me. That is wrong on so many levels, even for you."

She is laying into him while he sits there and takes it. Good, I hope it sinks in.

"You have it backward, Father, you are disrespecting me. I know if someone didn't tell you the truth, you would either have them killed or punish them in another way. What makes you better than me?" Her tone hardens. Still, I hear the panic welling up. She needs to tuck it down before he catches on.

My thoughts drift to how the mafia build themselves upon a law of honor. All members must abide by them. They set their own rules. But when the kingpin himself breaks them, everyone is expected to let it slide. At least that's what I'm taking from Sienna's statement. I took the same thing away from my phone call with Gabe this morning too. He told me to stand down once again and to keep quiet.

When it comes to business, I get it. Personal, those rules should not apply.

Lorenzo knew it was getting harder for me to keep this from her. I've been on his ass for days to tell her. Told him time and time again that the guilt was stretching me thin. Every time I called him, he said he would when he returned from New York. A trip he expected me to keep to myself. I have. I've kept it all bottled inside of me.

He betrayed me in a way that if I didn't trust Gabe when he told me Lorenzo is slipping due to the stressful worry, I wouldn't get past it. Still, it pisses me the hell off that he shoved betrayal in my face, then turned around and stabbed Sienna and me in our backs.

Worry or not, thank fuck I knew he was returning today because Sienna's razor-sharp eyes caught onto the fact I was hiding something. I was ready to tell her the second Lexi was asleep tonight.

I glance at the clock again—two and a half minutes.

"I've had it with you. Do you hear me? I've had it up to my ears with excuses. You'd better tell me everything you know about Luca right now. Test my patience one more time, Father. By all means, do it. I'll be the first person to walk away from you and never look back. What is wrong with you?" She's losing it. I can see her legs shaking, her hands trembling, her eyes clouding over with agony.

I feel her crushing ache inside my chest. So powerful, it nearly steals my breath.

"Test your patience? The last bit I had left flew out of the car window when Gabe told me you were out in public today. It's worrisome enough, allowing you to step out of the house to where I can't see you. What the hell were any of you thinking?" Lorenzo's body shifts toward mine.

And there it is, his beef with me.

Blood rushes to my ears. My heart batters against my ribcage. What the hell does he mean? If he thinks I'm going to lock her in a cage, he's mistaken. She's been in one for the last ten years.

I don't know what possesses me to glance at Seth and Rocco. It's another vibe that strikes me. One that has me checking them out from head to toe. Their faces are red, eyes crazed and focused on the front door, bodies stiff as a board. They look like they want to run through it and kill someone. And whatever, more like whoever they found is where they'd rather be. I'd bet every penny I have that person is at the warehouse in Houston with Aidan.

"I trusted you with my daughter's safety. You betrayed me once again." The accusation coming from Lorenzo should hurt. Right now, I don't have it in me to care. Instantly, I flip my attention back to him. His eyes are full of cold, burning rage. I've seen it before; it didn't intimidate me then. It doesn't now. It's how he shows dominance and conveys someone should fear him. The thing is, the more I study him, the more I see his stalling tactic for what it is. He's not afraid Sienna will crumble, he knows she will. It's him who is dissolving. The man who always serves fear like the emotionless dish it is doesn't want his daughter to see it in his eyes.

He is scared. That's a good thing. He just doesn't see it that way because he's used to being the enforcer. The man with the upper hand and he doesn't have it.

Tough goddamn shit. Behind the strength Sienna is building is his daughter, and she has overcome and harnessed some of her fear. And he needs to himself.

Whether or not he wants a shove in the right direction, he's getting it. It won't be tactful, and it won't happen here. It'll be with a good old heart to heart.

"You have a lot of things backward, Lorenzo. I didn't betray you. I took care of the woman who means everything to me. I'm doing what I can to bring life back into her—focusing on what she needs while you took off without a word, knowing full well I wasn't comfortable with keeping shit from Sienna. If anyone is disloyal, it's you. A member of our family is missing. Meaning, your loyalty lies with Sienna, me, my brothers, and yours. I took her out today so she could breathe. We've been out for walks while Lexi rides her bike. I will take Sienna out tomorrow if I damn well please. You will step back and let her live." Stretching my jaw, I keep going.

"You are going to tell her the truth. You are going to suck up not wanting to hurt your daughter, and you are going to go home, rest, drink yourself until you pass out. I don't care what you do, but you will not keep what we know from Sienna any longer. She's dying inside, no matter if she knows or not. While you cue her in, you might as well spill what you found out in New York. She said no more bullshit, she meant it."

My brain clicks into place. Either someone has spotted Joseph. There's been a threat or worse. That's the reason why he's bringing up going out in public. Otherwise, he wouldn't say a damn thing about it knowing security is within an arm's reach of Sienna. I'd take a bullet to my chest to save her.

The fuck does he think I'd put Lexi in danger too? He and I will be having words.

"You've been to New York?" Sienna's eyebrows pinch in confusion. "Oh, God. Is, is Luca dead? Is that what you've been keeping from me? He can't be, I would know. I would feel it. Please, someone, tell me. Is my son dead?" A soul-crushing screech escapes her trembling lips. It's a scream that attaches to every bone in my body and makes me want to curl into myself and die.

"No, La Mia Vita, he is not dead. I would never keep something like that from you, no matter if God himself asked me to." There was nothing I could do except let time stretch and slow-crawl as I get out of my chair to be by her side only to have Gabe haul me back by gripping my arms and twisting them behind my back when Lorenzo starts to tell her everything.

"He is not dead. Luca has been with a couple of men known as XYZ. They—"

"No," she screams again. It pierces me like a knife. "I know who they are. How can this be?"

She sobs into her hands. As much of a relief as it is to hear her let it out, it's tormenting when the tears drip between her fingers, and I can't wipe them away. Her breathing becomes ragged, gasping as her body trembles and shakes.

Shit.

I want her in my arms with her eyes on me. She needs me.

"Let me go, goddamn it." Her pain rips through me, tearing into my muscles.

"No, you let him finish this, son. He needs it to get back to the man he is. You'd do anything for your brothers, the same as I would for mine. Lorenzo needs to break in private with Sienna. You back down and give him his moment of weakness."

He isn't going to in front of her. Jesus Christ, am I the only one who can see that?

My heels dig into the floor, my eyes never leaving her wilting frame when he drags me out of the room, into the kitchen and through the back door to where he releases me.

"Fuck!" I growl. Kicking a chair clear over the side of the deck. My body pitches forward, hands resting on my knees. "This is killing us all from the inside out. What the hell did you find out? What did Lorenzo mean by he has been with XYZ? If you tell me my son is dead, I won't..." I'm losing my mind—sanity tumbling down a black hole of helplessness.

"He is not dead as far as we know. This is hard when a child is involved. Everyone loses their minds. It's hard as hell when you can't be here to take care of your own." I glance at the man who'd taken care of my brothers and me when we needed it the most. Gabe is a cold-blooded killer with a heart bigger than most. To look at him, you'd never guess he slit people's throats.

"I'm doing okay, old man. Sienna is too. Trust me on that."

"And you'll continue to do okay. Don't sell yourself short, Lane. You keep on doing what you've been and leave the rest to me. There's no man on earth prouder than I am right now. That was hard on you to let her go against Lorenzo. Get your emotions in check before I tell you what we found out."

I straighten when Seth and Rocco come through the door. Tension dripping off their posture.

Unease settles in my gut.

"No news is good unless Luca is home safe."

"True, but having the last two members of XYZ brings us closer to finding him. Until we do, Sienna nor Lexi leave your house. That's an order Lorenzo handed down that you will not betray. It's up to you to make sure Sienna obeys."

CHAPTER SEVENTEEN

Sienna

The disgust, dread, and sheer panic I'd been shivering from amplifies before Lane stops his SUV in the garage. Each step I take to get into the house stimulates that fear I tried so hard to push away. It quickens through my veins.

Sickness claws at my skin. Mind spinning a mile a minute at how evil and vile some people in this world are.

The silence driving here didn't come close to the maddening way my skin started to itch as soon as I found out what was going on. No, this time, I welcomed the quiet. It gave me time to think long and hard. To let my mother's loving heart weep for my son. It will continue until I know he's okay.

Visuals assault my brain—the downright terror of what Luca has to be experiencing churns the bile in my stomach.

Luca will never survive if he has to witness crimes so heartbreaking as to what those men do, but I'll pour every ounce of my love for that boy into making him whole if he comes back to me confused and destroyed.

And I will sleep at night with a smile on my face when Joseph is found and killed.

Hate and horror. Belief and hope. I've never held onto any of them as tight as I do now, especially hope.

Filth, unlike the hundreds of times Joseph had taken me savagely edges beneath the surface of my skin. It only took a second after my father told me for my heart to feel like someone shoved a dagger through it and set it on fire.

I lived with a man I knew was deranged, but involved with those men that used to freeze my blood when I'd hear about another abduction, it fuels the bitter hatred I have for Joseph.

He has a vicious heart out to destruct, and I want it carved out of his chest.

Images of what those men do to young girls, crawl at a snail's pace through my body. I never in a million years would have thought I'd end up married to a man that would do something beyond the realms of cruel to me, let alone rape others sadistically and with coldhearted intent.

I've never wished torture so severely as I do Joseph and those men. A bullet to the head would have been sufficient before. Now I want them to pay.

Scrambling through the house in the dark. I stumble into the bathroom, flip on the light, and fall to my knees in front of the toilet.

"Stay away from me," I scream at Lane when he enters, kneels beside me and pulls my hair away from my face.

He says nothing as I vomit, expelling the contents of my stomach until there's nothing left but an empty pit of revulsion. I dry heave until my throat burns.

Flushing, I push him away, turn on the shower, brush my teeth, and rinse the bitter taste from my mouth.

Tears spill over my cheeks as I strip out of my clothes,

step into the shower, lean my head against the tiles, and I sob. I cry for my son, for those girls, their parents. For Lane, me, and every person in this world who endures this kind of excruciating pain.

My heart is broken. The pieces may never fit together the way they're supposed to if Joseph allowed them to touch my boy. Worse, they will lay at my feet until the end of my days if he ends up being another victim never to be found.

So many emotions swirl with the steaming water as streaks of fire burn my cheeks—each one leaving a blazing trail of agony as I break out in tremors. Explosive anger blazes across my skin, and emptiness fills the void in my chest as the worst kind of thoughts pull and tug, trying to break that tightly woven thread holding me together at the seams. I can't let fear beat me over this.

I can't give up the belief Luca will come home.

I've come too far in such a short time to succumb to it.

I feel Lane behind me before the blazing heat of his hands take hold of mine and squeeze. Linking us together. Parents of a boy who is too young to understand any of this.

Worry.

"I'm sorry. I should have told someone what Joseph was doing to me." My words choke on another sob. I won't let it defeat me. Crying will not shove me in a corner full of pity.

"It's not your fault. I'm not leaving you alone, Sienna. Talk to me. You and me together, remember? I got you, La Mia Vita. You, Lexi and Luca, are my life. Don't lose sight of how far you've come, of how strong you are, how strong our son is. Let out those emotions. Cry until you can't anymore, then tell me what you need, but blaming yourself will eat you alive if you let it. Trust me on that." Lane's warm breath hits my ear. His voice softer than usual, yet holding a sharp command.

"I don't blame myself. I feel guilty. We agreed I have rights. There's no erasing this horrific one, Lane. I feel like Joseph has left a disease across my flesh that no amount of soap and water will take away. I can't begin to understand how people can do things like that to another." My throat clogs with sorrow.

I don't even care about my house or losing the things that can never be replaced. Not after hearing the double life Joseph led. There is nothing more valuable than those innocent victims' lives. Everything else is worthless.

Innocence stolen when it's a person's choice to give it away.

"Those girls will never be the same. They will never be free. If they're even alive." My father told me Aidan thinks the last victims they kidnapped are with Joseph somewhere. The thought of him keeping them captive, continuing the sick and twisted things those men do while having my son makes me want to die.

Despite the hot water, a cold shiver runs through my body, wondering what tumbles through those girls' heads. Is it wrong for me to wish them dead so they can breathe again?

Lane releases my hands, his comforting arms circling my waist, pulling me into a tight embrace. I turn into Lane, resting my head on his chest, letting the grief in my heart spill from my eyes.

More tears that I'd held back broke free. They streak down my cheeks in a rush.

Draining me dry.

If I'm going to make it through the seconds, minutes, hours, and days, I have to numb my brain. I'll die a slow death if I don't.

"We aren't wired the way psychopaths are. You could

beat yourself to death, trying to figure them out. Those men and Joseph aren't worth it. Luca is. Getting him home safe is. Healing him with your loving touch is. You have one, you know. I've seen it many times with Lexi."

Well, it doesn't seem loving right now. It wants to hit something. To take out the charring adrenaline that has seeped into my veins like hot lava.

"I need to become fearless because nothing can be worse than this feeling of hopelessness. I'm going with you to see those men. I want them to look me in the eye when I ask where my son is. I won't take no for an answer." My father told me about Lane killing one of those men. I know they have the other two held hostage somewhere. Maybe if they see me, they'll tell us where Joseph is.

Leaning his head back in the water, Lane releases a groan as rivulets cascade down his face and onto the corded veins in his neck, the ridged, bunched muscles at his neck and shoulders.

"I can't let you do that, Sienna. We've pushed your father far enough. He allowed us to talk to him the way we did because of what we are going through. He'll have someone drag you away, kicking and screaming before you take two steps through the door. Then I'd have to kill whoever touched you. Don't put that burden on him. He's hurting as much as you are, even if he did you wrong. If they know something, they will tell us before they die. You have to trust me on that."

Trusting him is about the only thing I'm sure of these days.

I won't ask Lane to help me reason with my father. I'll do it myself. I'll go behind his back. I'll sneak, I'll do whatever it takes to look those men in the eye.

"God help us all if we go against the wishes of Lorenzo

Ricci." My voice resonates with anger as the irritation toward my father owns every part of me.

My hands fist with the amount of fury coursing through me. I'm slowly dying thinking that those girls have endured physical pain, the profound agony that all you pray for is a miracle to drop out of the sky. To wish to die if no one will save you.

In an instant, my balled hands pound against Lane's chest. The chaos inside my body spins. A tornado is wrapping me into its destructive frenzy.

To take my frustration out on the man I'm falling further in love with than before isn't right, but it's liberating at the same time. He stands there and takes it. Takes my brutal beating over that damn tattoo that shouldn't be there. I slam my fists into him over and over, releasing those emotions that have dragged me down for years.

"I won't let my father, or you make my choices for me. No one gets to do that for me anymore. I want them to die! I want to look them in the eye and tell them they will never hurt another again. I know what it feels like to live in hell, and it is worse than anyone can imagine. They stole those girls' lives, raped them over and over. Joseph might have killed them, and their parents will never have closure. They didn't get a choice. I don't even know what to think when it comes to Luca. If I allow my thoughts to go to a dark place, I won't have the strength to get out of bed. I have to win this battle inside of me. God, help us all! Please don't let them have touched him. Please!" I'm rambling, and I don't even care.

The next thing I know, Lane's mouth is on mine, and he swallows my sobs. Our tongues tangle, our breaths mingle, his palms hold my face as if he wants to get closer, to inhale me. His cock hardens and presses against my stomach.

My body ignites like a match against the first strike.

"Sienna." He grabs both my hands, brings them to his mouth and kisses across every knuckle. It calms me when he does that.

"We should talk about what your father said, the things he wants."

"No. Talking isn't going to bring Luca home. I need you. Right or wrong, I do." I don't care if it's wrong to want Lane inside of me right now. I need to feel him.

He glances down at me, the unshed tears in his eyes, the desperation showing me he needs me as much as I do him.

"I don't want you to regret me if I take you right now. I won't be gentle. I don't have it in me tonight."

Both his hands smooth up my arms and wind gently around my neck. The man is trying so hard to maintain control. I want him to lose it. To get lost in me and me in him. There's no shame in what my eyes plead for him to do.

"How can I ever regret anything when it comes to you?"

He opens his mouth to speak, but I grip his cheeks, push up on my toes, and kiss him with everything I have. He yanks me against his body, hooks one arm around my waist as he takes a handful of my hair with the other.

Tonight I don't want his soft. I need his hard and demanding to make me feel alive.

"You wanted my voice, well, here's the one thing I've waited a decade to say. I'm falling in love with you. There hasn't been a day gone by where I haven't loved you. We're building. We're grieving, hurting, we are a mess, but we're those together."

He groans, and the heat of his stare has me going to my knees. I don't want him to say it back, not tonight. I said it because I mean it. I said it because I want him to know I'm not lost. I said it because our hearts have been linked since the day we met, our souls are now splayed wide open, and I will not let go of what we have.

I wrap my hand around his length and stroke. I lick across his head, both his hands palming the sides of my face.

"Jesus Christ, you don't get to say that and not expect me... fuck." He groans when I place my tongue on the underside of his cock and lick. "Fine, if this is what you want, then open that beautiful mouth and take all of it." His gruff voice stokes the fire he'd already set to my body.

I submit and open as told, gagging as he hits the back of my throat. Reaching up, I grab hold of his balls and give them a gentle tug.

"Shit, Sienna." He bucks his hips, losing control, gripping my hair tighter, and without pause, he fucks my mouth.

Possessively and relentless.

"Damn, that mouth feels good wrapped around my cock. Look at you on your knees, water spraying in your gorgeous face when it should be me on mine worshipping you. Touch yourself, make that pretty little cunt nice and wet for me."

I'm not a fan of that word. Coming out of him, it doesn't bother me at all. It's the way he is. A dirty talker underneath the kindest man I've ever met.

I'm already wet, and it's not from the water.

Reaching between my thighs, I slide my fingers through my folds and swirl my thumb across my clit as he continues to slam into my throat.

His mouth parts, those eyes staring down at me with so much love and adoration that I moan around him.

In a flash, he slides out of my mouth, lifts me to my feet, spins me around, places my hands on the slippery tiled wall, and bends me at the waist.

"You are so beautiful, so strong, so unforgettable. We are going to get through this. Don't doubt it. I got you, Sienna. Do you hear me?"

"Yes," I say around a gasp of pure pleasure when he slides the tip of a finger down my spine. Even though my heart feels empty except for him, I believe with everything in me that Lane Mitchell has me.

We will power this living, breathing nightmare together. When Luca does come home, we will be stronger than ever.

"We belong together, Sienna. I'm a goddamn weak man without you."

Tears sting the back of my eyes. Not many men will admit something like that. It only makes me care more. He skims his hands down my spine, grips a hip with one, drags the other to squeeze a handful of my ass before dragging a finger down my crack, circling the puckered hole.

Mouth drawing apart, I let out a breath when a long finger sweeps through my wetness, curving up into me as his thumb rests against my asshole.

I thrash as his finger pumps inside of me, and his thumb pushes inside. "I won't ever stop making you feel good. You want my cock, Sienna?" The rough grain of his voice skims along my spine, enhancing the need for him to fuck me. All I can feel is the tingle coursing through me; all I see are the sparks mixing with the water as he fingers me until I'm crying out his name.

"Fuck me, Lane, please."

He hooks a finger beneath my chin, tipping my head back, eyes hooded and challenging.

"It's going to be hard and rough. When we're done, I'm washing this sweet skin, taking my time, marking every inch of it with my tongue. There won't be a spot on you that I won't brand as mine. By the time I get to your pussy, you'll have forgotten your name, let alone the man who tried but failed to break my brave and beautiful woman."

"Then do it." I don't recognize my voice. That's what Lane does to me. He draws the raw and sensual need right out of me. No matter what's going on around me, no matter how worried sick I am, he's stroked this carnal side out of me that I missed as much as I'd lost me.

"Anything you want, La Mia Vita. I'm so hard for you." His words bring a smile to my mouth, and I bite my bottom lip in anticipation.

My back bows, a loud desirable moan rips from my throat when he suddenly slams into me, pulls, and plows back in.

Big hands clamp down greedily on my hips as he drags my body back to meet him with each hard thrust.

He pulls and slams and fucks.

I smack my hand against the tile in pleasure and scream loud enough that he clamps his hand over my mouth.

"Beautiful. Every inch. You have no idea how stunning you are." I can't talk; I can barely breathe knowing after tonight I was never going to be the same.

We both need this to bring us full circle to hold each other up from the ugly I know with everything inside of me is yet to come.

"Come on, baby, give me that pleasure."

His touch eliminates the pain of my past, and as the edges fringe closer and I let go, I grip onto the fact I'm not alone anymore. I have Lane back in my life, and he has me. Together we will carry the grief on our shoulders until the last people standing are him, our family, and our children.

CHAPTER EIGHTEEN

Lane

There were a few things I took from my mother turning her back on my brothers and me. To take care of those you love, and unless you are incapable of choosing on your own, you always have a choice.

Years ago, I did neither of those things when it came to Sienna. I lost her because of it.

I didn't hold on to my word as a man. I wasn't truthful, trustworthy, or reliable.

I was a coward, just like my mother.

My mother didn't try to fight for the people she once loved. She chose to fall in love with drugs, random men, anything that would stop her from facing the greatest fear of her life—the choice to be a loving single parent on her own.

Being a parent is hard enough; doing it on your own is tougher. Plain and simple, there's no tapping out. That's one of the few things I have in common with Lorenzo and no matter Sienna's age. He will always be a single parent to her. He's the first man she loved, but if he doesn't pull his head out of the well of regret he's drowning in, he's going to lose her. And no one recognizes that emotion better than me. It's an unpredictable motherfucker. An unforgiving shadow that'll sneak up any damn time it pleases. It's every drag down feeling rolled into one.

A tight-fisted little bitch that you can choose to kick the fuck down. I never did. I'm not about to add to the vise grip it has on me when it comes to Sienna.

I want it flushed out of me, and it won't be if I don't stand up for what my woman wants along with clearing the air while pushing Lorenzo in the direction he needs to go.

I'm not comfortable with locking Sienna away and making her obey like she some battered woman who doesn't have a say. She's been there. That was her hell.

Lorenzo needs to wake the fuck up, drop his power, and give Sienna everything she needs.

Right now, she needs his support.

As much as I don't want Sienna to come face to face with those men, I won't be able to look at myself if I don't fight for what she wants. If I don't convince the man I'm in hot water with as it is, that no matter what, Sienna has a choice, a voice and by God, he needs to back the fuck off and let her prove to herself that she can face her fear in the eye and stand tall while doing it.

Memories of Sienna and I flood into my mind as I glance into the rearview mirror and lose sight of my house when I turn the corner. From the first day I met her, the woman was like a torpedo aimed straight for my heart. She destroyed it for any other. I have that fiery woman back, and that's the way it's going to stay.

I hated leaving her curled up in a sleeping ball with those flaming locks a wild tangled mess spread around her from going to bed with it wet. What I hated most was standing over her while she held onto her phone.

She looked so small, so caged, clinging to the only lifeline she has.

For the time being, Seth is with her. His promise not to leave her side when I'm not around is as far as my conversation got with him, Rocco, and Gabe last night at Logan and Ellie's before I couldn't take hearing Sienna cry and scream anymore. I snatched her off the floor, with Lorenzo climbing my back for getting in his way and took her home without having words with him. Without knowing what the hell is going on with those men.

All of that plus a hell of a lot more brings me to now as I park my SUV and stare at a very pissed off Lorenzo through my windshield.

"Lane, you saved me a trip from coming to you. It's long past time I put you in your place. Inside now." He greets with zero impatience as I climb out with a smirk and face him.

His mouth sets into a firm line. Matteo is behind him with his arms crossed, jaw flexing tight. Eyes are likely shooting bullets into my head behind his sunglasses. I don't have to see his for him to be aware I'll drop him in a second flat. All he has to do is keep on looking into mine.

"For a man who continues to try and put me in my place when it comes to Sienna, I'd think the first thing out of your mouth would be asking how she is." I follow them into the house, shutting the door behind me. I know where my place is, and it sure as hell isn't to take orders from him or to be frightened by his bodyguard who never talks. If I'd hadn't heard him speak before, I'd think someone cut out his tongue.

"You wouldn't be here if she'd have lost her mind. I sure as hell wouldn't have allowed you to take her if I thought she had." He grunts and shakes his head.

Lorenzo turns around, narrows his eyes at me, slanting his head to the side as if he's expecting me to apologize for my behavior. He knows me by now, that'll never happen.

"At least we agree on something." I chose not to argue over his last sentence. It's a lie, he knows it. I know it. I would have plowed right through him to get her home.

Sienna is handling the news better than I thought. She's emotionally and mentally stronger. That doesn't mean she won't snap at any second. I'm here to avoid that.

"I'm not all that pleased you thought you could come to my house and hand my ass to me in front of Sienna. You got a problem with me, well here I am. Let's hash it out now." I grit my teeth when he looks me up and down, eyes set to dismiss me at any time. "Think you've handed both our asses in front of others to last a lifetime."

I'm not leaving until I've accomplished what I came here to do. To set him straight and for him to admit to himself, there's not a thing wrong with letting the right people see your fear. I see his more evident in the early morning light. The man needs someone to push him the way Logan did me.

Lorenzo is holding the weight of the world on his shoulders. All the while trying to remain tough as nails when it's okay for the roughest to crumble. That's the direction I need to push him in.

To drive him to the edge.

"You're playing with fire, Lane," he states in a cold and disconnected manner, not looking me in the eye. That's all the sign I need to prove my theory is right. Lorenzo never takes his eyes off from another when he speaks. He's ridden with guilt, buried in shame, and it's smothering him.

I hate that feeling. It strips you raw, dissolving your

common sense, and that is what it's done to Lorenzo. He can't think straight.

"I've been walking in it since I did the love of my life wrong. I'm burning in it right along with you. Let's cut the bullshit and get down to this talk." A voice inside warns me to bite my tongue. Under normal circumstances, I would, the same as I would never have gone off on him the times that I have. There's nothing ordinary about the situation we're in at all. Everyone is stressed. But Lorenzo needs to be pushed just a little further to see he needs to step off his throne and do what's right.

He needs to trust me when it comes to Sienna and let her stand up for herself. It's a lesson learned the hard way, and fuck does it hurt like a punch to my gut to be the one teaching him when the man has taught me more than he realizes.

"Sienna will never be the woman she's trying to be if you don't let her make choices on her own. She wants to see those men. She wants to work, and by God, you're going to let her. That woman has had enough of overpowering men to last her a lifetime." I might be one when we're between the sheets, but that's entirely different than uncalled-for-intimidation.

I shake my head when he goes to speak. "You think I'm power playing you when it comes to Sienna. That is the furthest thing from the truth."

He steps forward, shoves a finger in my chest, his eyes signaling he's on the brink of tears, while still holding some of the blistering anger inside of him. His self-control is slipping.

One step closer to the edge.

"No, you aren't trying to out-maneuver me. That's not the man you are. What you've done is overruled my decisions toward Sienna's mental state, you've derailed every one. If she's going to work, then you better be damn sure whoever is watching out for her is willing to take a bullet. The other demand, no way in hell. I suggest you shut your goddamn mouth and take it no further."

Her mental state? He's not giving her a chance to prove she can think on her own, and I get it. Whether he thinks I don't or not, I do. I would not want to fill his shoes. I hope I never have to. That isn't a bridge I'm crossing at the moment. I'm trying to convince a man who can't see past his grief that his daughter is fighting for her freedom to find out who she is.

"The hell if I'll shut up. You want to hand my ass to me, then go right ahead. While I appreciate you bending a little, you need to bend a little farther. No one, and that includes you, will tell Sienna what she can and can't do ever again. She doesn't deserve your wrath. She deserves to be treated as an equal." I toss her words in his face and keep right on shoving.

"Even if you were the king of the world, you will show my woman the same respect you show the men in your crime syndicate. I don't care if you bring ten men in here to tie me down, kick me in the teeth, beat me until I can't move, I won't stand for it. And don't throw; 'she's my daughter' in my face, and you know what's best for her. I know she is just as much as I know you love *her*. I love *her* too, Lorenzo. I've disrespected you for *her*. I've done you wrong for *her*." My irritation with him rages like an inferno. He's like a mule who doesn't take kindly to being pushed.

Well, too bad for him, I know what buttons to slam my hand down on. I'll hold it there until he gives in and budges.

"That attitude toward me is exactly why I was on my way to you. I don't want to have to force you to shut your goddamn mouth," he spits. For the briefest of seconds, I see so much bleeding emotion if we were alone, I would call him out on it.

My gaze lifts to Matteo, doing nothing to hide the stiffness threatening to crack my jaw.

"You lay one finger on me, and I'll blow your brains out." If Lorenzo thinks he can threaten me, then my attitude will take it out by pounding Matteo into the carpet.

Matteo's jaw tics, I can practically see the fury roll off his back as his chest heaves. I rough my hands through my hair, trying to compose myself.

"I've had enough of Sienna's opinions not mattering, Lorenzo. If we are going to talk about this anymore, we do it alone." Exhaling slowly, our glares spin into a tight ball. He can't read my mind as well as I can his. He's so close to the dam inside of him collapsing. I respect Lorenzo enough not to have him fall apart in front of anyone who will characterize it as a sign of weakness when to me, it's a man who loves his daughter and grandson so much he's slowly dying inside.

Lorenzo lost his wife. He's lived for years with the guilt that she took bullets meant for him. To this day, they never found out who it was. I can't imagine what that's been like for him. A slow dying death I'd assume and not knowing where Luca is has put a crack in his armor.

In front of our family, he needs to take that shield of steel off.

With a shake of his head, a slight smirk on his face, Matteo walks away without waiting for the nodding command. I could give a shit if I earned his respect, but something tells me I did.

"Perhaps I should have schooled you on my rules. I have

a list of them that maybe you don't quite understand. The first being you do not disrespect me."

"You're right, I don't. I don't care about your rules. I care about you. I care about Sienna. I care about getting my son back. I've never disrespected you in public. I'm not about to start now."

"You just did in front of Matteo." Although his sharp tone rubs me wrong, he's right. I won't blow smoke up his ass and tell him I'm sorry. Matteo knows him better than most. I've no doubt he recognizes Lorenzo's change. He might not speak unless he's told, but the guy isn't stupid. He would have never walked out on his own if he didn't understand exactly what I'm trying to do.

"I warned you, Lane, and yet you keep on. I don't owe you or anyone an explanation of why I do things the way I do. I don't answer to anyone."

That is where he is wrong.

"You owe it to Sienna. You owe it to yourself. You answer to her when it comes to what she wants. You let her fight back the way she chooses. The way you taught her. She wouldn't have made it through what she has if it weren't for the strength that you raised her to have. She stayed with a man to protect her own because you taught her it's what she should do, not because you couldn't uphold your duty as her father. You alone raised that woman to become who she is. A damn good one."

His facial expression switches into unrecognizable.

Fuck.

With him and his hundreds of poker faces, it's hard to tell if I'm doing the right thing or not.

"Those men could have come to you on their own to talk about giving Luca back. They chose to retaliate instead. Now their time has come to pay for their sins. You will let

Sienna have her say before they die, or she will live in a cesspool of guilt for the rest of her life. Is that where you want her? You want her trying to stay afloat like you? Those girls are not here to stand up for themselves. Sienna is, she's earned it. You will let her speak for herself and those girls." If she chooses to bring up Luca, then that is on her. I'll deal with getting her back on her feet if she falls.

"I don't want those men getting in her head. They are lethal. They will fuck with her mind with just an uncaring glare." His voice thunders, the vein in his neck is bulging, his jaw quivers, and when he finally meets my eyes, they are glossy with unshed tears.

Finally.

I feel like an asshole for pushing him. I promise, as a man of my word, I will hold on to his weathered hand. Him shattering, blowing that box of overloaded fuses, will never leave this room.

"I will cut out their eyes if they try."

"Goddamn you, Lane, you don't know what you are asking of me." He shakes his head again, clearly trying to keep himself in check.

"She can handle it, Lorenzo. I wouldn't bring it up if I didn't believe it. It's you who can't."

"You don't know what I can and can't handle. That is enough." His voice is a low growl through the agony of his guilty conscience clogging his throat, but it's earsplitting to me.

"You don't get to tell me when it's enough. Your heart is weeping, you don't think I see it, but I do, Lorenzo. You believe yourself weak if you cry. There's no shame in unmasking your fear when you feel like you've failed to protect the people you vowed to your entire life. What happened is not your fault. It's mine." A lump forms in my throat. It never gets easier, admitting that I did Sienna wrong.

"That's bullshit. I'm the one who placed Sienna's hand in Joseph's."

I've almost got him.

"I'm the one who hurt her. I'm the one who was too weak to choose her. I said I'm walking through fire with you, Lorenzo, I meant it. Neither of us will be the men she needs us to be if we don't let go of our regret. You and me, we need to lean on each other in the roughest of times. Trust me when I tell you that once you succumb to weakness, you'll find you're stronger because of it. Don't grasp for straws. Not with me."

The pride in his eyes stills me. I hope it's due to his faith in me and the choice I see he's about to make.

"You are a piece of work. A good man, but I won't lose it in front of you, Lane. That time is for me and me alone. No matter how old your child or children are, you want to shelter them from pain. That is something you can understand. You are a good father. A man I admire. A man I knew cared about Sienna the second you stood in my office and spoke for her. She can have her say because no man would stand up to me the way you have if they didn't love with their whole heart. No man would survive the punishment I would rain down on them if I didn't trust them the way I do you. The next time you step out of line, the consequences will cost you. Do I make myself clear?"

The disappointment I've had in him fades. I could stand here and argue, and it wouldn't do me a bit of good. My job is so close to being done here. However, I won't tuck my tail between my legs and succumb to his every command. Not without one condition.

"Yes and no. You won't keep Sienna in the dark when it

comes to our son ever again. She is the first person to know right after you. You promise me that, and you have my respect. You have my word that I'll shut my mouth. Otherwise, Sienna is in the middle. I'd walk away from her again before I'd come between her and you." I wouldn't, and that's something he knows just as well as I'll stand by her side when she meets those sick assholes.

With a twitch to his lips, he sticks out his hand to which I take.

"And I love her enough that I'd do the same to see her with a man that loves her the way a father wants his daughter to be loved."

Now that is something I believe he'd do.

Luckily, neither of us will have to find out.

CHAPTER NINETEEN

Sienna

When I first walked into my house in New York after being discharged from the hospital, the unquenchable heartache surrounded me as I laid in Luca's bed, crying on Victoria's shoulder, and begging my father to do everything he could to find Luca.

For weeks I couldn't get a grip on succumbing to the mercy of my emotions. They owned me. In a way, no matter if it's years from now, when Luca returns, they always will.

I was the mom who smelled her child's pillow, seized hold of his video game controller because I knew it was likely the last thing he held in his hand.

I felt the hurt of Luca gone in my heart until I wanted to die.

I was lifeless.

A part of me still feels empty, and every day I want to wake up and scream at God for allowing this to happen, but after two-hundred and seven days of not hearing his voice, looking into his eyes, telling him I love him and watching him learn something new every day, I don't feel as if I'm comatose anymore.

I don't know if it's because I'm infuriated that life can be beyond cruel to a child. Or the piece of my heart belonging to Luca has strengthened. But I've changed for the better and worse.

The devastating blow to my heart was different then. I was grieving the loss of the only person who kept me going. I'm still mourning. Little did I know that months later, my life would be different in the ways I'd dreamed it could be.

That I wasn't alone anymore, and the man I've loved most of my life was back just as abruptly as when I lost him.

Exhaling, I look up at Lane as he moves from my side to step in front of me when we enter the building blocking my view of Zackery and Yves. The remaining members of XYZ.

His hands go to my shoulders, and I tilt my head upward to meet his eyes.

"You good?" he asks, not an ounce of doubt in his tone. He's pledging his faith in me.

"Yes." My voice is steady, but I know once I stare into their eyes, it'll carry every octave from low to high to in between.

"You have a handful of men at your back, you say the word, and we go home." Lifting my hands, he kisses my knuckles. All I can do is nod because right now, all I can think about is how in less than twenty-four hours, my heart has braced itself for a brutal attack I know is coming after years of it being bruised and battered and torn and ripped and stomped on. It's a mystery how the stubborn organ refused to stop thumping when it should have died the day I woke to find my son was taken from me.

But it hasn't.

Maybe it's because I'm stuck in a giant bubble my prick

of a husband has placed me in, and every day I've fought with the love I have for Luca not to give up. Waking every morning, knowing I have a choice to let the oxygen deplete from my lungs or to continue fighting against the emotions that want me to lay down and give up.

Maybe it's due to falling asleep cocooned in the arms of the man who restored my faith in myself only to force my lazy eyes open to another morning of no word from Joseph or Luca. The devastating weight of what I learned last night charging through my mind like a bull seeing red.

Maybe it's when I noticed Lane sitting across from Victoria at the kitchen table. The man trying to console her by telling her none of what was going on is her fault. Her body stiff, her eyes full of unshed tears, and her apology for not coming to me sooner written all over her face before she let the words slide out of her mouth.

Maybe it was when she cried and cried in my office today. Her guilty conscience for keeping quiet so real and raw that it made me angrier that Joseph is hurting people I love, and I'm over it.

Perhaps it was the phone call from my father this afternoon telling me I could talk to Yves and Zackery, and I'm so pissed that Aidan was able to find them when the worthless authorities couldn't.

Or maybe I've finally gone crazy right along with the combination of all those things, but sometime during that time, I've built a cement wall around my heart while placing it in the palm of Lane's big sturdy hands.

I'd be lying to myself if I didn't admit I'm frightened right out of my ever-loving mind, and it's not from fear. It's because these men have brought out a part of me I always knew existed. I'd just hidden it away.

I'm a lot more like my father than I thought, and I will

use what I observed when I was younger, what I learned from taking a man's fists to my body, from being raped and abused and from being a mother who will do anything she has to do to cleanse my soul along with giving it all I have to get them to talk.

Everything about my son's disappearance has changed me. Everything about the way I looked at myself in the mirror this afternoon after Lane called to make sure I wanted to do this has changed.

The depressing look still haunts my eyes and the insecurity, the dwindling hope, and conflict that my son is not okay will be there until I see him, but after everything I've been through with Joseph and these past months, I've changed from hating myself, hating violence to downright wanting to take these men's lives.

I won't, my father, Lane, none of these men who stand at my back would let that happen. I will, however, make sure my voice blares in their ears while they rot in Hell for all the women's lives they stole and left them without one of their own before they took their lives.

A coldness unlike I've ever felt before chills the room when Lane moves out of my way, and I get my first look of Zackery and Yves.

My gaze lands on Zackery. His smile produces dimples in his cheeks and a warmth to his eyes, despite the blackness within their depths.

I can see how he might lure a young girl with that look of charm. He doesn't look a day over twenty, either. Dark blonde hair, deep brown eyes. Very little facial hair. All hidden behind a slippery cold-hearted killer. A man who the Devil stole branded his soul the day he was born.

And I know him. His real name might be Zackery, but

to me, I know him as Damien Hart. Our accountant. No wonder every dime we had was gone.

I know them both as I swallow and glare at Yves. Picture Clark Kent and men working on Wall Street, and that's the way I described my driver.

My driver, I talked to about many things. My driver, who Joseph suddenly insisted I have. My driver, who took my son back and forth to school and spoke with him as if he cared. My driver, who I can't look at anymore. My driver, who I want to kill with my bare hands. My driver, who seemed not to be around when my family came to visit.

How fucking convenient.

Joseph insisted he'd drive us wherever we went when my family would come to town. So much clicks now, yet not enough for me to call checkmate.

A slow breath leaks from my lips. Shock wanting to mold itself into my skin.

No.

For many reasons, I'm not about to let it, not here anyway.

"Well, well, did they bring you in as our last meal before we die? If so, you're stuck with me. Yves likes little boys," Zackery says with a taunting smirk. Several hisses and swearing come from behind me as I walk sturdily toward them on legs that feel like limp noodles.

I block everyone out of the room except the three of us. Not that I even know who is here besides Lane and my father, nor do I care.

I'm not letting on I know them just yet. I want them to squirm in the wooden chairs they are strapped down tight in before the life is sucked right out of them. Plus, I need them alive to get things off my chest. I contemplate wondering if I should or shouldn't. Am I prolonging the possibility of finding out where Luca is? Will they even tell me a thing?

"You already know he likes little boys, don't you, Sienna? After all, he drove yours around all the time. It's good to see you again," Zackery whispers low enough for only me to hear.

Without so much as a fuck you, I draw back my arm, and bitch slap him, feeling the sting at the back of my hand.

His eyes water. A devious smirk setting firm in place.

"Come on, mommy dearest. You can do better than that. Hit me until you scream. I bet you're a screamer. A sexy piece of ass as you loves it rough and dirty, don't you?" His voice rises with that comment. Loud enough for everyone to hear. He wants to play the game. He wants to anger the men behind me so they kill him. He better prepare to lose because this mother isn't the weak woman he thought me to be.

Not anymore.

I throw my head back and laugh. I should be frightened over what these men could do to my mind if I didn't know them. They are psychopaths: serial rapists, pedophiles, and murderers. I'm not scared in the least. Not like they'll soon be.

"You shouldn't talk about what kind of woman I am in bed in front of my father. Learn your manners. Or, didn't mommy and daddy not teach them to you?"

Zackery's eyes narrow, and he swipes his tongue over his teeth.

I want to rip his throat out.

"Did I strike a nerve? It's my understanding your parents disowned you the day you both were kicked out of college. Cut off trust fund boys with no money and nowhere to go. Boys who disappeared out of fear of going to prison. Is that why you formed XYZ? For the money? It's too bad you can't take it to hell with you. The Devil doesn't care about money. To him, you'll be another corpse he'll fuck in the ass, but you'll feel it. Every day you'll feel the flames that will burn you over and over. You mess with fire, you're going to get burned. Isn't that what they say? You messed with the wrong family, asshole."

His chest heaves, and he cast his eyes away from mine.

His first mistake or second. It depends on if you count the fact he was caught. Either way, he's going to die with the sound of my voice forever ringing in his ears, the knowledge his family cast him aside.

I don't know much about their families. Only the bits and pieces my father and Lane told me on the way here. I'm using what I have to my advantage by hitting them right where it hurts.

"You'll never know if I fucked with anyone in your family or not. Untie me, and I'll show you my lack of manners, bitch. Tell me, are you a fighter or do you lay there and take it? From what I hear, you lay there like a dead fish. It's a damn shame a woman as gorgeous as you can't find pleasure from a dirty fuck," he whispers.

I say nothing. That doesn't mean I'm not trembling inside, that his malicious words aren't hammering on the wall in my chest.

"I'd make you scream for more. One little pill would have you grinding your pussy against my dick. You, though, I'd make you fight me. Instead of begging for me to fuck you, I'd make you beg for me not to. I'd tie your hands to your ankles and fuck you until you bleed. I love it when we first take them, and they fight. Love to fuck them roughly until I've had my fill." Zackery shrugs, head tipping to the side to stare at everyone behind me before flicking his gaze at Yves, who has yet to say a word.

He better not speak either until I tell him to, or Lord only knows what I'll do.

Yves is agitated and nervous, though. Drawing it out by tapping his fingers against the wooden arm of the chair. Funny how he'd do that on the steering wheel as he drove through the streets of New York. I didn't give it much thought. I figured it had to do with the crazy traffic.

How wrong I was. He's nervous and pissed about something. Knowing my husband, he's behind Yves's anger. It's the nervous part I've yet to figure out.

I won't let Zackery see he's struck a nerve with me too. That, of course, I laid there and took a man raping me over and over. Any woman in her right mind would. As hard as it is to think about, I would have given anything at the time to have a pill to make me want it. Unless he's lying, it'll make me sleep better at night knowing those girls might have been out of their heads while being raped. It's the coming down from whatever high they were on, the aftereffects of not knowing what runs through their minds that will forever haunt me.

I draw my hand back and bitch slap Zackery again across his cheek, provoking a string of curse words out of his filthy mouth.

"I'm not the begging type. Since you love it rough, should I untie you, strap you down to one of those tables behind you and shove the hammer waiting to pound a nail through your pathetic dick up your ass? If so, by all means, try to terrorize me again. By the looks of you sitting there in nothing but your boxers with nice deep cuts across your chest and arms, your legs shaking from what looks like someone took a torch to your flesh, I'd say you are suffering without a pill to take over your body. To numb you from the pain that has to hurt. You have no power here, boy. But by all means, please taunt me more. I'd love nothing better than to smile while watching you beg." I lift both brows and dare Zackery to say he knows me. In a way, I wish he would, so I could watch him die.

I take a seat across from them. Crossing my legs as I do. Bile swirls in my stomach, my throat suddenly dry. My gaze flits between the two, not quite sure what I'm looking for, but I study them the same way I did every man from my bedroom window when I was younger.

A smile works its way to the corners of my mouth as I sit forward, resting my elbows on my knees, and glue my eyes to Yves.

"There's a lot to be said about men who hide things from people. I don't mean that in the way either of you might think." As I lean in a little closer to Yves, I watch him with eyes wide open, the mask that I wore every time I slipped into the back of the car long gone. Yves isn't wearing the one he did for four years while he chatted with Luca effortlessly, played catch many times with the football while they'd wait for me either. Nope, he's a wide-open book.

I see a scheming son of a bitch who pulled the wool over not only my eyes but his partner next to him.

It's a little too late to save him, but he can bet before he dies, he'll give up everything he knows.

"Cunt, please don't try to get into our heads. You'll fail. We know we're going to die, but you'll never know if your son is dead or alive. You'll never save the bitches we killed. You'll never save yourself from a lifetime of mental distress. You want to dangle your sweet, caring mommy body in front of us to get us to talk, by all means, spread your long legs, and maybe we will."

I sit back in my chair, pondering how to address Zackery. His gaze slides up and down my body. Eyes are flaring in lust. He's looking at me like a shark circling its prey. One bite and he'd rip me in half, just like Joseph used to look at me.

He's examining me to see how far he can push until I crack like an egg. He won't be able to. I broke a long time ago, and I'll soon heal because I'm not leaving until I find out where my son is. Zackery doesn't have a clue, but Yves does.

I remain stone-faced and stoic. Luca isn't dead. With every breathing fiber in my body, I know he isn't. Those girls aren't dead either. No. Joseph is on the run, and he has those girls. He's why they got caught. He fucked them over. What does Joseph have up his sleeve? What is he doing with those girls, and where is he going?

Here. My husband is coming here—panic tremors through my body. Joseph is so close I can smell him, and so is my son.

I swallow down the urge to flee, to run off somewhere, anywhere so Joseph can find me. The need to protect anyone else from harm slips into my veins like a healing drug.

I won't let Joseph near anyone I care about.

"You'd like that, wouldn't you, Zackery? You'd like to tear right through me the way you did those girls. You'd like me to believe my son is dead when we both know he, nor those girls are." I manage to spit out my words without letting the tears drip from my voice.

Luca, hold on, my sweet boy.

That panic tries making its way to my bloodstream. I harden it right along with those tears. They turn to ice.

"You have no idea what I know. I might not take my

money to hell. You bet your sweet little body I'll take what I know about Luca with me. You must be deaf or dumber than a box of rocks if you didn't hear me the first time. I'm not saying shit. Bring on the big guns, sweetheart. If you are going to go up against me, you better be packing something bigger than a slap to my face and words that don't mean shit to me. Otherwise, you are wasting the last bit of air I have left." Those eyes of Zackery's hold more than he's letting on. As empty as they are, he doesn't want to die any more than Yves does.

Well, that's too damn bad. He's disposable to me. I want him out of my face so my uncle can work on Yves.

"Oh, I'm packing alright, and it's not a gun. You are scared out of your mind not knowing how you're going to die. I bet those girls you stole thought that every single minute of the day. You need to do better than that if you want to play with me, boy."

Anger snakes through my gut. I need to know where Luca is right now. It's time to move my pieces across the board.

"Call me boy one more time. Yves loves it. It's his favorite word." Hardly. Yves's favorite word is shit. Because that's what he has to be doing right now, is shitting his pants. He's about to get tortured to his death.

"You're good at trying to get in my head, asshole. I'm better. Especially when you two boys are sitting on death row with the clock ticking down."

Sucking in a breath, I prepare myself to get Yves to talk. Strengthening my resolve that wants to scream at him as I claw his deceitful eyes out.

"It has to be tormenting to you both. Knowing you'll never touch another girl. Never claim another mind. Never feel the control you need to hurt them. Then again, men like you have never felt pain so excruciating in your entire lives except for the nights you laid in bed missing your families. I bet you hated not being able to watch your sister walk down the aisle, Yves. Did you know she's expecting her first child? I'll be sure to friend her and her child. I wonder what she'll say about you when we meet for lunch. I bet it rots your gut that you didn't get to say goodbye to your father when he died, Zackery. How does that feel to be a disappointment to the people who once loved you?"

With a tsk, Zackery shakes his head while Yves finally shows his true colors by letting out a barking laugh like a wolf howling at the moon.

My gaze immediately snaps to his.

"Fuck, you are better than the old man behind you who tried getting us to talk. It's too bad for you, I don't give a fuck about my family anymore. Kind of like I don't give one about your son or you. I will give you a little reprieve since you have guts. No one has hurt your son. Not physically, anyway." Through clenched teeth, he growls.

His so-called reprieve grates on my spine enough to coax me into standing and punching him right where it hurts a man the most.

In his balls.

As far as I'm concerned, he doesn't have any.

I grip Yves by the hair, denying him the right to bend forward. "You should know that the old man will play with you before he takes your life. You will bleed to death before he shows mercy on your rotten soul. Don't fuck with me when it comes to my son. You have five minutes to tell me where Luca is, or my father is going to make a phone call and put a bullet through your sister's head." He isn't. Yves will never know even if the next words out of his mouth aren't something I want to hear.

"Fuck you, cunt. You must think I'm stupid." His eyes scream that he's sorry. Mine yells it's too late for him to have a guilty conscience. His life might have been saved if he had stopped the car at any time and told me he was getting me out of hell.

Then again, there are many lives he took to spare him the luxury of living. The videos he was a part of. The parents left behind always to wonder what happened to their daughters. The hell they will live with for the rest of their lives with no closure. No chance to watch them grow up to become everything they wanted to be.

"No, but you are. Now sit there and stew on what I said." I give a condescending motherly pat to his cheek, and turn toward Zackery, needing to get out of here and breathe.

"How about you, asshole? Do you want the same, or don't you give a fuck either? Explain to me how three men who grew up in good homes, loving parents, no sign of abuse, would deprive others of their spirits before they had a chance to spread their wings and fly? If you don't, the men behind me will prolong your death. They are like you, only better with mind games. They could spend days in here while chipping away at your flesh a little at a time."

A flash of silver hits the corner of my eye, my uncle swinging it back and forth between the two. I step back several feet. My heart is thrashing against my ribcage. I might never get answers if my uncle doesn't catch on to what I'm doing and shoots Yves instead of Zackery.

"A man never kisses and tells. If you don't like my answer, then you, right along with them." Zackery pauses with a lift of his chin and a vindictive grin that causes me to freeze in place.

I can't describe his stare other than it's like staring at a leopard wondering if he's going to play with you or attack for nothing more than a midnight snack—a bona fide monster who gets off on rooting around in people's heads. The expression causes every hair on my body to rise. "Can go fuck yourselves." Kicking his head back, he spits at my feet.

I flinch at the same time being grateful when a gunshot rings out and hits Zackery in the chest, propelling him backward, landing on his side with a heavy clunk of wood and blood. For a few seconds, he holds that smirk until my uncle kneels beside him, grabs him by the throat and drags him out of the room, leaving a trail of blood behind them.

I turn around, my eyes landing on my father—the man who taught me to stand on my two feet.

"I know this man. I know the other one too. Zackery pretended to be our accountant. He doesn't know a thing about Luca's whereabouts. Have Uncle Gabe kill him quickly. This one, he was my driver. He knows everything, Father." I raise my hand and slap Yves across his face so hard his eyes water. "He was playing follow the leader with Zackery until Joseph came along with a proposition he couldn't refuse. I don't know what it is, but once it's beaten out of him, I don't care how you kill him. I want him to suffer until he bleeds to death."

CHAPTER TWENTY

Lane

There was only one other time besides the day I learned Luca was my son that my life came to an abrupt halt. Where everything about the way I viewed things changed. It was the day I found out Lexi was mine.

At first, I wasn't sure if she was mine. I denied it. I was a selfish bastard, after all. A Mitchell who always got what he wanted, and it wasn't a kid. When the paternity test came back with its nearly one-hundred percent accuracy that I was her dad, I knew I wanted my daughter even though I was afraid.

From the day she was born, my little girl was the greatest unexpected gift. This piece of me, I didn't have a clue how to take care of, let alone hold, soothe, and feed. I'd never changed a diaper. I went to bed and woke when I pleased. But the first time I held her, this little bundle of pink staring up at me with blurry eyes was the moment my life would change forever.

For the better.

The first few months of learning the ropes taught me to

have patience. My baby was a crier. Face turning red from holding her breath, screaming at the top of her lungs when she wanted someone to hold her. When she wanted her food, her diaper changed, she wanted it now, and no one could lull her the way I could.

I used to think of Lexi as this delicate flower waiting to bloom. She hasn't opened to her full potential, and when she does, this miracle is going to change me again as well as change herself.

They'll be no more sneaking into her room. No, she'll likely be the one sneaking out of the house to meet up with some little punk thinking thoughts that'll get certain parts on his body chopped off.

I won't always be around to protect Lexi from some asshole, thinking he can hurt her. That thought slays me as nothing else could.

But I've done everything I can to make sure she's safe now.

I've been lucky she hasn't seen the criminal side of anyone she loves these past six or so weeks. I've made sure she's stayed clear of it all. I want her full of excitement and to strive for those possibilities in life. I never wish for danger to surround her. You'd think any parent would even if the child in question wasn't biologically theirs.

No child should have to live with danger surrounding them. From what I understand, thanks to Sienna remembering whose blood she has in her veins, that's exactly where Joseph is heading.

To place my son in more danger.

Because of it, I needed Lexi to soothe me every night since, even if she's asleep. To give me a little calm before the storm, and there's one brewing. It's been building violently.

Ready to destruct and destroy.

With all the information Aidan and Gabe gathered about Joseph, and with how chaotic our lives have been, I came in here tonight to not only calm me but to quietly tell my girl that I'm sorry I've neglected her these past few weeks. I'm sorry I haven't been around much at all. I don't think she'd know the difference with how much time she's been spending with Ellie and Braxton during the day. Then with Sienna and Victoria at night. It's me who needed to reassure myself I'm a damn good father to this little girl who taught me the meaning of unconditional love.

The kind of love that only a parent would sacrifice their life, happiness, and lives of others. That's what Sienna did for ten years. That's what she's been doing this week by not letting her phone out of her sight. If possible, she's clutching onto that thing harder than before, taking baths instead of showers, stuffing it inside her bra while watching movies, and cooking dinner. Small things she doesn't think Seth or Victoria will notice. They have and reported it to me. Worse, she's been going to work even with my change of heart of asking her not to.

She's waiting on that damn phone call from Joseph or Luca. I still don't think they'll call, but I want that phone. If by chance she's right and he calls, or they do, they're going to talk to me. Tonight, I'm playing dirty. Whatever it takes to get my hands on that phone.

I trust her with everything except sneaking out if he calls.

I've done everything I can to have an eye on her at all times when I'm not around. I've set up more security from here to the restaurant, to Logan's.

Lorenzo, Roan, and several other mafia leaders have made calls, worked with their corrupted government allies by getting men close to the border to stop Joseph from crossing into Mexico as Yves told us he'd planned. Hell, they even have them at the Canadian border. People are everywhere.

Not a stone unturned. Still, I know desperation when I smell it, and it's pouring out of Sienna. That scares the everloving hell out of me. Of course, I had to check to make sure she's been here every night before I get my Lexi fix. And it pisses me off more at Joseph, at her, at the whole goddamn world.

Joseph is near. We all know it.

I can feel the warning he's close rippling in the air. Tonight it's working its way through me like poison.

As if several of my senses are on high alert. I can taste Joseph's starvation to get his hands on my woman. I can smell his obsession to obliterate her. I can hear how he wants to imprison her by threatening to kill Luca if it chains her to him for life. He isn't going to leave the country without Sienna. I know that for a goddamn fact.

It's been prickling at my skin since I stared into Zackery and Yves's eyes. It was like standing in front of four deep black holes you knew were dangerous to peek into. However, as soon as they saw Sienna, a bolt of white-hot lightning broke through the blackness. Giving me the perfect view of the men they were.

I saw pure unsympathetic evil. I wanted to rid them of their misery myself, but they weren't the blood I want on my hands.

I want Joseph's, and by God, I'm going to have it before he drains Sienna's out of her again.

My woman is back. The other half of my soul—my tough warrior queen, who I need to sink inside of and be the sneaky asshole I am to make her forget about her phone. I haven't been inside her all week. I've walked, driven, ran through the streets of this city and surrounding ones with Rocco, looking for the van Yves told us Joseph is driving. He not only has my son; he has several girls, making it all the more important we find him.

Trying to find a white cargo van is like searching for a needle in a haystack. It's unsettling to the brink I'm physically and mentally exhausted.

"I love you, sweet girl. You own a part of my heart, and soon you're going to meet a boy who shares it with you," I whisper, knowing full well this little jumping bean will open her big loving heart to Luca. She'll probably drive him crazy with Ariel talk and command he be her best friend in the way she does everyone else.

As I watch the rise and fall of her chest, no place else makes me remember that I'll do everything to make sure my kids have the kind of bond I have with my brothers.

Lexi stirs, her eyes opening wide. She rubs them, nose scrunching in confusion before shooting upright holding onto her doll. She's about to whip up one of her windstorms while half asleep.

I break out in a grin, her little girl sweetness wrapping around me.

"Hey, princess, I didn't mean to wake you. I missed you so much. I had to come in here before going to bed."

She blinks, a little disoriented from probably wondering why she's awake when the only light in her room is coming from her Little Mermaid nightlight.

"Daddy, I tried my hardest to wait up for you. We watched *Beauty and the Beast*. Sienna made sweet tea. I loved it, and Victoria didn't. She said she's a Yankee and they don't put sugar in their tea. I asked her what Yankee meant, and she said it's a word used for people who live in the states by New York. I don't even know where New York is, but I told her she's crazy if she doesn't put sugar in her tea. Uncle Seth drank his without making one of those funny faces. You know the one where he makes his lips look like a fish, and his nose gets all wrinkly. He even gave me a hug, a kiss, and a secret. They aren't as good as yours. I love you so, so much. You don't have to miss me, not when I'm with Sienna, Victoria, and Uncle Seth. And guess what. Victoria is working at The Grill House now."

At that moment, where most kids are between awake and asleep, my child starts yacking her mouth. It won't surprise me a bit if she doesn't talk in her sleep. I wouldn't want her any other way.

"Is that right? I'm glad you had fun with Sienna. You like her, huh?" I knew Victoria started working for Sienna. They make a great team.

Lexi's arms squeeze tight around my neck, her body melting into mine as every muscle in my body loses the tension I've been holding for days.

"I love her. Someday she's going to be my mommy. I know it…" Her voice trails off at the end. My girl falling right back to sleep against my lurching chest, pounding like a madman at her words.

"She will, princess. Someday she definitely will."

Sienna and I aren't there yet. Along the way, I'll give her everything in life she deserves. Keep those promises I made years ago about loving her with all I am. I haven't come out and said the words yet. She hasn't brought it up either. Not that I don't feel it or want to. The timing, plus us not seeing much of each other, hasn't felt right.

I kiss the top of Lexi's head, adjust her back under the covers, placing her doll next to her, and pause at her doorway to glimpse one more time at the rise and fall of her chest before closing it partway.

It feels like hours by the time I make it to my bedroom to find my other girl standing in the middle of the room. Hair piled on top of her head, phone at her chest, breathing in hope and heartache.

It fists my gut seeing her this way.

"What if I'm wrong and Joseph never calls? What if he slides right past us and gets deep into the Mexican Cartel? We'll never get Luca out of there." She huffs out a loathing breath.

No, we won't. There's no negotiating with the cartel. I learned that from Gabe after Seth bitched and moaned about me going out to look for Joseph.

I have my reasons. Mostly, it's the father in me along with missing years of Luca's life that need to make sure Joseph knows that no matter what kind of pollution he's put in my kid's mind, I'll make damn sure I'm the one who erases it all by loving that boy as much as I do Lexi.

"Our story doesn't end here, Sienna. We're beginning, damn it. Don't fall backward. Don't doubt your father's ability to catch Joseph before he gets close enough to the border to cross it. Show me that woman who stood in front of those men. Show me the mom who spared her happiness to keep our son safe. Let me see her."

Her eyes shy away for the longest time, then touch back on mine.

She's frightened out of her mind. Yet here she stands to expose so much of herself by the expressions glaring off her stunning face, drawing me like a moth to a flame.

And, damn, do I want to feel the burn.

Love. Want. Hope. Need. Scars. They radiate.

I could do without those scars that she doesn't let anyone but Victoria and me see. I could do without the distrust I have chipping away at me that Sienna will go to Joseph and disappear if it meant being with our son.

Still, I've waited for this day. A damn lifetime it seems for Sienna not to show a scrap of guilt or fear. Even though the waiting for Joseph to call is driving her crazy, every morning I wake, I've seen it slip out of her a little more.

She reaches me in a second flat, instinctively I grip her face in my hands, my fingers delving in her hair until I find the clip she uses to pile it on top of her head. Dropping it to the floor, I yank her head back, mouth stopping a breath away from hers.

God, her smell and the warmth of her body consumes me as I pull her into me. Captivate and trap me. Haunt and calm me at the same damn time.

"Every time I've ever looked at you, I see my life. I see this woman with a brave heart. I see someone who has fought her way through life and kept her beautiful soul intact. I am addicted to you."

I take her mouth. Slow and soft, comforting in ways that words would never be.

Waves of greed twist in my stomach when she bites my bottom lip, taking over the kiss. My infatuation with this woman is nothing but a craving that will never leave my system. When she whimpers into my mouth, the animal in me takes over, and I devour her mouth.

Palming her ass, I rock her against my hard cock as I back us toward the bed, positioning her the way I want her. My eyes bore into hers as every detail of our future flashes in my mind. Without breaking our connection, I take her phone out of her hand and blindly place it on the nightstand beside my bed.

She doesn't protest, which is a damn good thing. If she

did, we'd be arguing instead of fucking. It's a bastard move, and I don't feel an ounce of regret or guilt for doing it.

We'll fight after, I'm sure, but that's fine by me. It's a fight she's not going to win. I'm going to keep her here with me, safe and by God, we will be bringing Luca home. I won't stop until we do.

"Your heart and mind are the most beautiful things about you, Sienna. This body, this temple I'm going to worship, is the body of a goddess. And your face..." I shake my head. "Can't wait to wake up every morning to it for the rest of my life."

The very first time I saw Sienna Ricci runs through my mind. *"That's Lorenzo's daughter? She's hot." Logan dropped the remote to the video game, jumped up to greet her while I sat there staring at a profile made out of a molded perfection.*

With my head cocked to the side, all I could see was a thick braid of red, and it jolted me. I felt this energy float through the room. To a young kid, it was a weird feeling that I wanted to happen again and again.

Swear to Christ, when I got my first glimpse of her face when she looked down at me, I thought an angel was standing in the doorway. She was more than pretty. She was beautiful. Someday she was going to become mine.

For minutes, I stand towering above her, loving how her smile increases when she roams my face, my chest. About drops me to my knees when she swipes her tongue seductively across her plump bottom lip when her eyes land on my crotch. Her dark lashes flutter, and once she bites the corner of her mouth, I lose my ever-loving mind.

I'm desperate to get inside of her.

Sienna's breath hitches as I whip my shirt over my head, and my hand dives to the button on my jeans.

"Clothes off. Spread those legs and lie back, Sienna, because the instant you come in my mouth, that's all it's going to take for me to sink inside of you. We never talked about protection. Are you on birth control?" I tug my jeans off, not once taking my darkened gaze from hers as she drags her shorts and panties down her legs, grabs the hem of her tank top, and slowly pulls it over her head, baring those lush tits.

"Yes." Good to know. Although coming inside her and having it take root would be alright with me.

Hooded eyes drift down my chest, across my tattoo, and go wide when she sees my cock.

I drop to my knees. I'll gladly do this too for the rest of my life.

"Fuck, baby," I mumble, dipping down, mouth close to her wet pussy. I grip her hips and pull her into my face. Her feet jump to my shoulders with the first swipe of my tongue. I eat her like the temptation she was years ago, a man who couldn't wait to get to the core because he knew once he did, he'd commit the most pleasurable sin to man.

To fuck and devour.

My tongue explores her clit, hardening the little bundle of nerves until she moans. I curve my finger inside of her, a feverish finger fuck that adds to each long lick across her swollen clit.

I fuck her pussy like a man gone wild, and I watch her through the barely open lids of my eyes as she grips the sheets, her ass lifting in the air, and when she comes all over my mouth, it's all I can take.

With hands that itch to roam every inch of her skin, I gently place her feet on the edge of the bed, lean in and palm her breasts with manic movements, tugging both nipples until she arches her back, and tips her head to the side. My mouth waters to touch the spot where her pulse hammers. I trace it with my tongue to where her panting breaths steal mine when my lips seize her mouth in a kiss.

I could feast on her mouth for days. Weeks, even.

Pushing up, I position her legs back over my shoulders, line up my throbbing head to her wet slit, and thrust inside her. Her answering whimper when I sink to the hilt is as sweet as her body. Grabbing her ass for leverage, I lift slightly and slam into her, going as deep as I can get. She releases a sigh that is both relief and anguish. Those emotions are swarming through me, too, as I drive in and out of her.

I'll never have enough of the woman.

"Lane, don't stop. I'm almost there." Her walls clench around me, muscles in her ass tightening in the palms of my hands while her breasts bounce in time to my thrusts and Jesus Christ, it takes all my restraint not to let loose and come.

Sweat drips down my temples as I pick up my pace, pounding into her. Every thrust rough. "Come, for me, Sienna," I whisper.

Our eyes lock when she comes undone, a roar ripping out of me as I empty inside of her, tightening the binds that had always connected us.

"Hold me, please?" she asks after we catch our breath, and I slip out of her. I wrap my arms around her, holding her close.

"My arms were made to hold you."

She says nothing, but I feel the weight of her slight smile. There's nothing else I can do except hold her while we wait. It's the worst feeling in the world not being able to take away her pain.

Pure torture.

Burrowing my face into her hair, I close my eyes and breathe her in. I'm waiting for her to ask for her phone, but the question never comes. I don't know how long we lie here, but eventually, her breathing evens out, and I know she's drifted off to sleep. Rolling over, I reach for her phone, tuck it under my pillow and turn back to hold her as close as possible.

Guilt. I feel it as I start to drift into a deep needed sleep knowing we'll have a blow-up in the morning. That'll be the perfect time to bring up the reasons why I love her.

A little while later, I jolt awake, blinking hard a few times, waiting for the dark room to come into focus. With nothing but the moonlight filtering in through the window, I can see that her side of the bed is empty. With a feel of my hand, I determine it's also cold. Sitting up, I flick on the light, slide my hand under my pillow to find her phone still there.

"Sienna," I holler, slipping on my jeans, running through the house, panic ringing in my ears when I can't find her anywhere.

Where is she and why would she leave without her phone. She'd wake me in an angered frenzy to get her hands on that thing.

Unless she played me for a fool, and Joseph already called her.

Motherfucker.

CHAPTER TWENTY-ONE

Sienna

An instinct. They are, at times, so hard to explain. For days the one settled in my stomach has been guiding my very existence. Or, maybe it's the part of my healed heart that will forever live in pain, reminding me if I listen and it's wrong, everything in my chest will hurt forever.

I don't know, except I chose to follow it to listen to my inner voice, and it led me to the rooftop of the restaurant.

If it's right, then Joseph has known what I'd been up to, where I work, live, and who I've been with as I suspected all along, and I hope he's been biding his time for that perfect opportunity to catch me off guard.

It's a dangerous game to play when many lives are at stake. The only weapon I have if this were to backfire in my face is I'm not the woman I used to be with Joseph. He's going to think that one look at him will jar back years of abuse, he's going to threaten me with Luca. He's going to touch me, and I'm going to obey. The mere thought of Joseph putting his hands on me after what he's done to those girls doesn't come close to having him touch me after Lane has.

It's a sad thing to admit and swallow.

It's going to feel like choosing death over the man I fell in love with quicker than when my father taught me how to ride a bike.

Joseph will rape me, beat me, and punish me, but he will never own the part of me he covets the most. He will never have my heart.

"Please don't let it get that far. Please give us a miracle here. Let us get caught at the border." I nearly double over and let the buckets of tears fall when I feel the ghost of Lane's hands, the warmth of his breath glide over my skin. It will linger on me forever.

I straighten my spine. I have to take this as far as I can to save Luca, and now there are young women involved. Even if their lives are never the same again, I need to help them the only way I can.

To escape.

Lane knew it might come to this. I led him to believe it wouldn't. I don't know what my chances are of him forgiving me. Slim to none. But he'll never turn his back on our son. I've said and known that since the day I found out I was pregnant. I will cling to that belief, along with my hope until I figure out a way to demolish Joseph's plan to work with the traffickers of drugs and sex slaves in Mexico. I cannot allow my son to be brainwashed into degrading women.

Fighting past the lump in my throat, I try to talk to Luca. This time I'm afraid if I try to speak, I won't be able to keep my sobs silent any longer. That's the last thing I want Joseph to hear if he were to show up. So I stand here, with my heart breaking, wearing the mask I've worn for years without making a sound.

I placed that appalling mask back over my face days ago, and so many times, as Seth shadowed me, it nearly slipped out of place.

I wanted it to fall to the floor and smash to smithereens so everyone could see for the time being I'd given up on hope. So they could see how I was barely able to breathe. It never did until I slipped out the door, scaled alongside the house, and ran until I knew the coast was clear. From there, I walked for what seemed like miles until I was able to hail down a cab, and the minute I stepped out of it and onto the curb, I secured it back in place.

That was an hour or so ago and still nothing from Joseph. If he doesn't show soon, there'll be nothing left in me, not one more day.

"I'm right here, Joseph. All alone, where the hell are you?" I whisper. "Where is my son?"

He needs to get here before someone figures out where I am. If I had one wish granted to me right now, it's that they aren't awake yet, and the thought of Lane, Seth, my father or anyone showing before Joseph scares me more than having him touch me because my husband will be trigger-happy and shoot anyone on sight to get what he wants.

As soon as the thought crossed my mind to come here the other day, I knew it was my desperation calling. So I moved through the days on autopilot. Working and keeping the same expression around everyone. Pretending I was okay when I'm anything remotely close.

I'm desperate, reckless, and what I'm doing is risky. Joseph could kill me, and Luca could be lost in the world forever.

I don't know what else to do.

And I left without making peace with my father. Oh, God, he's never going to forgive himself.

Panic sets in when I sense I'm not alone—my heart slams into my ribs. Emotion burns my eyes as the footsteps coming from behind me get closer. My nerves had already been prepared and wired, and now they shoot off like a flare.

I don't know if I want to smile that he's here or cry.

"I know the sound of your feet, I've heard them for years. One foot lands heavier than the other. You have this walk that lets people know you are a man of power and strength. I'd be glad to show you how to sneak up on someone the right way if you'd like." There's no sarcasm coming from me, no wanting to turn around and yell and scream. It'll do me no good and make matters worse than they already are.

"Sweetheart, I can be as quiet as a mouse if I have to be. Like all the times I stood above you and watched you sleep when you were a little girl. I used to stare down at you with wonder at what good I did to deserve you—my precious angel. Sienna, you are the only thing good in my life. With that, you gave me a grandson. Even though what you thought you were going to do by coming here was out of emptiness inside you. It was not a wise move. I'm proud of you for it. It shows I did one thing right raising you. But as your father, I can't have you sacrifice your life without sacrificing my own." His tone is soft, thick with emotion.

My father hides his soft side well. It's wide open at the moment. A vulnerability I'm afraid to turn around and see.

Swallowing hard, I release a slow breath, shake my head and take a step back, squinting my eyes as I watch the glowing white of the moon give off light in the inky sky.

"I used to watch Luca sleep too. I'd give anything to

watch him again. I love you." I don't know what else to say. My father isn't going to leave. Joseph might have decided to torture me mentally for the rest of my life and not show. I should have brought my phone. I left it for Lane in hopes that if Joseph did show, he wouldn't have Luca with him, allowing him to find a way to call, and he could save himself and those girls.

My father wraps his arms around me. I close my eyes and drop my head back against his shoulder.

"I love you more. So much more than the way I treated you. Forgive me." He's in so much pain. I hear it even when he tries to hide it.

"I already have." I surrender a sad smile, wanting so badly to turn around and let my father hold me. I can't seem to move. The emotions inside me have drained me dry.

"I would have done the same thing you were planning on doing if someone took you away from me. Grief and desperation make us do crazy things. When Lane called, in a panic, I must add, the first thing that ran through my mind besides getting to you before Joseph did was, I never told my daughter that she is more like her mother than she is me. Sacrificing takes courage, Sienna, and if my child is willing to give up her life to be with her son, then who am I to stand in her way. But what kind of father would that make me be if I let her go? Not the type I promised her mother after she sacrificed her life to save yours."

He isn't helping contain my tears. They fall freely for so many reasons I can't express. If I ask if Lane is here, the numbness around my heart will subside. Lane is my life as much as I'm his.

He's my salvation. My anchor. The other half of my soul. Without him, I'm numb. He loves me, and neither of us came out and said those three words in the right way.

God, I've made so many mistakes.

"I don't know how to go on without Luca any longer. I don't know anything anymore. I'm tired of Joseph controlling my family. Of hurting everyone I love. I want this to be over. Why can't this be over. I tried so hard to let Lane be enough to get me through this. He's not enough. No one is. I love you, him, Lexi, everyone with all that I have, but I can't live without my son any longer. I can't do it anymore, father. I'm dying a little more every day inside. My veins feel strangled; my heart is bleeding. I'm so scared I'll never see Luca again. I just want him back." I'm trying so hard not to fall to my knees and sob, but I'm falling apart. The last thread is flying away.

"Joseph isn't coming. The sun is going to rise soon. He won't show when it's light out." No. My predator husband likes to strike in the dark.

He wants to clip my wings to ensure I never take flight.

"This is all my fault. Everything everyone is feeling is my fault. The torturous pain that won't ease and let us be." I will never find that woman I had a tiny glimpse of while facing Yves and Zackery again. She will be lost forever without Luca. A floating feather that briefly touches the ground before once again being swept away.

"You're right, wife, it is your fault. The death of your father's will rest on your shoulders, the same as Luca's, the same as Matteo. I hated killing Matteo. I kind of like the loyal fucker. When we leave, baby, don't look at him, there's a knife stuck in his throat. The poor schmuck is bleeding like a stuck pig. Bastard didn't even squeal. Hands out to the side and step away from her, Lorenzo. Sienna, if you don't get your ass over here where you belong by the time I count to three, I will shoot our son right here."

The muscles in my father's arm tense and tighten around me, and he growls at Joseph's word.

"You're lying. You've always been a liar. Luca isn't with you. He would have warned me before you even came through the door."

Luca is not with him. I know this in the deepest part of my heart. He would yell, no matter what.

"Shoot me then, that's the only way you'll get her out of my hands. Rest assured, you won't make it two steps out the door before your blood splatters the sidewalk." Anger escalates the emotion in my father's words. I pinch my eyes shut as he turns around to face my ruin in the eye while grabbing one of my hands and squeezing to the point it hurts.

Mistakes. If anything happens to my father, I won't live through this one either. I will surrender to my unwanted death.

"You can't do this, Father. I won't survive if anything happens to you. I lost one parent this way, please don't make it both." God, where is Uncle Gabe. Seth, Aidan? The rest of the security? Joseph is one man, he can't kill them all. Unless he already has. Oh, God, what have I done?

"Hmm. You're right. I am a liar. Release my wife, Lorenzo. One."

A gunshot pings off the floor at my feet.

"Let me go, Father, please!"

He doesn't. Another gunshot goes off. My father slumps forward—both of us falling to the floor with him landing on top of me.

Blood soaks through my shirt, my father gasping for air.

He doesn't ask me to believe in hope. He doesn't tell me to be strong.

He says nothing at all.

CHAPTER TWENTY-TWO

Luca

My mom told me a lot of times I could be whatever I wanted when I grew up. I just shrugged and said, 'I know' while I rolled my eyes and went back to doing whatever I was doing. Most of the time, it was playing video games, working out math problems, or practicing on my tight spiral throw with my football. I still can't figure out how to get that throw right. I'm going to figure it out just as I'm going to figure how gravity can slow that sucker down to make it spiral around as many times as it does.

I haven't held a football since before I learned the kind of person my dad, who isn't even my real dad, was. I have to stop thinking about him as my dad. Joseph is a monster. Way worse than the ones I've seen on movies, my mom would go crazy if she knew I snuck and watched them on television.

Let me tell you, I'm not even mad at my mom for keeping it from me, not after the things I've seen and heard. Things I never want to tell my mom, no matter how much she tries prying it out of me.

I don't know what I'm going to be when I grow up or why I'm sitting here wondering about it. I know for sure I won't be a man like Joseph. If I'm going to hurt someone, they'll deserve it.

Like him.

He should have someone do to him what he's done to these teenage girls.

Chewing on my lip, I look out the window wondering why my mom is in Texas. Joseph said she got a job at a restaurant. Well, he didn't tell me that. I overheard him telling Yves. That's how I found out Lane Mitchell is my real dad.

The monster named Joseph doesn't know I know these things. I heard all about my real dad one night when I snuck out of my room, and from what I put together, Lane doesn't know about me. That makes me mad at Joseph even more for hurting my mom.

I wonder if Lane likes football and if I go to him like my mom said, will he watch me play? I wonder if he likes math the way I do. Maybe he loves another sport better, and he might teach me. I wonder if he lives here, and that's why my mom came to Texas. I don't know, but the man I imagined in my head wouldn't hurt my mom the way Joseph did.

A squeaking sound coming from the back has me turning around and pointing the gun Joseph placed in my hand toward the noise. He told me to shoot the girls if they tried to escape. I didn't want the gun. I didn't want to shoot anyone but him. I want my mom. He said he was going to get her. But I don't want her anywhere near him ever again.

He hurt her, and she's probably worried sick about me too.

I hate him.

I stare at the girls slumped on the floor of the van.

Hands and feet tied together with thick heavy chains. Black hoods Joseph had me place over their eyes when we stepped out of the crappy motel are covering their heads. Why I had to do that, I'll never know, these girls never make a sound, they never look at me. But I know they are scared. I know they've had terrible things happened to them, and I know I have to get them out of here.

Eight of us slept, showered, and ate in that room for days, and I watched them like a hawk. They sweated, they shook, and they shivered. They sat like dogs on the floor. Shoving food in their mouths like they were starving, and they look it. Skin and bones and eyes that seem too big for their faces.

They slept on the dirty carpet floor—my dad, I mean Joseph, and I each had a bed. I barely slept.

And, just like the girls, I never said a word. I haven't spoken since I woke to find myself in the very spot that they are. I wasn't tied up or beaten like I've seen my dad, Yves, Zackery, and Xander do to these girls.

Yves, who I learned, is an evil man just like Joseph, tried getting me to talk. He would lick his lips when he looked at me. One time he touched my leg, but Joseph told him he was never to lay a finger on me again. I'm not sure why Joseph yelled at him. All I knew was Yves isn't a good man.

I played dumb the entire time like I was in shock or something. I kept my mouth shut, ears and eyes open, waiting for the minute to do the one thing my mom told me to do. She said run, Luca, and I have to run. I'm afraid to leave these girls in case Joseph comes back. He will hurt them more than he has. He might even kill them.

Some of the things I heard I don't think I can repeat to anyone ever in my life. I want my mom and me to start over.

She promised we would. Maybe with my real dad. He has to be a good man, or she wouldn't have told me to get to him.

We haven't seen Yves, Zackery, or Xander for a while now. I hope my grandpa and Uncle Gabe found all three of them and killed them.

I wasn't starved or screamed or hurt either. I was left alone in a room and played video games, watched movies, and became very, very angry, wishing I had a phone to call my mom. I wanted to tell her I was okay. I wanted to tell her I was going to find a way to get these girls and me away from the bad men. I wanted to tell her I didn't cry once. Not even when Joseph said she was dead.

He's stupid if he thinks I believe that. He's even dumber for trusting that he has me scared enough that I won't get help.

I swallow, open the door to the van, and I run like my mom told me to.

I'm going to protect her from the monster and save these girls.

CHAPTER TWENTY-THREE

Lane

"I said, turn around and walk, son. You might have gone mute on me, Luca. I know damn well you can hear. I gave you an order to stay with those girls. You better hope for your sake; they are still there. If they aren't, I will shoot you, drag you back here and lay you next to your grandpa's body. I should say the hell with you and do it anyway. You were a pain in the ass to keep safe from Yves. You'll be an even bigger one trying to get you to do what I tell you once we get to Mexico. Now hand me the gun, son. If you don't, I'll break your throwing arm."

What in the fuck?

Chills spread over my sweat-covered skin as I come to an abrupt halt at the top of the stairs. Those words are the third time that's happened to me. Twice when it's come to Luca. There won't be a third time, and never again, when it comes to the voice that has controlled Sienna.

That voice needs to be gone. It is the only way Sienna will ever be entirely free.

Every muscle in my body escalates to high alert. Luca

isn't supposed to be here. By the sounds of it, he didn't listen to Victoria when he called her. She told him to get back into the van and wait for Aiden to find them.

And what the hell does Joseph mean by mute?

I don't have time to think about it.

My mathematical brain has been counting down the minutes since Gabe and I parted on the sidewalk in front of the restaurant after Aiden called to tell us where Joseph was, along with him having a bad feeling something happened to Lorenzo. Which, by the sounds of it, he was right, then I have four minutes to remain calm and keep them on this roof while I wait for Gabe to break into the building next door and shoot the motherfucker. Not the brightest plan to do in front of a child. We had no idea Luca was up here.

Fucking hell. Panic strikes my system. The damage this would cause to Luca hits me head-on. The kid has been through enough.

The ticking clock in my head reminds me I could be running out of time. I have to do what's needed to keep my family alive.

The door leading to the roof is open enough to give me a clear shot. I'm not wasting another minute. My family might not have one to spare.

Silently, I step forward, pausing briefly when I notice Matteo slumped against the wall. Eyes vacant. Dead. I was hoping he'd be alive. Should have known he wouldn't be if he didn't greet me with his gun the second I landed at the top of the stairs.

"PLEASE. You can beat me, break me, do anything to me, just let Luca go, Joseph. I am begging you to let him go. Let me touch him. Let me touch my baby. Can't you see he's scared? We'll go wherever you want. He'll listen. He'll talk, he'll do whatever you say. Please let me touch him, Joseph. Oh, God, please." A hiss follows Sienna's begging, but it's the loud smack against someone's flesh, a tiny whimper, a thud and a scream that hits my spine like a serrated blade scraping across my bones that has me making a split-second decision to let myself be known.

Gun drawn, my pupils widen as I slowly push through the door, and my fingers tug at my stomach to pull the trigger and rid my family of the fear they've lived with long enough. I can't—my internal debate about pulling the trigger and splattering blood all over my son pumps anger and hostility through my veins. My emotions are too goddamn high to do it.

Tears threaten to blur my vision. I shove them away. It takes me a second to register what I see. Joseph yanks Sienna off the ground by her hair, and places her in a one-armed chokehold. A knife at the base of her ear. Her cheek is bright red, eyes bulging the harder he squeezes. His other arm is stretched out taut and tight with what I assume is a gun pressing into my son's forehead. Luca's shoulders are shaking. His back is to me, a gun dangling at his fingertips.

Jesus Christ, my nine-year-old son has a gun in his hand. Just when I think this nightmare can't get worse, it does. He has to be scared out of his mind, yet he stands tall with his feet planted on the ground.

Whatever is going through your mind, son, do not lift that gun.

It's probably a damn good thing I can't see the expression on Luca's face because the one on Sienna's is painful enough as I flick my gaze toward her. There's guilt, worry, anxiousness, and relief, but the heartbreaking tremor of her lips, the outstretched arms that are shaking worse than I've ever seen, is what undoes me.

She wants Luca in her arms. No doubt thinking about how she's missed him. How badly she wants to run her fingers through his hair and all other things she's told me. Goddamn you, Joseph. I hope your trip to Hell is the beginning of endless torture and suffering.

Glancing left to where Lorenzo lies on his stomach, I can hardly make out through the semi-darkness how much blood is underneath him. From the shadows still covering half his body, I can't tell if he's breathing either.

He might be dead. He might be trying to hang on. He might not have the minutes we need to save him.

My head spins, stomach twisting and turning as realization sets in. I'll die saving my family if that's what it comes to. If I do, then mine and Sienna's love story will live through our children.

"Shut up, bitch. The next time you beg, it will be on your knees. Luca, if you want your mom, then drop the gun and do what I tell you. I don't want to kill you, son. You are my boy. I love you, but I will kill you before I kill your mother. You have thirty seconds to turn around, or I'll shoot you." There's a slight shake in Joseph's tone. The son of a bitch is borderline nervous, as he should be.

And my woman stands there with tears running down her face—tears of absolute heart-wrenching, agonizing pain.

I die a little right here.

"I'm not dropping the gun, and I'm not your son. My dad's name is Lane. When you had me locked in a room, I dreamed he was a superhero, and he was going to save me and my mom and those girls. Let my mom go, and I'll do whatever you say. I'll go to Mexico, and I'll help you. I'll be the best gunman you and the militia have seen. I'll train every day. I promise to make you proud. Just let my mom go."

Mute my ass, my son has proven he's a Mitchell by sacrificing his young life for his mother's. It'll go ignored by Joseph. To me, it's everything—an even more stubborn, sneaky, and sacrificial male to the batch of Mitchells.

Mine.

My mind spins, and my heart fills. I'm no superhero, but I'll die trying to keep that thought in Luca's mind forever if need be.

Bitter laughter coming from Joseph closes down what Luca said in my thoughts. That proudness, though? It belongs to me.

"Is that so? Your superhero isn't coming to save you. If he were, he'd have come with your grandpa. If he were a superhero at all, he wouldn't have ever let your mother go in the first place. Or fall into my hands to where she became the obedient little queen I beat her into being. You had me fooled, son, by not talking. I'd show you how proud I am of you standing there, proving how good of a soldier you'd make if we weren't days behind getting those girls across the border and into the hands of the men who bought them."

Yeah, those words snap those parental emotions out of me for the time being. Deep down into the darkness, I go. Adrenaline pumps through my veins. That split-second decision is upon me. I only hope Luca doesn't turn around out of curiosity to look at me.

Keep those feet rooted right where they are, son. If you turn around, I'm afraid Joseph will shoot you in the back of the head.

"That is so, asshole. I've had enough of Satan answering his disciple's prayers when it comes to my family. It's about time someone answers theirs. You'll have to go through me.

From where I'm standing, that isn't going to happen. You stole my son from his mother. Whatever proudness, I'll take credit for it since Luca has my blood running through his veins. Not yours." I pause, taking my glare off the cocksucker and direct it at Sienna.

"Sienna, look at me." My voice comes out rough, demanding and on the verge of pissed the fuck off. I am, but not at her. I need her to think I am before she falls farther into waves of shock that sweep her too far out of reach.

Come on, show me that face. Show me you are still here with me. Show me you trust me to get you out of here safely. Look at me so I can silently tell you to elbow the son of a bitch and give me a clear shot to blow his brains out.

"La Mia Vita," I plea one more time before I'm left with no other choice except rattle Joseph's chains enough that he turns his gun on me.

She won't lift her head. I'm not sure she even knows I'm here. She stands there, trembling, eyes transfixed, pleading for our son's forgiveness.

"Well, I guess your superhero showed, after all. Let's see which one of you he chooses to save." The gun cocks. Sienna's eyes go wide as do mine when Joseph presses the tip of the knife into her neck. Blood trickles, and her arms fall to her side.

My life flashes before my eyes. All the things, the memories, the having each other's backs, the love I have for my brothers reels slowly. The day my little girl was born, the way she curled her tiny fingers around my pinky the first time I held her. The promises to the love of my life I never kept. I planned on keeping them through our second chance, but I also promised I would die trying to get our son back to her. Our son, I may never get to tell him how proud I am to call him mine.

If I die, I'll go knowing my family will be safe.

"I choose them both. Sienna is mine. She tells me that every night. Luca is a Mitchell, that is something you can never change. It'll be me who buys him his first car—me who coaches his football team—me who teaches him to be a man. Me, who helps fix any damage you've done to him. They are my life. I'll take them on family vacations, picnics, barbeques, while you rot in Hell, asshole. I'm not walking out of here without either of them. You, on the other hand?" I shrug, leaving the rest of my statement to linger until my phone vibrates in my pocket that Gabe is in place.

I've done lost count. It has to be well past four minutes.

Shit, Gabe, where are you?

"Fuck you, Lane. She's my wife. Not your life. Luca might have your blood, but he's my son. He's going to do what I tell him from here on out. If you're lucky, I might not convince him to snatch your little girl someday and bring her to me. I'll train her before selling her to the highest bidder. Wonder if she'd like living in Russia, Dubai, or maybe here in the states where she's right under your nose?"

My heart catches in my throat, making it hard to breathe. Sweat drips down the side of my face, heart racing so fast it wants to explode. Lexi is my life too, and him speaking about her fuels me on by pure rage.

If the prick thinks he can rattle me better than I can him. He'd be wrong. As in, hurry the hell up Gabe, wrong.

"That won't ever happen. I believe that with all I am, Luca will play you as long as it takes to free him and his mother if you were to get past me. He won't change his way of thinking. Any guess why? Refresher, Joseph, he's my son. Mine, in case I haven't made that clear. You've known it all along. My blood shows in him by standing in front of you. You shoot him. Then I shoot you. It's called a standoff, dumb ass. Sienna, I love you. I love you so damn much. Love our son, our life we are building. Joseph doesn't have the power to break how much we love each other. He never has, he never will." Now is the time for her to hear those words. It's all I have left to make her feel me. Feel that unbreakable bond.

Her barely open eyes shoot my way. There she is, right here with me where she should be.

I strain to remain calm, not to let Joseph know he doesn't have her as he thinks.

"You love her? It's a little late for poetic words. As you can see, Sienna is doing what I say. Baby, tell him to drop his gun and get the hell out of my way. If you don't, I'll blow Luca's brains out."

Sienna flinches when Joseph presses the gun a little farther into Luca's head, nearly knocking him to the floor. If he fell, it would be a hell of a lot easier to save them both. My little hero keeps standing, despite the urine that starts dripping down his legs.

The bottom of my feet catches fire, urging me to take off in a sprint and grab hold of both of them.

"Your wife loves another man. She always has. She's been staying with me, doing a damn good job at this restaurant. Loving on my daughter as if she were her own. Sienna could be pregnant with another Mitchell baby right now, as far as I know. She's her own person, but she belongs to me. You found out about me and her, and it altered your plans. You were hoping she'd die so you could take my son with you to Mexico. That was your plan all along. When you realized she wasn't dead, you were going to leave her to wonder for the rest of her life until you found out about her and me. Am I right?" I know I am. I know my son could pay the price for provoking him too. My gut tells me wrong. It didn't let me down when I hopped on Lorenzo's plane to get to Logan after I'd found out his enemy was out of prison earlier than we thought. It was a good thing I listened to it. My brother was lying in a pool of blood. He'd been shot.

It gnawed away at me like it is now. Joseph wants to kill me as badly as he wants Sienna. He hates me as much as I do him and he knows well and good I will shoot him at the same time he does me.

It won't get that far, not when my brave beauty is waiting for the sign from me to finally set her free. I just need Gabe to hurry the hell up so I don't chance to die in the process.

Hold on, son. Hold on.

"Ah, so the superhero is a mind reader too. I'd clap, but as you can see, my hands are deciding which one to kill. If I choose to let Sienna live, if she is pregnant, then I'll make damn sure she never sees it. I will take the baby from her the minute she delivers. I gave Lorenzo until the count of three to back away from my wife. I'll do the same for you. Drop your weapon. One." His laughter rakes across my nerves.

Come on, Gabe. Damn it.

"Fuck you, Joseph. If you think I'll drop my weapon and let you waltz out of here with my family, you are crazier than I thought." Spit flies from my mouth as I shout behind clenched teeth. My nerves are worn out. My finger presses a tinge on the trigger.

"They are my family. You fucked your chance all to hell and then stormed in like some white knight thinking you're going to steal her away. Fuck off, Mitchell. I raised Luca. He'll do what I say when I say. When I tell him to jump, he'll ask how high, Dad. You call my son yours again or attempt to move. I'll slice her throat at the same time I blow

Luca's brains out. They'll both die along with me. You'll live in Hell for the rest of your days knowing you didn't save them. The choice is yours. Now drop your gun and move out of my way. Two."

My vision blurs, the floor shaking beneath my feet.

I slightly nod, praying Sienna saves us all.

"No, you will not take another thing from me, Joseph. Run, Luca." My heart pounds as Sienna hikes up her arm quicker than the speed of the bullet that hits Joseph in the back of the shoulder holding the gun.

Gabe. Thank fuck.

Joseph drops to his knees. The gun and knife clatter to the ground. I spring into action, go to sweep up Luca, but Sienna beats me to it, and she starts to run.

Every part of me seizes in that fatherly desperation to look, to touch, and to make sure the two of them are alright.

"Sienna, stop. Seth should be here by now with a doctor to look at Luca and you. You stay with him." It doesn't take long for her to heave out a sigh of relief. Agony gone.

"I love you, Lane Mitchell," she says through tears that keep sliding down her face.

"I know." I wait until I can't hear her footsteps before starting to count. Ten seconds. One for each year of her pain.

After what she and our son have gone through, it's a shame not to drag out Joseph's torture for just as long. My family needs me more.

"Unlike you, who is only smart enough to come up with bullshit, half thought-out plans, Sienna thought quick on her feet by coming here. You don't have her the way you want her; you never had her at all. She's mine. All of her is. And those girls, they are on their way home. I could give you a choice to have me kill you, or turn you over to the cartel, but I won't. You never gave Sienna one. Rot in Hell, Joseph."

With a groan, he reaches for the knife only to have me stomp on his hand, the sound of his bones crunching puts a smile on my face.

"Fuck you. Sienna will never recover; neither will my son." He snarls and raises his head to look me in the eye.

"That's where you're wrong. Dead fucking wrong."

The sun is rising. It's a new day, a new beginning.

I place the gun at his forehead and pull the trigger.

EPILOGUE

LANE

Fourteen months later

"Illegal hands to the face, number eighty-one on the offense. The result is a fifteen-yard penalty. Repeat third down."

"Bullshit," I mutter, wanting to tell the ref to shove his call right up his ass.

"Fifteen yards? What do you think this is, the NFL? It's junior league football, that should have only been five yards, and you know it. What about roughing my quarterback by the defense before he threw the ball?" The entire game, I've kept my temper in check. Trying to set an example for my team. Mostly for my son. But that penalty was a crock of shit.

The foul was on purpose. I can't get my running back, Eli, to keep his free hand down when he's carrying the ball. He's quick on his feet, can weave past most defenders, but he has the attention span of a gnat when it comes to listening to what I say. He's mouthy. A spoiled punk and one of these days, Luca is going to lose what he's worked so hard to keep contained by punching the kid.

I don't want today to be that day.

He's thrown a near-perfect game, and the weight falls on the quarterback. But if Luca wants to continue playing, he needs to control himself, or I won't let him play until he does.

I get his frustration. I see the anger because there are days I still feel it. It took me a long ass time for it to simmer. It didn't matter my family was all together. My boy was hurting. Sienna was crying all the time with worry once I told her Luca wasn't okay.

We were a mess. Finally, Sienna started counseling, so did I, and eventually, the four of us went together. The only one still seeing a therapist is Luca. "Come on, son, do not get in Eli's face. Let me handle it," I mutter under my breath.

Now would be a good time to call time out, but before I do, I pay close attention to Luca as he squeezes his free hand into a fist, puffs a breath out into the air, bows his head, and I can barely make out the movement of his lips as his teammates hurry in for a huddle.

He's counting. That checks my temper, makes my decision not to make the call right there, and replaces it with pride.

I rough a hand through my hair, turn toward the stands to see my new bride, daughter, and every member of my family sitting there watching Luca's first football game. Including Renita, Norah, Victoria, and Lorenzo. The man, thank fuck, is all smiles, paying attention to Lexi as she stands in front of him, likely talking his head off about her dance recital tonight. Good thing too; otherwise, he'd be concerned over Luca.

He made peace with himself, like the rest of us. Watching him now, able to interact with my girl after taking a bullet in the stomach. How he's enjoying his role as a grandfather, including to Lexi, he's the happiest he's ever been. Especially after last night when he placed Sienna's hand in mine.

We were married at Logan and Ellie's. Luca by my side, Lexi by Sienna's, all four of us smiling. One of the best days of my life.

I glance back at my wife, my eyes telling her Luca has this under control.

At least I hope he does.

Hope. Confidence. Anticipation. Patience and unconditional love have played a considerable role in adjusting our family to not only Luca's recovery but also Lexi's understanding of having a brother.

In the first couple of days, Luca wouldn't speak to anyone except Sienna. It took him four days after we found out Lorenzo was going to survive before Luca would even talk to me.

I'll never forget the first conversation we had. The minute Sienna stepped out of the room to talk to the nurse, my son looked me in the eye and asked me the question that proved what I already knew about Luca.

How much he loved his mom. How much he was a Mitchell clear to the ivory of his bones.

"Do you love my mom? I mean, really love her? You'll never hurt her, right?" he asked, his lips quivering.

"Yes, I love her, and no, I will never hurt her." I saw his belief through the tears he couldn't control. They fell hard and fast.

"Is Joseph dead?" He wiped the tears away from those mournful eyes. They kept right on falling.

My hands were itching to hold him. To mend, to bond, to take away, to carry his pain.

On top of never wanting to hear that man's name again, I hated he was mourning Joseph's death.

I understood it better than he knew—different circumstances than when my mother died. Still, she was my mother. I didn't want to think she didn't give a shit about me. It stung. To this day, it does.

"Yes." I leaned forward, resting my elbows on my knees, because fuck, I wanted to drop to them, open my arms wide, and gather my son up.

The ball was in Luca's court. I'd wait on my side as long as it took for us to get to know each other. This kid, this remarkable, brave boy, was so confused. It was going to take a while.

The waiting was going to rip my heart out again too. The result of him healing will be worth the wait.

"And you're my dad? Is my name going to be Luca Mitchell? I have a sister?" He stood from beside Lorenzo's bed and started slowly walking toward me. Wavering. Hesitating. Pretty sure my heart overflowed with every cautious step he took.

"Yes, son, I'm your dad, you do have a sister. Her name is Lexi. I'll never hurt you either. I promise." That's one I won't break. "You can call yourself whatever you want, Luca. I won't make you do anything you don't want to do. I'm not that kind of man. I'm one that loves you. I'm one that will support your decisions, within reason. I mean, come on, buddy, you are only nine. Although, I will love you no less if it's one I don't agree with." The slightest grin tugged the corners of my mouth. I had to force it to not pull into a full-fledged smile when one lifted his too.

"I'm almost ten."

"I know. A little secret about your sister. She'll want to make your cake." Shit, I couldn't wait for these two to meet.

"Lexi, Luca, and Lane Mitchell. We all start with an L. If you and Mom get married, she'll be the odd one. I want to be Luca Mitchell. Can I be called that?"

Fuck yes.

"Yes." I chuckle. Knowing Sienna will get a laugh out of being the oddball in our family.

"Do you like football?" He was within my reach—just a few more steps.

"It's my favorite sport."

"Can you throw a spiral?"

"Well, I'm no Tom Brady, but yes, I can." I lean down and pick up the football I brought from home. It's beat all to hell. "This was my brother's and mine when we were younger. Sometimes we play catch on the beach. It's yours now." He looks from me to the ball and back again at least a dozen times before he takes it, cradles it under his arm. And then he broke out in sobs as he climbed onto my lap, wrapped his arms around me and held on for dear life.

Mine.

This kid with a million scars I was going to do everything I could to heal is mine.

There was a lot more said that day and the days that followed.

Luca and Lexi took to each other quickly. Luca pretended to be okay in front of everyone, especially Sienna. I saw it though, that anger building—the need to get it out before it erupted.

I handled it with gentle hands, a loving heart, and the father-son bond I let Luca take the lead in us having. It started with him coming to me for help with his math homework. Then once we picked back up on Saturday being Lexi day, he asked if Sunday could be his. We now get together with my brothers, Gabe, and Lorenzo, if they are around, and watch football all day.

Lexi had a million questions. We tried to explain and answer them the best way we could. I couldn't lie to her. Of course, we left out the girls, XYZ, and everything having to do with them as well as Sienna living with abuse. We told her Joseph kidnapped Luca out of hatred toward Sienna and left it at that.

As far as the girls go, Aiden tells us they are adjusting as best they can. That's all they can do.

Turning back around, I hold my breath while I wait for my son to get his anger under control before the play clock runs out, forcing me to call a time out.

I'm not calling a time-out. I'm putting confidence in my son's hands.

Unease stirs through me as the team approaches for a quick huddle, Luca calling out a play.

I watch my son take the snap, running the same play as the previous one. As the coach, I should have my eye on the entire offense, but I don't. It's glued to my son, who is placing his confidence in Eli.

That's my boy.

Luca places his index finger on the seam, thumb underneath the back of the ball, remaining fingers across the laces, and he brings his arm back for the perfect spiral throw to which Eli catches and scores.

Today, we lost by two touchdowns.

And that's okay.

I'm proud of how far my son has come with controlling his anger over the past fourteen months, despite the time he spent in hell on earth.

I know he still has a ways to go before he's as okay as I want him to be, but I'll be here at his side every step just like his mother and Lexi will.

THE END.

Please continue reading for an important message from the author.

EVEN THOUGH MY story is fiction, the NCMEC says 203,000 **children are kidnapped each year** by **family members**.

If you suspect a child is in an uncomfortable situation, please call 911. You can remain anonymous. It could be a false alarm, but you could be saving a child, a parent, a sibling from living a nightmare.

As a young girl, a family member tried to kidnap me. A true story I will leave at saying it didn't get that far. I was scared, though. Afraid I would never see my mother or my siblings again. And I had nightmares for weeks.

THE BELOW INFORMATION has been copied from The Nation Center for Missing & Exploited Children.

In 1984, John and Revé Walsh and other child advocates founded the National Center for Missing & Exploited Children as a private, non-profit organization to serve as the national clearinghouse and resource center for information about missing and exploited children.

Unfortunately, since many children are never reported missing, there is no reliable way to determine the total number of children who are actually missing in the U.S.

When a child is reported missing to law enforcement, federal law requires that child be entered into the FBI's National Crime Information Center, also known as NCIC.

According to the FBI, in 2019 there

were **421,394** NCIC entries for missing children. In 2018, the total number of missing children entries into NCIC was **424,066**.

This number represents reports of missing children. That means if a child runs away multiple times in a year, each instance would be entered into NCIC separately and counted in the yearly total. Likewise, if an entry is withdrawn and amended or updated, that would also be reflected in the total.

During the last 35 years, NCMEC's national toll-free hotline, 1-800-THE-LOST® (1-800-843-5678), has received more than **4.9 million calls**. NCMEC has circulated **billions** of photos of missing children, assisted law enforcement in the recovery of more than **311,000** missing children and facilitated training for more than **365,000** law enforcement, criminal/juvenile justice and healthcare professionals. NCMEC's Team HOPE volunteers have provided resources and emotional support to more than **71,000** families of missing and exploited children.

National Center for Missing & Exploited Children

Charles B. Wang International Children's Building
699 Prince Street
Alexandria, VA 22314-3175
800-843-5678

ABOUT THE AUTHOR

USA Today Best Selling Author Kathy Coopmans is a Michigan native where she lives with her husband, Tony. They have two son's Aaron and Shane.

She is a sports nut. Her favorite sports include NASCAR, Baseball, and Football.

She has recently retired from her day job to become a full-time writer.

She has always been an avid reader and at the young age of 50 decided she wanted to write. She claims she can do several things at once and still stay on task. Her favorite quote is "I got this."

Release notifications- text Kcoop to 21000